My Painful Duty

Ben Vizard

Copyright © 2020 Ben Vizard

All rights reserved.

All rights reserved. No part of this book may be reproduced in any form or by any electronic or mechanical means, including information storage and retrieval systems, without permission in writing from the publisher, except by reviewers, who may quote brief passages in a review.

Published by Independent Publishing Network

Printed in Great Britain

Although every precaution has been taken in the preparation of this book, the publisher and author assume no responsibility for errors or omissions. Neither is any liability assumed for damages resulting from the use of information contained herein.

ISBN 978-1-80049-208-0

Have you forgotten yet?

Look down and swear by the slain of the War
that you'll never forget.

Siegfried Sassoon

Chapter One

1919

England

Click. Click. Click.

Hansen watched the ink stamps rotate slowly in their rack. His eyes, gritty with weariness, lost focus as he watched, and he could no longer see this mundane object for what it was. Instead, there was something in its shape and in its sound that put him on edge. As if it were something to be feared. A surge of adrenalin forced its way through his chest. Instinctively he swallowed hard to hold back the rising nausea. The idea was so ridiculous to contemplate, he put it down to tiredness, and let his eyes droop for a moment to clear the image.

Bang.

With a start his eyes were wide open again, and for a moment he couldn't place the sound, only to realise, stupidly, that it was just the ink stamp being brought down smartly on the document. The clerk looked askance at him.

'Excuse me, Major Hansen?'

'I'm sorry, what did you say?'

'I was just saying I need your signature, here, sir, if you wouldn't mind?'

Hansen took the pen being offered. His writing hand began to shake, and he steadied it with his left. He was more than usually aware of the clerk watching, and the others queuing patiently behind. He took a long breath and scrawled his name, although it was barely recognisable, and dropped the pen.

'Thank you, sir.'

Was there a faint smile on the man's face, or did he imagine that too?

'You are entitled to wear your uniform for a period of one week after today, Major.'

'A week?'

'Yes, sir. Here also is an advance of your pay, war gratuity and clothing allowance. Can I ask your destination, sir, so I can issue a railway warrant?'

An easy enough question, but at this moment to answer it was a struggle. Where else could he go? Home.

'Exeter. Make it out to Exeter please.'

'The West Country, eh? Very pleasant,' said the clerk, smiling.

'I'm sure it will be.'

He tried to return the smile, but a swell of nausea caught him off guard and it was all he could do to control it, sweat seeping down his neck.

'All done, sir. Have a nice life.'

He took the documents from the clerk and stood stiffly. A sharp pain down his left leg made him wince. Head spinning, he turned and made his way outside for fresh air.

A young soldier swung the door open for him and saluted eagerly. He nodded back in acknowledgment, his hat under his arm. Green as they come, he couldn't be more than sixteen, and hadn't even been taught how to salute.

As he reached the top of the steps a chilly gust of wind caught him. He enjoyed the coolness for a moment, feeling the breeze dry the perspiration matting his hair. He tried to focus on something else, but the image wouldn't leave him. Round, metallic. That click sound. He forced himself to hum a tune to distract his mind. Whatever the image was, he knew he didn't want to see it.

'Richard, is that you?'

Hansen turned to find the familiar voice and almost collided with its owner. Ernest Crosse, his old padre. He hadn't seen him since France, a year ago at least.

'Steady, old chap!'

'Ernie! I'm sorry, I was somewhere else for a moment.'

'Somewhere pleasant one hopes?'

'Of course. Not for a clergyman's eyes!'

'Just my luck. Are you finished here?'

The same warmth in his voice, the same puffy face behind round glasses. A bit greyer perhaps. He clasped his hand and shook it. His friendly face felt like being rescued from drowning.

'It looks that way. Four years and it's come down to a few bits of paper and a third-class railway ticket.'

He folded up the collection of documents and stuffed them into his tunic pocket.

'Going home?'

'Going to Devon, yes.' He couldn't bring himself to call it home. 'How about you?'

'Well, it's the most remarkable thing. I've been offered an opportunity in New Zealand as it goes. To be headmaster at a school.'

'A headmaster? Are you qualified?'

'Yes, it's curious, they seem to place more emphasis on moral fibre than on actual teaching experience. Or indeed any sympathy for children.'

'And your head for mathematics has always been lamentable.'

He could see Crosse being a mentor, but if it came to discipline, it might be closer to a sarcastic barb than ten of the best from a birch.

'If any management of money is required, we'll be closed in a month. Still, it's an exciting thought to go to the far side of the world.'

'I'm pleased for you.' said Hansen. Except he wasn't. 'When do you leave?'

'In about a week or so. I thought I'd while away some time in London, spending my pay, such as it is.'

'What was that about moral fibre?'

Crosse chuckled. It was never a big belly laugh with Ernie. More of a short explosion that forced its way out. Most of the time he would just cock his head to one side and offer a sideways smile, sucking on his pipe, as if waiting for a round of applause. It was a sense of humour formed in war, and not always appreciated by his superiors, who felt he lacked the dignity appropriate to a clergyman. But they hadn't been where he had.

'You know, if you like we could probably put you up,' offered Hansen. 'Exeter has a fine cathedral, and I know how you like a good cathedral. Plus, it sounds like you'll need to save your money.'

Crosse deliberated, unlit pipe drooping from the corner of his mouth. He struck a match and held it to the bowl.

'Such faith! It's a tempting prospect though. And if you're volunteering to mooch round a cathedral just to have me along--- well, I can't say no, can I?'

He clapped Crosse on the back, and they shuffled off down the steps. Once upon a time he would have bounded down, eager to move on to meet the future. But now he grimaced with each step and his knee creaked like an old man's. What kind of worn-out shadow was this to return to the 'real' world? At the age of four and twenty, to feel so old. As if a lifetime had passed. He knew he was clinging to Crosse like a lifebelt. Anything to avoid returning home alone. And for some reason the imminent loss of his uniform bothered him. Why only a week? He wasn't one to show off, but to be without it felt impossible. This lousy, scratchy, dirty thing was who he was now, and that, more than anything else, shamed him.

***

'Weren't you one of the first to sign up?' asked Crosse, as they stretched out in the empty train compartment, puffing away on his pipe once again. Hansen nodded. 'And you're only getting out now?'

'There was still work to do.'

Crosse assented. He knew better than to pry. For every man who had been eager to escape the trenches for home in November, there had been another who had clung on for reasons of their own. Another winter and another spring had come and gone, but he'd been finally told to go.

'I could ask the same of you.'

'I go where I am called,' replied Crosse, somewhat sanctimoniously. There was that little tilt of the head.

'I've never known anyone with less of a calling,' teased Hansen, but immediately wished he had caught the words before they had left his mouth. Crosse smiled good-naturedly, but it was clearly a joke too far.

He looked out at the English countryside, bathed in sunshine now. Untouched. Lying in his bunk and listening to the guns, it had been something of a comfort to visualise these places. Like the picture on the wall when he was a child of a bucolic scene in the mountains of Switzerland, where he'd spent hours of his imagination roaming in the alpine meadows. He sometimes imagined the sea lapping on the shore at Sidmouth, or the meandering river Exe where he'd fished. The gentle hills and the dappled woodlands. A dream of the world he was fighting for. At times he felt calmed by it, but now as he saw the reality in front of him, he had to force himself to release each breath, caught in his throat. He couldn't sit back in his seat. He was fixed with the notion that he was waiting for something, like the eve before battle. But there was no battle to fight.

As he tried to calm himself, he noticed the click of the compartment door opening and he turned in a rush, ready to push off from his seat, one hand instinctively on his revolver. The old lady entering was so startled she dropped her basket and, in a fluster, stooped to pick up the bundles that had fallen.

'I'm so sorry, I was just going to ask if I might join you gentlemen,' said the lady, dressed in an elegant black frock.

'Of course', said Hansen. 'I do beg your pardon if I startled you.'

He dropped painfully to his knees, helping the lady to pick up her purchases and seeing her to a seat. She thanked him for his kindness, more out of politeness than anything else, and he sheepishly resumed his seat on the other side. Crosse peered at him over his round lenses, chewing on his pipe with an expression that gave little away.

Hansen returned to his thoughts of home. The question of what he would do now was one he had turned to again and again, but with no answer. His studies at university had never interested him, and now even the feeling of obligation that had pushed him was missing. He tried to consider what his father, and most especially his mother, would think and could summon only indifference. Nothing could sting a new emotion beyond the all-encompassing fog that was suffocating him. He realised his knuckles were clenched together and he slowly released them, angry red marks persisting on his palms, slick with sweat.

He needed sleep desperately, but his mind raced on. He checked his watch - barely mid-morning - but drew the hip flask from his pocket anyway. The warm taste of the whisky eased things a little, and he leant back into the seat and closed his eyes. If sleep wouldn't come, at least he could pretend and avoid the feeling that the others were looking at him.

Chapter Two

September 1915
Loos, France

He looked straight ahead, fixed on the ladder, his hands gripping it tightly. The guns pounded, like his heartbeat. Now was the time to say something encouraging to his men, to steel them for the fight. But there was no chance of that. Any eloquence he had was hiding from him, and in any case, he wouldn't be heard above the thundering artillery.

Then suddenly, silence. Hansen looked up to the sky and muttered a half-remembered prayer. Who there could be listening? Surely God was as deafened as the rest. But it gave him determination. As much as fear filled every pore, he had to admit to an equal measure of excitement. Dawn's light was tingeing the sky above him pale pink. There was nothing left to think about. Everything now was about doing. 'Show no fear' the Captain had said, 'you must lead'. He gripped the swagger stick under his arm. Useless. It would make him an obvious target. And yet there was comfort in it.

He drew his revolver and stood as tall as he could manage. He forced a smile onto his face. He knew it was false, they knew it was false. But his men responded to it. At least, most of them did. The lad next to him was crying silently, tears running down his face. Hansen looked away. He couldn't blame him, and if he went over the top despite the tears, he'd have done his duty. What could any of them do but that? To stand and keep moving forwards, that was all that was asked.

He checked his watch for the hundredth time and this time saw what he longed for and dreaded - six o'clock. Whistles began to sound distantly and then more and more along the line. Hansen put his own whistle to his lips and blew for all he was worth. And then he climbed.

He reached the top first and scrambled to his feet, dazzled by the rising sun. His breath steamed in the cold air, and the empty space seemed vast, flat and featureless, impossible to cross. The German lines erupted in gunfire, like a crash of thunder, flashes of tracer fire merging with the sun. But it could not hide the machine guns' devastating effect. Like a macabre game of skittles, they swept away lines of men. And Hansen walked on.

He looked to his left and saw only dead and dying. His men, shorn of memory, shorn of honour, shorn of life. And Hansen walked on.

The Highlanders, on their flank, followed their piper, who somehow evaded death, but led his followers forward, like scurrying rats, to be blown to pieces and cut apart by shrapnel. And Hansen walked on.

By what miracle he remained unscathed, Hansen didn't know. The rifles picked off his tear-stained comrade as he turned to lead him on. Shot through the throat, he could do nothing for him but leave him to drown in his own blood.

The standing order was just that - to stand and walk and not to run and hide, but many of his men were running now to find cover. There was no shame in it. Why would anyone wait for the inevitable? For himself, fear was gone, or at least quieted, by the desire to reach the enemy line. A foolish, reckless desire to get there, though he had but little idea of what he would do when he reached it. If he reached it.

He stepped away from barbed wire in his path and his feet went from under him. Before he could throw out his arms he'd landed heavily on his back, sliding and sliding into a water-filled shell hole. There was an agony of scratching to win back control as his body spun, unwilled, down the bank. Finally, his feet landed on a branch and disturbed a nest of rats, who scurried across him and away. Momentary disgust was replaced by relief when he realised he'd stopped short of the water. It might be any depth and in this mud he might never have got free. He kicked against the branch to get purchase, but only then did he realise that it was curiously covered in green serge. Slowly he noted the thumb sticking out of the mud, partly stripped of flesh.

He felt faint and wanted more than anything to be somewhere else. He crawled, clawed and clambered desperately. The German guns seemed a better prospect at that moment than being there with 'it'. No longer a person, not an object. It had no name.

As he pulled himself to the edge, a machine gun raked the ground and kicked up mud into his face. He covered his head, waiting for everything to pass. As he lay with his arms over his head he could imagine staying there. Perhaps no one would notice? Then he thought of the weeping soldier, whose name he didn't even know. These men had followed him into this madness, and he couldn't betray them now by seeking a place to hide. He must lead, and to do that he must walk on and show them he was not afraid. Maybe they would believe it, and gain courage. That was surely all he would be able do for them, so he should, for as long as he could.

Seized with a new determination, he threw himself forward. The enemy guns had not found their mark yet, and with every step he began to believe that they wouldn't. An insane confidence gripped him. A certainty that he would get there. Captain Harris appeared from the smoke ahead, shouting encouragement. He couldn't hear what he was saying, but he hurried towards him. He'd fought in South Africa. Harris would have a plan.

He began to jog but like in a dream the Captain seemed always just out of reach. The din of the battle was unbearable. Gunfire, explosions, shouting, screaming. Then out of the noise came a new shrill whistle. He turned his head to locate it, in time to see a shell arc into the ground ahead of the Captain. A great force hit him like a hurricane and the noise stopped.

He gasped, the sounds of battle returning around him. A suffocating weight on his chest. Every limb ached and he could barely take in a breath. His head pounded and he could taste the tang of iron in his mouth. He looked up at a flight of birds crossing the now-blue sky. He envied them. Gradually the weight dissipated, and he could breathe again. His chest ached but he could roll onto his side. He searched for Harris. It was a strange shock to find only empty space. Perhaps he'd gone ahead, he told himself, but he knew it was futile. There was no one to lead him now, he must be the leader for real. His men would be looking to him and the other lieutenants, if any others were still alive.

Suddenly he was furious. Angry for the death of his commanding officer, but angrier still that he must do this, barely a man, not even in his majority. Not ready.

'Devons!' he screamed. 'To me!'

He searched for every head responding to his call, scattered and hiding. He waved them on, and they came. Bit by bit they followed. Whether through habit, through discipline or through stupidity, they followed.

Then the German line was right there. He could see people moving. Machine guns were destroyed, but there was still rifle fire coming. He ran towards them, readying his revolver. A figure climbed onto the edge of the trench and levelled a rifle at him. As if aiming at a paper target with a fairground pistol he sighted the German and pulled the trigger. The figure sprawled to the ground and slid back into the trench. He'd imagined what it would feel like to take a life, if that's what he'd done, but there was nothing to feel.

He reached the top of the trench and found Germans fleeing in all directions.

'Grenade!' he shouted to a soldier near him, who launched bombs, one after the other, into the trench. The explosions thudded against the trench walls and stopped the running Germans. Hansen slid down the ladder and surveyed the scene. All quiet.

Then he felt like retching. His legs caved beneath him and his head was too heavy to carry upright. He wanted to fall to his knees, he wanted to sleep, he wanted to scream. But he must lead. Soldiers around him were looking for orders. Should they go on and press the attack, as the handbooks said? The thought of it was unbearable. His woolly brain searched his memory. 'Hold until relieved' was all he could remember.

Sergeant Cairns trotted down the trench towards him. Thank God!

Chapter Three

1919

England

Hansen snorted awake. For a moment he thought he was in the dark of a dug out, before the train freed itself from a tunnel and sunshine splashed back into the compartment. He was becoming used to being wrenched back from sleep by his dreams. It left him feeling more tired than before, his body fighting to release the nervous energy from his system.

'Where are we?' he asked Crosse, who was reading the paper.

'Salisbury, I believe.' he replied, without looking up. 'Wonderful cathedral in Salisbury.'

Hansen turned to look out of the window. Their elderly companion had left. Either she'd reached her stop or more likely, was reluctant to be in the same compartment as him.

'Goodness me,' said Crosse. He tutted and sucked his teeth. 'Things in Germany go from bad to worse.'

Crosse tossed his paper away and re-lit his pipe.

'Many would say they deserve everything coming to them of course,' he continued. 'He who lives by the sword and all that. But I can't feel so unkindly. We are all God's creatures.'

'They suffered as much as we did,' said Hansen. 'Perhaps more. And we're all guilty. "It is forbidden to kill; therefore, all murderers are punished unless they kill in large numbers and to the sound of trumpets."'

Hansen arched an eyebrow towards Crosse.

'If you're going to test me, you'll have to up your game' said Crosse, puffing rapidly on his pipe.

'You can play for time if you like.'

'I know it.'

'Of course you do. It's just the name that escapes you.'

'A French philosopher?'

'It couldn't be any other.'

'It's not Descartes?'

'You're right. It's not.'

'I know! It's Voltaire,' cried Crosse, in triumph.

Hansen nodded, smiling. He felt immediately guilty. These intellectual games had always been enjoyable, and he and Crosse had used them to distract each other during the worst bombardments, but now anything that brought him pleasure brought an equal amount of self-reproach.

"'All is for the best, in this, the best of all possible worlds,'" said Crosse.

'I'm not having that' replied Hansen.

'The quote, or the sentiment?'

'Either. Both.'

Hansen stretched out. Now there was something strangely reassuring about the compartment. Enclosed. Safe. He took a deep breath. Would that he could stay here. With Crosse as well, there was an ease. There was an understanding, a shared experience. There was no need to hide those experiences, so there was no need to share them. They could just be. He'd forgotten when they'd first met. Crosse had just always been there in the background. Always jolly and at ease. It could be raining shrapnel and you'd half expect him to raise an umbrella and comment on the weather being unusually inclement. Hansen had leaned on his stoicism many times, drawing on that strength to keep up the façade for his men that he feared nothing. He wondered at where it came from. Was it God-given? Is that what faith could do for someone? Perhaps it was resignation – a simple result of long suffering and experience. There was nothing left for him to feel, so he didn't.

***

The train eased into the platform at Exeter St. David's and the clump of doors being opened and closed began to rattle through the train. Hansen pulled his case from the rack, turning his back on the window.

'Pleased to be back?' asked Crosse.

'Of course,' said Hansen, forcing a smile.

Perhaps if he said it enough, he'd begin to think it. It seemed churlish to feel this way. This had been a happy home for him in so many ways, but it felt so distant he could barely recognise the man - the boy - who he remembered being here.

They climbed off the train and walked up towards the cathedral. Crosse had convinced him to make a stop there first, and he had been easily persuaded, partly because it meant putting off the moment when he would have to be in that house again.

Every turn they made threw up memories that were both warm and unpalatable. They passed Northernhay Gardens. He'd walked out there with Madeleine, in the long summer of 1913. He knew his mother wanted them to form an attachment. It was a good match in her eyes, and she was beautiful, certainly. Green-eyed, with a tall, elegant figure, but my goodness she was dull. Her conversation bored him, and he couldn't see himself marrying someone who would do little more than chatter about afternoon tea and the latest fashions.

The museum. He and his cousin Sebastian had spent long afternoons here studying the fossils and the strange specimens in jars. They had been curious about everything. As close as two brothers, there was nothing that they could not investigate and study. To learn everything there was to learn about a world that seemed vast and fascinating. And most of all, full of possibility. He couldn't feel that now. He caught his breath, a shiver running from his heart to the pit of his stomach. Some memories were best not to consider.

They walked on and reached the cathedral. Crosse scurried around examining everything and produced chalk and paper from somewhere to take brass rubbings. He was in his element. For Hansen it might once have been fascinating, but he struggled to engage himself in anything of interest. The history, the beauty of the architecture, the stories behind the memorials. None of it caught his attention. At length he took a pew and waited.

'Honestly, you are the worst, Crosse,' he called, his voice echoing. 'The architect couldn't know it better than you by now.'

Crosse scampered across to where Hansen was sitting.

'They didn't have them,' he said, to a look of puzzlement on Hansen's face. 'Architects. Not really. It was a job that could take generations.'

'I know how they feel,' replied Hansen, like a bored child.

'I don't think following your father into the family business is quite the same. If that is what he expects of you?'

Another of Crosse's tricks. He remembered everything about everyone in his regiment. He would pull out little nuggets of personal information about soldiers Hansen barely knew. He couldn't remember even telling him that his father was a solicitor, much less that he was expected to follow the same path.

'I know he'd like it, but I can't see myself in that world now. It's so -- conventional.'

Crosse sat down on the pew next to him and pushed his spectacles down his nose. Hansen responded like a pupil ready for a lecture.

'You do know that anything you do now will seem "conventional", in your words. What we have experienced, to be that close to death, and to be so alive. You won't find that again.'

'You think I want to be back there?'

'You tell me. But life doesn't stop because the war has. I'm considering how to inspire snotty children with the life of St Augustine. You need to do the same.'

'I have no interest in St Augustine,' said Hansen, smirking.

'You know what I mean. You could return to Oxford.'

'To study law? No.'

'To do anything you like. You've done your duty. You've looked after your men. Now take care of yourself.'

'I take it back. You're made to be a headmaster. It's late, we ought to get going.'

Crosse made a great show of adjusting his spectacles and nodded slowly. They began to walk down the aisle. He was right. There was no longer a unit to look after or for him to give orders to. There was something reassuring in being able to do that. Civilian life would be messy by comparison. He ought to think of himself and his own future. But there was that feeling again.

They passed through Bedford Circus and across Southernhay to the tidy row of Georgian townhouses that he knew so well. He looked up at number 14. He could see the window where he had leaned out to shout to Sebastian that he had been accepted for Magdalen College, and there was the step where they'd said goodbye before this all started.

'Looking at it won't change it,' said Crosse, breaking in on his thoughts. 'When were you last home?'

'Not long enough.'

Hansen approached the door and pulled the bell, which jangled somewhere inside. As he waited, he realised he was holding his breath, and tried to relax his shoulders. The door opened and Emily, the maid, looked up wearily, expecting just another visitor. Then her eyes widened, and she smiled. Such a smile it made Hansen grin in return.

'Oh my! You're back, sir!'

Hansen nodded dumbly. He found it hard to believe that this was the little girl he'd known before. So timid and afraid, he'd felt protective to her then, like she was a younger sister. Much though his mother disapproved. But now he struggled with what to think. He couldn't help but find her beautiful, with her dark eyes and olive skin, and that smile. But so thin too, and there he felt protective again. Flour was smudged across her chin and he longed to gently wipe it away.

'Hello, Emily. How are you?' he ventured.

Then she embraced him in a rush, as if compelled to act on an instinct she had held back. And it was delicious. The warmth, the smell of her skin next to his and the feeling of closeness flooded through him. He wished for it to last, and then just as suddenly, she pulled back, embarrassed.

'I'm sorry, sir. Forgive me, I wasn't thinking.'

'It's alright, I'm pleased to see you as well,' he stammered.

Chapter Four

1913

Exeter

The house looked imposing as she took in the full height of the building. Mr Creighton held her arm tightly as they climbed the steps, as if worried she might run. It was the last thing on her mind. She could barely think at all. Everything had happened so fast. In the workhouse at least she had friends. Now she felt totally alone, cast into a place she didn't know. Was she really expected to look after this whole house? It looked twice as tall now.

The door opened and a lady stood there, ramrod straight. She looked her over and then turned her attention briskly to Mr Creighton.

'This is the girl?' she asked him.

'Yes, ma'am. I promise she'll give you no trouble.'

'We shall see. How old?'

'She is just thirteen, ma'am. A good worker by all accounts. Her name is Emily.'

'Teeth?'

'I beg your pardon?'

'Does she have her own teeth?'

She didn't wait for an answer and turned quickly to Emily and pulled her mouth open to examine her teeth, much as one would do for a horse. She shrugged and seemed satisfied.

'Very well. I shall take her on trial for a week, Mr Craven.'

'Creighton, ma'am. Certainly, as you wish.'

'Well, good day. This way, girl.'

She turned and was back indoors in a flash. Emily stood stupefied for a moment, before Mr Creighton pushed her forward.

'Go on! Follow your new mistress. You're lucky to have such a position. Behave yourself, I don't want to have to return here for you.'

And then he was gone too. Emily went passively inside, looking around her at the showy decoration and gaudy objects on display. Her new mistress stood waiting with a list in her hand.

'I shall expect you to complete all of these tasks daily. There are others which you may do less frequently, but for now I wish to see you accomplish these satisfactorily. You shall call me Mrs Hansen or ma'am. Any questions?'

It was a question to which clearly no answer was expected, as she handed Emily the list and swept off towards the parlour.

'The first thing you can do is bring me some tea.'

She paused at the door and turned back, fixing her cold eyes on Emily.

'The response you are looking for is "yes, ma'am."'

'Yes, ma'am.'

The door closed and she was left alone. Emily could feel a rising panic as she studied the list. Where even was the kitchen? Nothing was said of where she should sleep, or her wages, and she was too terrified to ask. She tried to order her thoughts. This was no different to looking after her mother. She needed to work things out and tackle tasks one at a time. 'First things first and the rest will take care of itself,' as her mother had always said. She swallowed hard.

The kitchen proved easy to find, but lighting the stove took time, and every moment she worried that the fearsome Mrs Hansen would descend from on high and throw her out. It was at least warm in the kitchen and that was comforting. She knew other girls who had returned to the workhouse from placements with families where they had proved unsatisfactory, for whatever reason, and none had found another, to her knowledge. Bleak as she felt, that prospect was worse.

Unsteadily, she carried the tray of tea things upstairs, measuring every step on the unfamiliar staircase. She checked everything again. Surely there was nothing missing? She reached the door to the parlour and stopped herself just in time from going straight in. She balanced the tray uneasily and released a hand to rap gently on the door. A voice from inside bid her enter, with poorly concealed impatience, and she went in.

'It is almost noon, girl, so long have I waited.'

'I'm sorry, ma'am.' It was the only possible response.

'Be quicker next time. I shan't be at home for luncheon, so you can make a start on your other tasks. I shall be checking. You may go.'

***

She could no longer feel her hands as she worked away, scrubbing the doorstep. The water was getting cold quickly and her fingers were red and numb. She'd swept all of the rooms, made the beds, cleaned the grates and the windows and beaten the rugs. And there was the evening meal to prepare yet. To distract herself, she'd been considering the lot of other servants she knew. Mrs Rouncewell had been with Lord and Lady Dedlock for fifty years, but the idea of still scrubbing steps in her sixties was too unpleasant, she could barely conceive of it. Mrs Fairfax had been related to her master Mr Rochester, much good it did her. Then there was Mrs Reynolds, who was happy enough, praising Fitzwilliam Darcy to anyone who would listen. It seemed an unlikely state of affairs, but perhaps she would earn Mrs Hansen's respect in time. The difference was that they all had company in a big house. The more she thought, the more alone she felt. Tears formed in her eyes and began to trickle down her face. Her mother would have held her hand and smoothed her hair. She smiled at the memory, but it only made the pain more acute.

'Hullo! You must be the new maid,' said a friendly voice behind her, 'unless you're a kind stranger cleaning our step for a wager or something?'

He chuckled at his own joke. She turned quickly and stood up to curtsy to him, doing her best to hide her tears. He was tall and imposing, but with twinkling eyes. A second man stood a few paces behind, staying quiet.

'Yes, sir. I mean, yes, I am the new maid.'

His face fell with concern.

'I'm sorry, it was a poor joke. Are you quite well?'

'Yes, sir, thank you,' she replied, unable to look up at him.

'I don't think you are. Look, come inside, it's bitterly cold out here, and I have gloves on. You must be chilled to the bone?'

'I must finish my work, sir.'

'That can wait, surely? Come on.'

He took her by the arm and gently guided her inside. The warmth of the touch took her by surprise. He took her into the parlour and made her sit by the fire. Then he took off his gloves and raised her hands to the fire. She could barely feel his touch, but it spread a warmth through her whole body.

'That's better,' he said, smiling. 'It would be bad luck catching hypothermia on your first day, wouldn't it?'

She wanted to thank him. In fact, she wanted to hug him. But this was enough, to feel that someone cared. She felt she could be Mrs Reynolds now. By and by he released her hands and stood back.

'I'm being terribly rude, aren't I? I haven't introduced myself. I'm Richard. Richard Hansen. And my skulking friend is my cousin Sebastian. He's often round here, even though he has his own home to go to.'

'Good day' said the other man lightly. 'Don't mind Richard, he fancies he's a comedian.'

She could see a similarity in their features - both blonde-haired with blue eyes - but Richard had a confidence his friend lacked. She was enjoying the warmth but began to feel uncomfortable at being so comfortably ensconced by the fire.

'Might we know your name? Or it will be difficult to converse,' teased Richard.

'Emily, sir.'

'Welcome, Emily,' he said, smiling warmly. 'I hope you'll be happy here. Ask me if you need anything. It must be all very new. Is this your first position?'

She nodded. She tried to guess their ages. Perhaps eighteen? They both wore the same tie, which must be their school. That would be happiness, she thought, to still be in school at their age. Her own education had been basic, but her mother had always encouraged her to learn in whatever ways she could. She had told Emily stories from as early as she could remember, which, she later learned, her mother had recalled from having read them in books.

One of the few gifts she had ever been given was a book, which she prized.

'We should go, Richard. Best not to keep the ladies waiting.'

Richard twisted his face in mock dismay.

'Of course. Afternoon tea at Deller's,' he explained. 'Have you been there?'

'No, sir.'

An odd question. Why should she have been there, where an afternoon tea would set you back two shillings! Still, it was nice to be treated as an equal.

'It's very pleasant. Will you be alright if we leave you? I'll be back for dinner.'

'Yes, sir,' she replied, before realising she had no idea when dinner should be. 'Could you tell me, sir - what time shall I serve dinner?'

He smiled. 'At seven. Just hit the big gong over there and we'll all come running! I actually just stopped by to get a book for Madeleine.'

He went to the shelves on the other side of the room and plucked a volume straight off. He noticed her curiosity.

'Thomas Hardy. Tess of the d'Urbervilles. Not that she'll read it. See you later.'

And with that they were gone. The door slammed behind them and Emily was left alone by the fire. It was tempting to remain there a little longer, but Mrs Hansen might walk in at any moment, and there was no way to explain this. She stood up and dusted off the chair. Time to get back to work, but perhaps it wouldn't be so bad, if some in the family cared about her wellbeing. She started back towards the front door, but she couldn't help but notice the books now. Shelves of them, covering the walls. There must be hundreds. She examined them more closely. There were some she recognised, but many more were new to her. History, religion, science, art, and many more. Novels and poems too. She wondered who Madeleine was. How wonderful to be brought a book as a present. She was certain she would read it if someone did that for her.

The clock in the hall chimed. Four. There was still so much to do. She turned back to the door and resumed her scrubbing.

***

At seven she rang the gong and the family assembled in the dining room. Sebastian had joined them and Thaddeus Hansen, Richard's father, had come in from the office shortly before. She wasn't sure what to make of him at first. Dressed in a sober charcoal suit with Victorian mutton chop whiskers, he was an intimidating figure as he hurried past to get dressed for dinner. When he returned in white tie and tails, she was bringing the soup into the room. On seeing her he grinned broadly, immediately disarming her initial impression of him.

'Good evening. I'm so sorry I'm late. I was detained at the office. You must be our new maid.'

'Emily, sir', she replied, with a respectful bob.

'Capital. We need someone to keep us in line, don't we Richard?'

'You do, Papa, certainly.'

Thaddeus let out a huge guffaw and took his place at the table, under the watchful eye of his wife, who narrowed her eyes and knocked his elbows off the table with a quick swipe.

'Thaddeus, she's a servant.'

'Yes, Mary, my dear, I'm sorry. I'm just being friendly.'

'Please stop.'

He made a gesture to indicate he was buttoning his mouth and winked at Richard and Sebastian, who stifled a laugh. Emily began to serve the soup and went to Richard first as he was nearest. He flicked his head discreetly towards his mother and hissed in a whisper:

'Ladies first. Then my father. Let them serve themselves.'

She nodded in gratitude and he smiled back. She made her way around the table and held the bowl for his mother to serve herself.

'How is Madeleine?' asked his mother.

'She's well enough I believe,' replied Richard, somewhat testily. 'Although we spent more time discussing the health of her horse, her dog and other four-legged creatures.'

'Don't be facetious, Richard. She's from a good, respectable family. She's a good match for you.'

Richard opened his mouth to reply, but seemed to think better of it, and turned his attention to his soup instead, which Emily had just finished serving. Emily left the room and went down to the kitchen. When she returned to clear away the plates Sebastian was addressing the table.

'His estate demands much of his time and it's taking its toll on him I think. I've always said I will return there if he needs me, but he says no.'

'I'm sorry to hear it. I've asked my brother many times if I can assist, but to no avail as you know. He's stubborn. Still, I'm very glad you are here, Sebastian.'

'I haven't mentioned my visits here, uncle. I don't want to get caught in it.'

Thaddeus nodded in understanding and wiped his mouth with his napkin. Mary Hansen noticeably rolled her eyes at this, before turning back to Sebastian.

'He wishes you to better yourself, which is laudable. It's a great opportunity for you.'

'Yes, I'm very aware of it, Aunt Mary.'

Sebastian dropped his head, as if weighed down by the thought. Emily studied Richard, who had a look of serious contemplation. He looked from Sebastian to his father, then noticed her attention. He flashed a smile, restoring a facade that he seemed embarrassed to have momentarily dropped.

***

At the end of that long first day Emily fell into her bed and lay for a moment, just appreciating the relief on her aching muscles. She noticed the quiet first. Aside from the gentle tick of a clock from the kitchen, it was silent. Many times she'd wished for a moment of quiet in the noise of a dormitory, but actually she would have preferred the distraction now. She tried to think of the room around her as 'home', but she struggled to think she would ever be genuinely comfortable there. She envied Richard. She would give worlds to be in his place, with a professional career mapped out, whether he was happy about it or not. She snapped herself back. Her mother would tell her off for dreaming of impossible things, before breakfast or at any other time. 'It's unjust,' she would say, 'but that's the life we have.' It became a refrain which Emily tired of hearing. It was true that the things she dreamed of - education, travel, security, real happiness - might be unreachable. But a part of her wouldn't let go of them. That would be real failure. But it was becoming harder to find a chink of hope, and today it had felt further away than ever, until he had held her hand. She tingled at the memory and closed her eyes.

Chapter Five

September 1915
Loos, France

Hansen steadied himself as Sergeant Cairns came towards him. What he really wanted was for Cairns to make the decision for him, but that would never do.

'Sir, are we pushing on?'

No escape now. He'd have to call it.

'Well---' he began, weakly.

'It's just, some of the lads are for going on, come what may, but I was saying to them that you'd want to dig in, that being the sensible thing to do. These young boys get a rush of blood, don't they?'

'Indeed. Though I like their spirit,' he temporised. 'Please organise a watch and the others can rest. We will hold here and await new orders. And take a roll call.'

'Yes, sir.' And with a click of the heels, he was off.

Sergeant Cairns was a 'Mons man'. He'd been in it since the start, and a professional long before that. He was perhaps fifteen years older than Hansen and steady as a rock, or at least he appeared to be. He could never feel the way Hansen was feeling now.

He wanted to find somewhere to sit before he passed out, as he believed he was about to do, but with soldiers milling about this was easier said than done. He forced himself to march down the trench, receiving salutes as he went and taking his time over it. It was affected for the benefit of his men, and he wondered how many other officers were simply acting the part. Corporal Allen made his obeisance and offered him a mug of tea.

'Thank you, Corporal.'

He took the mug and automatically began to raise it to his lips, before realising that his hand was shaking noticeably. He looked around him to check if anyone had seen. He couldn't tell. They seemed caught up in their own affairs, but he couldn't be sure. They would never be that obvious about it, but behind his back they'd share a laugh about the officer who got the wind up.

'Roll call complete, sir,' broke in Cairns, who returned to Hansen's side without him noticing. It was as much as he could do not to jump in surprise.

'And?' asked Hansen.

'45 present and correct, sir. Of which, eight walking wounded. 46 missing, including Captain Harris, sir.'

'Thank you, S'ant Cairns.' He'd known it of course, but to hear the official report struck home.

'Here, sir.' To his bafflement, Cairns was offering him a handkerchief.

Hansen looked up from the handkerchief and followed Cairns' eyes to his sleeve. In quiet horror he realised that blood and gore, sticky and thick, was trickling from his sleeve onto his hand. His trousers were stained as well. He took the handkerchief and started wiping the remains of Captain Harris from his hand, as if it were something he did routinely.

'Have you organised a watch?' he asked.

'Yes, sir. I thought perhaps Lieutenant Peters should take first watch?'

Peters was even younger than he was. In fact, he suspected he was underage. He couldn't have him issuing orders while he lazed on a bunk.

'No, I'll take the first. Which other officers do you have?'

'None, sir. As far as I know.'

'Very well. Will you take a watch as well?'

'Yes, sir.'

The realities of war, that he could leave the death of comrades so unremarked. But it couldn't be otherwise. It would have to be for others to do the grieving. He imagined a distraught mother, sweetheart, wife, children, and then wished he hadn't. He began to walk down the trench in search of a quiet space to think, but Cairns followed at his heels. He realised he should have dismissed him, but he'd look a fool if he did so now.

'I want a firing step on this side,' he ordered, turning to point at the back of the trench, which had become the new front line.

As he pointed, he noticed a soldier, busy taking the boots off one of the dead Germans. It might have been the man he himself had killed. He couldn't be sure, but either way the thought of robbing the body disgusted him. He pulled his swagger stick from his boot and rapped the soldier hard on the knuckles. The soldier turned to confront his attacker, but quickly shrank away when he spotted the officer's uniform. It was harsh. They all did it, even though technically it was frowned upon. German kit was often better, and if not, he could sell it. He wouldn't win friends by being seen as a jobsworth, but he couldn't help it. Without some code of conduct they would be as bad as the enemy. The atrocities in Belgium were fresh in everyone's minds, and he needed to know the moral high ground was theirs. Or that God was on their side, as the padre would put it. Here he was now, shuffling along the trench, sharing a joke with some of the men.

'I'll see to that, sir,' cut in Cairns. It took Hansen a moment to remember the order he'd given.

'You've got to give the squareheads credit for knowing how to build a trench, sir. The bloody thing is lined with concrete.'

Hansen winced at the term. He had never liked it. Cairns was looking around admiringly. He was right though, it put the British trenches to shame. More worrying that they were digging in for the long haul.

'You wouldn't be thinking of complaining about the accommodation, would you Sergeant?' said Hansen, forcing himself to affect a nonchalance that he didn't feel. 'Provided at great expense by His Majesty's armed forces?'

'No sir, not <u>thinking</u> about it, as such,' replied Cairns, with a twinkle.

'You should see the dugouts,' interjected Crosse, who had now joined them. 'Hot and cold running rats.' He cocked his head to one side and took his round glasses off to clean them, much good it would do them.

'Carry on, Sergeant,' said Crosse. Cairns came to attention and moved off to begin barking orders at the men.

Hansen tried once again to lift the mug of increasingly cold tea to his lips, and once again his hand shook visibly. Crosse noticed and discreetly pulled out a hip flask.

'I find this improves the taste of army tea no end.'

He poured some whisky into the tea, which Hansen steadied with both hands before gulping some down. He could feel a warmth in his throat which eased the tension in his muscles.

'Thank you.'

Crosse smiled in acknowledgement and then nodded towards a group of officers approaching.

'I think you'd better report, Richard.'

The party included Major Dawes, the battalion commander, whom Hansen had only seen at a distance up to this point. He was a short man with greying hair and an elaborate moustache hanging on his top lip, his jaw jutting forward like a bulldog. There was also a captain he didn't recognise, who was looking through a periscope, and several other lieutenants. He guessed the butcher's bill for officers had been high across the whole line. Crosse took the mug from him, and Hansen tentatively approached the officers. Major Dawes noted his approach and turned to him as if trying to place the name of someone he had once met at a disappointing party.

'Lieutenant?' asked Dawes.

'Hansen, sir. Reporting for 'C' company. Captain Harris is dead.'

Dawes nodded, examining something under his fingernail.

'Continue.'

'Company at half strength, sir. 45 present.'

Dawes turned to the group, gesturing extravagantly with a sweeping motion to the trench around them.

'Thank you, gentlemen. We're not going to hold this. Prepare for orderly withdrawal. I want to clear out before they realise how few we are---'

The captain with the periscope turned back suddenly.

'Counter-attack, sir!'

'Damn it,' said Dawes. 'Very well, stand to.'

The others rushed off to their units, leaving only the captain. Hansen was rooted to the spot, unsure of what to do next. The captain smiled at him.

'Better get back to your company, Lieutenant… Hansen, is it? You're in command now, like it or not.'

'Yes,' replied Hansen, to both comments.

'I'm Captain Martin, by the way,' said the captain, shaking hands. 'Duncan.'

'Richard.'

'Well, good luck.'

Captain Martin turned on his heels and made off, leaving Hansen to return to the company of men who would now be looking to him. This was the time to counter-attack, before they had made the trench secure. Without even a proper firing step in place it would be a scramble to respond and his depleted and exhausted company would be facing fresh troops, keen to catch them off guard. Tactical knowledge slowly began to come back to him, and he could see the landscape in front of them with crystal clarity. It was suddenly obvious where he needed to place machine guns to create a killing zone and how he needed to organise his troops. He moved with certainty for the first time and a new wave of energy galvanised him.

'Stand to!' he shouted as he made his way along the line. 'Lieutenant Peters!'

A slender lad, every inch the George Arthur to his Tom Brown, he scrambled his way towards Hansen, looking fired up. He was not short of courage, that was clear.

'Peters, I want your platoon to fix bayonets. Spread out down our line and I want your men to turn back any enemy that makes it through.'

'Yes, sir!'

He turned the other way and found Sergeant Cairns and Corporal Allen busy turning boxes into an improvised firing step.

Two soldiers from his own platoon, Privates Veale and Challacombe, were manhandling a machine gun into position.

'Challacombe, Veale, I want that Lewis gun set up from here for flanking fire.' He pointed to a communications trench running at a right angle and towards the advancing enemy. 'Intersect with B company.'

He deployed others to cover the communications trench itself, and there was soon a steady rat-a-tat of machine gun fire. Now it was their turn to feel the teeth of mechanised war. On they came, and down they fell. It seemed unsporting somehow. Where was the honour in lurking behind sandbags like a coward and firing 400 rounds a minute at an enemy who had nowhere to hide and nothing to protect them?

***

The day wore on and they came again and again, wave after wave. He lost count of the fallen. Three times a scattered group made it into the trench and Peters' flying platoon rounded them up and dealt swiftly with them. The boy exchanged blows with a German twice his size and finally forced his bayonet through the man's ribs. He seemed unsure how to react when the giant fell dead at his feet. Half delighted, half shocked, he turned to Hansen looking for some guidance. All he could do was nod and order him to continue the fight.

The sun set and the attacks continued. Hansen's small force was shrinking steadily and if this kept up, they must surely retreat, or die trying. He rubbed his eyes and looked for the thousandth time through the periscope. The remnants of the last foray were seeking cover, or were they? They seemed to be turning back and running.

'They're falling back, sir!' said Veale

'Got them on the run now,' chipped in Private Challacombe

'Steady, Challacombe,' replied Hansen. 'They haven't chucked it up yet.'

But he had to conceal his own delight for the sake of appearance. It did seem they were turning tail and running for cover. Sergeant Cairns collapsed beside him, out of breath.

'Major Dawes' compliments, sir, we are to hold here and not pursue the enemy.'

'Very good.'

As if they could if they wanted to. Hansen uncoiled himself from his position and tried to stretch his limbs. He realised he hadn't eaten all day and he was suddenly ravenous.

'Have the men eaten, Sergeant?'

'No sir, we haven't managed to organise anything.'

'See to it.'

Cairns saluted and scurried away. It might only be tea and iron rations, but it would do wonders for morale, and he was hungry enough to eat the tin. Food and sleep, in either order, was what he most desired in the world, but it would have to wait. He found his way into what looked like an officer's dugout and discovered a gramophone with a record still in place, and a filled pipe resting beside it. Had their owner run, and was he missing them now? Or was he one of those lying outside, bootless and lifeless?

'I see you've found yourself a comfortable billet.'

Hansen turned to find Captain Martin in the doorway.

'What were they listening to?'

'I'm not sure,' replied Hansen.

'You look contemplative. What were you thinking about?'

'I was just wondering who they belonged to.'

'Some fellow who is missing a good smoke right about now, I should think,' said Martin, lightly. 'I don't know about you, but I'm in need of a drink. Hot work, all this.'

Martin pulled a silver hipflask from his pocket and unscrewed the top. He handed it to Hansen, who noticed an inscription in Latin around the top: '*Quod me nutrit me destruit*'.

'What nourishes me, also destroys me' said Martin, noticing his interest in the words.

'A bit bleak, isn't it?'

'Perhaps. But accurate. Finest single malt is a noble destroyer in any case.'

Hansen took a swig and gratefully felt the whisky burn the back of his throat. He handed the flask back to Martin.

'Here's to your first show, Richard.'

'Is it always like this?'

'I wouldn't know,' replied the Captain, taking a long gulp.

They sat together in silence, sharing the flask between them. Hansen examined the record sleeve. It was a recording of Schubert. Symphony number four. It was a piece that his father enjoyed. They often played it when Sebastian visited, at his cousin's request.

A distant clanging broke in gradually on his thoughts. The noise became louder and somehow more urgent, travelling down the trench towards them. Then it became clear that the sound was a gong, the signal for a gas attack.

'Gas helmets are called for I think,' said Martin languidly, as he stood and began to unpack his own. Then he was off and running down the trench towards his men. Hansen followed him out, just as a sickly green fog began to flood across the top of the trench.

'Helmets on!' he shouted, needlessly, as his men were already scrambling to get the coverings over their heads. It seemed unlikely that such a thing could protect them, but it was all they had.

Then in horror he realised that young Peters was coughing, unable to untangle a gas helmet which was in any case too big for him.

'Sergeant,' he called, as he saw Cairns making his way along the line, checking that the others had secured their masks. 'Watch for the enemy.'

He turned his attention to Peters. The young man was panicking and failing to see that the helmet was inside out. Hansen grabbed it from him and gave it a sharp flick to reverse it. Then he pulled it out and forced it onto Peters' head. He could feel the chlorine gas burning his throat and his eyes were beginning to stream. The mask was too loose, so he ripped his lanyard from his revolver, took the other end from around his neck and tied it around the young lieutenant's neck to secure the baggy helmet in place, pulling it tight, so much so that he thought he might throttle poor Peters. He began to retch, but only when he was sure the contraption was secure did he put his own on. It was little better inside, the canvas close against his face and the metal tube cold in his mouth. He took a difficult breath and searched around him, seeing little through the tiny eyeholes.

With shouts and screams, shadowy figures appeared from the mist, but it was impossible at first to understand what was happening. Then the distinctive outline of a pickelhaube helmet confirmed his fear. There was no need to issue orders, his men were resisting as best they could. Private Veale was swinging a trench club at one. Sergeant Cairns was wrestling another, his sheer strength pulling the German off his feet.

Hansen drew his revolver and then in a sudden flurry an enemy officer had him by the throat and he was grappling, desperately trying to force the hands from his neck. The grip tightened and he felt his own strength ebb as the immoveable force continued to hold fast. Through the fogged eye holes, he could see a figure, masked as he was. There was no sign of humanity, no sign of pity behind the glassy eyes. Was this what it felt like? To drift away from consciousness, like moving further and further from shore. He felt calm enough to just let it happen, but he must lead.

He twisted his leg around in a wrestling move he had last deployed at school and just for a moment had his enemy off balance. The grip loosened and he ripped the arms away. He sucked air in and took the initiative. His revolver was locked in the grip of his assailant and he forced it by turns, pushing it towards the other man so that the revolver rested against his chest, the barrel pointing up. It took all his strength to hold it there as he edged his thumb free and pulled back the hammer. Their hands were shaking with effort as he finally reached his aim and squeezed the trigger.

A loud concussion and a gust of air rushed upwards as all tension was released and Hansen fell forwards onto his attacker. They landed together on the ground, but the man's hands were still locked onto his. Blood had splattered across the eye holes and the German's helmet had a huge gash ripped into the top. What was left of his skull was leaking out. Hansen let out a huge breath and tried to pull himself clear. As he forced the man's grip away from his own the German's canvas mask began to shift away, revealing an eye, lifeless and dilated, of the deepest blue. Seized with a need to know the man he had ended, he pulled the mask back.

He choked, unable to breath. It might have been the gas, except that it was rapidly dispersing now, and his own mask was still in place. He ripped it from his face and tried to take in the air, but it was no better. Someone's arm was around his shoulder now, holding him up.

'It's alright, sir, medics are coming.'

Chapter Six

1919

Exeter

Emily rolled the pastry again, puffs of flour tickling her nose. She was already behindhand, and Mrs Hansen would not be pleased if dinner were late again. She silently wished for no disturbances to delay her further, and just as she did, the doorbell jangled behind her.

She cursed under her breath and wiped her hands, resenting every step she took towards the front door. If it were the grocer's boy again, who somehow always refused to use the back door, she would send him packing and enjoy doing it.

She reached the front door and wearily pulled it open, ready to vent her temper on whoever stood on the other side, but all was forgotten when she realised who the visitor was. Excitement overtook her and she couldn't stop herself smiling from ear to ear. She was sure she looked like a crazed lunatic, but the delight was real.

'Oh my! You're back, sir!'

He nodded back slowly. He obviously did think she was mad, but she was so relieved to see him, that she didn't care. Now he was smiling too.

'Hello, Emily. How are you?'

The same smile as that first time they'd met. Then she'd wanted to hug him for the kindness he showed her. She hadn't, but now she couldn't stop herself. She wrapped her arms around him and felt his warmth again. The relief at knowing he was finally safe. But she could feel his awkwardness, and she knew at once this was madness. She pulled back, embarrassed.

'I'm sorry, sir. Forgive me, I wasn't thinking.'

'It's alright, I'm pleased to see you as well,' he replied, with ill-concealed embarrassment. 'I'm pleased to see all of you.'

Emily realised that Mrs Hansen was standing quietly behind her. Without looking she knew the expression she must have. A restrained contempt and disgust. Emily backed away, avoiding eye contact, and stowed herself in the porch.

'Richard,' said his mother.

'Mother,' he replied stiffly, smile gone now.

His mother inclined her head slowly to allow Richard to gently kiss her on the cheek.

'We weren't expecting you.'

'Things have been rather hectic. I'm sorry that I couldn't wire ahead.'

Emily watched in astonishment. After four years, risking his life, this was all his mother could say? There must be some feeling, some love there, and yet there was no outward sign. He could have been a passing stranger. She wondered at the reaction if it had been her own mother, and rather enjoyed the thought of what that reunion would have been like. She would have hugged her close just as he had. She smiled at the thought.

'And who is your friend?' said Mary Hansen, looking at the little round-faced man standing behind Richard, cleaning his glasses.

'This is Reverend Crosse. He was the padre in our battalion.'

'Delighted to meet you Mr Crosse. Won't you come in?'

'Thank you, you're exceedingly kind,' replied the little man, with good grace.

Emily went back inside, and the others followed. She took their coats and bags and stood back. He looked older, there was no doubt about it. The sparkle in those eyes seemed to be dulled. Was it so surprising? More than anything she wanted to sit and talk to him, like they had before. Those times when he would come down to the kitchen to chat about this and that. He would talk and she would listen, mostly, just pleased not to be alone. Maybe he was too.

They went into the parlour, and Emily followed, ostensibly waiting for instructions, but equally, to stay close to Richard. He noticed her watching, but whereas previously that would have occasioned a kindly smile or a joke, now he turned away.

'Emily, make yourself useful, girl. Fetch some tea and then you can make up Mr Richard's room for him, and one for Mr Crosse as well, if you're staying Mr Crosse?'

'If it's not too much trouble?'

'You're very welcome.' She turned impatiently in Emily's direction. 'Well?'

'Yes, ma'am.'

Emily turned and made for the door.

'She's a good girl, but not very bright.'

The door closed behind her.

***

Emily rolled the hot water around the teapot slowly to warm it. 'Not very bright' she repeated, to herself, quietly seething. She threw the water into the sink and nearly the teapot with it. She stepped back and took a deep breath. There was nothing to be served by getting angry. So many times she'd dreamed about choosing just the right words and venting her frustration. Storming out of the house and throwing her apron in her face. Count to five and twenty, she told herself, like Tattycoram, though it might do as much good.

Emily approached the door to the parlour, her temper little repaired, carrying the tray of tea, and stopped to knock on the door. Without waiting for a response, she pressed down on the handle and stomped into the room. No one there was speaking. The new guest, Mr Crosse, was searching the ceiling for something of interest. Mrs Hansen was examining the pleats in her skirt, and Richard simply sat there, looking ahead. His expression was so pitiable that her temper vanished. She could sense something. Something that she struggled to put her finger on. She'd seen it before when he'd tried to conceal a sadness, but what was worse now was that he couldn't hide it. She placed the tray carefully on the table.

'Ah, tea. Shall I be mother?' said Mrs Hansen, like a marionette jerked back into life once more.

'I wish you would,' said Richard, under his breath, but loud enough for all to hear.

Emily took some tea to Mr Crosse and Mrs Hansen poured a second cup. Emily moved quickly to pick it up. She turned briskly to take it to Richard, but she hadn't heard him approach and delivered the hot tea straight down his front. With a yelp he began cursing to himself and Emily moved to help him wipe it off.

'For goodness' sake! I wish you'd stop fussing!'

Richard pushed her away with an unexpected forcefulness, and she lost her balance, steadying herself on the table and knocking over the other cups in the process.

'Mind what you're doing, girl!' shouted Mrs Hansen

'I'm sorry, ma'am.'

The Richard of old would have been quick to apologise, if he would ever have reacted in such a way, but there was no apology.

He simply sat down heavily in his chair and looked away. She could feel her face getting hot with embarrassment as she tried to clear away the mess, with Mrs Hansen tutting at every clumsy attempt.

'I'm suddenly quite tired,' said Mr Crosse abruptly, rising from his chair. 'I'd like to see my room if that's possible, and perhaps lie down?' He touched Emily lightly on the arm. 'Would you show me?'

'Of course, sir.'

'We shall see you for dinner, Mr Crosse,' said Mrs Hansen as Emily led him towards the door. Mr Crosse nodded and shot a brief but intense look at Richard, who looked up momentarily from his chair.

Emily led the clergyman towards the stairs.

'This way, sir.'

But Mr Crosse stopped and took his glasses off, waiting in the hallway. From where they stood, they could hear the conversation continuing in the parlour.

'I hope you won't drive the maid off,' said Mrs Hansen. 'It's not easy to find help nowadays. Every girl thinks to have a career.'

'I need a real drink' responded Richard, with a clink of glass indicating that he had helped himself from the decanter.

'Will you be going back up to Oxford?'

'Today?' he replied curtly.

'Don't be flippant. I meant when you've --- properly settled back in.'

'I don't think so.'

'You'd waste your father's investment?'

'Is that what it is? A waste is what it is for certain.'

There was a thump of a glass on the table, and Richard stormed out, slamming the parlour door behind him.

'Waste, waste, waste---'

He turned to notice them, and his eyes met Emily's. There was a hint of a half-smile for just a moment that seemed to suggest an apology of sorts, and then he turned and walked out of the front door, closing it behind him.

***

'I'd like to raise a toast,' said Thaddeus Hansen. 'To my courageous son Richard, and our new friend Mr Crosse and their safe return. May the enemy have learned well the might of the British Empire!'

Emily returned the wine to the sideboard as Thaddeus raised his glass expectantly. Crosse took his glass and joined in good-naturedly. Mrs Hansen stiffly followed suit, while Richard remained stone-faced, draining his glass. Emily took the wine to him to refill his glass. He looked up at her, as if to say something, but she looked away quickly.

'Richard, it's so good to have you home,' said Thaddeus.

'Thank you, Papa.'

There was warmth in the reply. But submerged behind something else. An apathy that seemed to rob him of all the energy that had been his defining characteristic. A love of life and all the possibilities it offered. Possibilities for a future that he dreamed of and could make real, while she could only dream.

'You don't seem yourself,' said his father. 'Is the wine not to your liking? It was recommended to me by my great friend Sir Francis Acland, you know?'

'I'm fine.'

'Sir Francis Acland, the politician?' cut in Mr Crosse. 'Do you know him?'

'Oh yes, I know him well.'

Richard threw his head back with a sneer.

'You met him once.'

Where once upon a time this might have been a playful joke, this time it was said with a bitterness that she had never seen before. His father could not help but look hurt.

'I… well. He was kind to me and was good enough to suggest this wine.'

It was sad to see the old man brought so low, as silence enveloped the table. There had always been something slightly absurd about him, but he meant well. Richard had always been comfortable in his own skin. The middle-class gentleman who knew what it was to be that person. It was something his father aspired to but had never quite mastered. She had heard him speak of humble origins, but Richard had never been so unkind as to throw light on them like this before. Richard caught her eye and she realised she was scowling at him. He looked down and took another swig of wine while Emily returned downstairs.

Some time later she returned to the dining room to find Thaddeus, composure restored, entertaining Mr Crosse with one of his courtroom stories. Richard turned sharply as she entered the room, as if startled, then tried to hide his reaction and turned back to his glass, which he was studying, glassy-eyed. His father tried to draw him into the conversation.

'Richard, you didn't tell me that you are to be awarded a medal. I had to find out from Barraclough. He read about it in the paper. What is it, the Distinguished Service Medal?'

'Order,' said Richard, barely looking up. 'Distinguished Service Order.'

'You didn't say, Richard,' said Crosse, with a genuine look of admiration. 'That's quite an honour!'

'It's nothing. They hand them out to staff officers.'

'Hardly. DSOs don't grow on trees you know. What was it for?'

'An action on the Italian front,' said Richard. Emily noticed the corners of his mouth turn up slightly, as they always had when he was embarrassed by a compliment. He cleared his throat and took another gulp of wine. 'We took a machine gun emplacement.'

'I think you're being modest,' said his father. 'From what he told me it was more than that. The report said single-handed?'

'I did my duty, we all did.'

'Well, I don't know,' said Thaddeus. 'If I won a distinguished--- wotsit, I'd be telling everyone who'd listen.'

'Will you receive it from the king?' asked his mother

'I don't know.'

'I'm sure not many at Oxford will have such an honour,' said his mother with considerable relish.

Richard drained his glass and sat with his eyes closed. He looked ill suddenly, as if he might be sick, but the others hadn't noticed. Emily was forced to leave the room once again, carrying her concern with her.

***

Pausing on the stairs, Emily took a moment to rest. As she did so a half-remembered thought came to her. Something she had read. 'Would you like to live with your soul in the grave?' She put it aside just as quickly. If that was Richard's path, the thought was too troubling. And in any case, he would never see her in the way Heathcliff had seen Cathy.

She pushed the door open into the dining room. Port was being passed around and Richard was filling his glass, slumped in his chair. His attention was turned away from the decanter by his name being called.

'What?' he enquired of his father.

His mother cringed at the coarse response.

'Pardon, Richard.'

'I didn't say anything,' said Richard, drunkenly amused by his own joke, while Mrs Hansen quietly clucked her displeasure.

'I was asking what stories you can tell us about the war.'

'They're not stories Conan-Doyle would tell, Papa.'

Something of the old twinkle was evident now, released by the alcohol from whatever was smothering him.

'Our generals could have done with Sherlock Holmes, eh?' said his father. 'He would have sorted them out. No, but I just want to hear about what you got up to.'

A pleading, hopeful look on his father's face was shut down with a simple shake of the head from his son.

'Well. As you like.'

'Mr Hansen, I should explain,' said Mr Crosse. 'We soldiers are odd souls. For us it's about the unit, not the individual. The best officers, and if he doesn't mind my saying, I include Richard in this, they only think of their men. At the risk of giving him a swollen head, I once saw your son rescue another officer who was unable to secure his gas helmet, at great risk to himself---'

Emily turned to Richard, expecting to see the look of embarrassed pleasure once again curling his lips. Instead, he seemed to be struggling to breathe and was as pale as the tablecloth which his head was about to touch. Instinctively she went to his side of the table, unsure of what to do. He was pouring with sweat and looked ready to pass out. His hand was touching the stem of his glass, and there was a noticeable tremor in it.

'If he hadn't intervened, I doubt Lieutenant Peters would have survived,' continued Crosse, oblivious.

'Can we talk about something else,' said Richard, with difficulty. 'Please?'

He had made an effort to raise his head from the table, but it fell back quickly. The others now took notice and Crosse stopped what he was saying. From where she was, Emily could see Richard's eyes were screwed up tight. Not knowing what else to do, she poured him some water and put it into his hand.

'I'm sorry old man,' said Mr Crosse. 'I didn't mean to embarrass you.'

'I think you've probably had enough to drink' said his mother, with little sympathy.

Crosse slowly took off his glasses and made a show of cleaning them, but with one eye fixed on Richard.

'Mr Hansen tell me about your work,' he said while peering through the lenses. 'You're a solicitor I believe?'

'Indeed,' replied Thaddeus. 'Not very interesting I'm afraid. Some conveyancing, boundary disputes. I do a lot of agricultural work. I wanted to serve in the army when I was a boy, it was the traditional thing for second sons to do where I grew up. But my health was always a little fragile you understand.'

'I'm sorry to hear it,' said Crosse, half-listening.

'Will you see something of our city while you are here, Mr Crosse?

'Yes, that's my intention,' he replied, replacing his glasses finally and smiling a little as he noted Richard's colour beginning to return. 'It's a beautiful city.'

'Yes, I'm sure we can show you something of it.'

The padre nodded appreciatively as Emily began to gather up the plates and returned to the kitchen.

***

Hours later Emily had finally finished cleaning up and was making her way upstairs to lock up. She registered the hallway clock striking midnight and yawned, almost in response to the lateness of the hour. She turned to go into the parlour, which was dark save for a lamp turned low. As she stooped to extinguish it, she was startled by movement in the chair next to her. Richard shifted into the light, a nearly empty decanter of brandy next to him. She pulled back.

'I'm sorry, sir, I didn't realise anyone was still up.'

'Just barely. Though somewhat horizontally.' He giggled at his own joke.

'I'll go, sir, unless there's anything you need?'

He picked up the decanter and looked through the glass at her.

'What does anyone need? "Someone to love and someone to love you, a cat, a dog, and a pipe or two, enough to eat and enough to wear, and a little more than enough to drink; for thirst is a dangerous thing!"'

She couldn't help smiling in recognition. He surely didn't remember that it was her favourite book. In her minds-eye she could see the younger Richard sitting on the kitchen worktop complaining that Sebastian couldn't see the merit of such comic novels or comic operas, and then going on to entertain her with an unaccompanied verse or two from HMS Pinafore. Maybe that man was still there.

'I think you should sleep, sir.'

'"To sleep, perchance to dream. But in that sleep of death what dreams may come?"'

He stared at her intently and in his eyes there was a depth of sadness she couldn't measure. This angry man was broken. Desperate. It was painful, and the happy drunk was suddenly pathetic and lost.

'What do you think of me, Emily? Truthfully?'

How could she be truthful? In all honesty she was so very sad for him and wanted him to know it.

'I couldn't say, sir.'

'I think you can, but you're a good girl. Too good for me. I could change that---'

He fumbled to his feet and moved unsteadily towards her. She backed away and found herself against the wall as he moved close.

'You're as pretty as any French girl, you know, and I knew my share.'

'I don't want to know, sir.'

His lips were close enough to kiss now.

'Don't you? Haven't you thought about this? In your kitchen, all alone? In your room at night?'

This was torture. Of course she had, so many times, but this was wrong. She hated him for wanting her now, like this, and hated herself for still wanting him.

'Not like this.'

'No, it's not very gentle, is it? But then gentlemen don't do what I've done. Why shouldn't I be what I am? A savage.'

But his eyes made a lie of what he said. She couldn't believe he could be so totally reversed in character. 'Someone to love' – was this what he meant? But she couldn't give him this, it would ruin her. No job, if Mrs Hansen found out, no life. For one night. His hand touched her waist and pulled her closer. His other hand caressed her face, tenderly, despite his claim.

'I want to help you, sir.'

She wanted to scream out, to run and hide. And at the same time, to touch him as he was touching her.

'Then come with me.'

He took her hand and began to sway towards the door, pulling her with him. The strength of his grip frightened her. She couldn't resist him.

Richard reached for the stairs but lost his footing and fell. He lay in a heap, struggling to get up and it occurred to her that she could leave him there if she wanted. But she didn't. She looked down at him and offered her hand, pulling him up with all her strength. They climbed the stairs together, one by one, and she had to prop him up with each step.

At the top he scratched at the door to his room for at least a minute before it finally flew open and he staggered in, collapsing onto the bed. She could have turned away, but she followed him inside and closed the door behind her. Her hands shook as she began to pick at each button on her dress.

"'Sorrow, I baptize thee in the name of the Father, and the Son, and the Holy Ghost,'" she muttered to herself.

She turned again to the figure on the bed. He had not stirred. Then there was a snort and he turned onto his back in a drunken sleep.

She put her hands to her face as tears began to form. She fell into the chair beside the bed and watched him sleep. She saw herself in a white gown lying next to him and chided the little girl of her imagination for her naiveté.

'No angel,' she said to herself quietly.

She pushed his legs onto the bed, took his shoes off, and placed a blanket over him.

Chapter Seven

1919
Exeter

Gas swirled around him. Dark figures loomed at him from the mists and the revolver felt heavy in his hand. Try as he might, he couldn't cock it, and it began to feel heavier and heavier, until he could no longer hold it.

A figure grabbed for him from the darkness and he turned away, but his feet stuck into the mud and he was wading, an inch at a time, the hand getting ever closer. He cried out for help, but no words would come. No words. He fought and fought to get free.

And then he jerked upright in a panic, terror seizing him. As he left sleep behind the fear began to subside, and gradually he could make out the room around him in the half-light of dawn. His heart slowed as he saw the pictures on the wall of his childhood room. He breathed again and wiped sweat from his top lip. His other hand was still held tight. He turned over to find Emily sitting next to him, holding his hand in hers. Her eyes betrayed concern. He wanted to tell her she should not worry, but his mouth was cracked and dry. She handed him some water and he drank gratefully.

'Thank you. What time is it?'

'The sun's just coming up,' she replied, turning away from his gaze and looking out of the window. 'It's about five.'

'Did you ---'

He wasn't sure how to ask the question, or even what he was asking.

'I must go. Work to do. Try to sleep.'

She got up to leave, but their hands remained locked, neither letting go. After a moment she gently disengaged her hand and went to the door, turning back to look at him, the morning light playing across her face. He smiled and she went out, closing the door quietly behind her.

He wrenched himself from the bed, his head gently swirling, and a hammer pounding in his skull, and staggered to the door, falling onto the frame. His knee ached. As he opened it there was the sound of another door closing and he looked around. But Emily had gone.

***

At the breakfast table Richard nursed his head. His father was slicing into a piece of steak. Hot fat ran freely as he tore his knife into it and smeared it with mustard, and Richard's stomach turned over at the thought of it. At the other end of the table his mother spread marmalade onto toast and eyed him cautiously. Crosse was drinking his third or fourth cup of tea and dissecting a kipper.

Emily approached with a pot of coffee and poured him some.

'Have some. You'll feel better' she said quietly.

As he picked up the cup, he followed Emily with his eyes, and could see his mother also watching her intently.

'Fresh coffee please, girl,' ordered his mother.

'Yes, ma'am.'

Emily went downstairs and Hansen tried to force his brain to recall the previous evening. There was a hazy memory of holding Emily in his arms, but it was not a warm recollection, like the moment on the doorstep. He winced at the thought. What had he become that he would abuse her trust like this? He had always tried to protect her, but that was all for nought if she feared him now.

'I hope you get this, whatever it is, out of your system' said his mother.

'What do you mean?'

'I don't think we need discuss it here. The sooner things are back to normal, the better.'

She left the table. The implication was obvious, but it seemed unlikely she could know anything. Unless she'd seen them.

What would that mean? He got up awkwardly from the table and pursued her into the hall.

'What are you trying to say?' he pressed.

'I think you know,' replied his mother. 'Emily was in your room early this morning.'

So, she had seen.

'I don't care what you do in that regard.' She shifted uncomfortably. 'But I will not have this sort of behaviour in this house. And I will of course have to ask her to go.'

'No!' he protested. 'It is not what you think. Emily is entirely innocent in this. I simply had too much to drink and she was helping me upstairs. I fell asleep in the chair.'

His mother searched his face sceptically but seemed to believe him. It wasn't exactly a lie. For all he knew, it could be true. If only he could be sure.

'Very well,' she said at last. 'But you know as well as I do that the silly girl has always---'

She looked for the right word.

'---esteemed you. I won't have gossip spread around. I've spent years training her to be modestly efficient, but I can't have people thinking such things about her. It would reflect badly on me and your father. If I find out that you lied, she will be gone, with no reference.'

'Without a reference she wouldn't work again.'

'That's for the best if she should spread rumours about us. But of course, you wouldn't lie to me.'

She tilted her head and looked up at him with narrowed eyes.

'Would you?'

He shook his head. One lie to compound another. If it were a lie. She sighed heavily, convinced for now at least. Then she turned and went upstairs.

It was true that he suspected Emily was sweet on him at one time, and he'd even played on it a little when he was younger, teasing her with his attention. He found it endearing in a way, but she had been a girl, and it was no more than a girlish infatuation, if it were anything at all. Outside of being a servant, she was like a younger sister, and the thought that he might have wronged her troubled him greatly. He had felt so out of control since his return home, and the shadow that he felt lurking behind every corner was beginning to cast its shade over others too. He didn't know if he'd ever been a good man before, but if every man had a Mr Hyde hiding within him, his was surely ruling him now, and it scared him.

He descended the stairs carefully and could hear Emily crashing around in the kitchen. It was what she did when she was upset. He almost turned around, but he couldn't leave it like this. He stood in the kitchen doorway and watched her. She was drying plates, lost in thought. Was she thinking about last night? Hating him?

'Stay away' she said quietly.

'Did you say something?' he asked.

The question startled her, and she turned and dropped the plate she was holding, flushed with embarrassment.

'Excuse me,' he said. 'I didn't mean to make you jump.'

He bent over to help her, his knee tightening painfully. He took a sharp breath and grabbed it with his hand. He felt useless.

'I can manage, sir. Is there something you need?'

'No, I. Well---'

He dropped gingerly to his knees, but she began to back away from him. His head dropped, despairing. Her response was surely enough to tell him what he wanted to know. Or rather, what he didn't want to know. Shame filled him.

'Please don't look at me like that.'

'I don't know what you mean, sir.'

'Like I might---'

He stopped, unable to complete the thought. It was too horrible. He searched her expression, looking for a clue. There was fear there, he sensed, but something else too. He stood up painfully and turned away.

'Coming back here, it's not the same. Except it is, or I'm not. Whomever you thought I was---'

It was useless, there was no way to justify it, and it all seemed hollow, like so much meaningless talk.

'This is a good job, sir. I don't want to leave.'

And worse. Now she was in fear of her job, because of him. At least he could set her mind at rest on that score.

'That's not what I meant at all. There's no danger of that.'

He moved towards her again, but again she flinched away. Then he realised that this was her place. He was intruding.

'Carry on,' he said, as if addressing one of his soldiers.

He turned and walked back upstairs. He could feel her watching him go. He turned back and tried to sound as casual as he could.

'I meant to say. Ernie – Mr Crosse – has asked for some tea. Would you be able to bring some up? Tea for two.'

'Of course, sir.'

***

In the parlour Hansen sat alone in the same chair as the previous night. He started to rehearse an explanation, but it became clear that the only way he could explain his behaviour was if he understood it himself. Perhaps he should just continue as if nothing had happened. She had. But he couldn't be such a coward. He must lead.

He looked at the decanter beside him. Almost empty. A noble destroyer indeed. He picked it up and poured the remainder into a pot plant. As he sat back down, there was a gentle tap on the open door and Emily stood in the doorway, carrying a tray of tea things. He could see her noticing the empty decanter in his hand and he swiftly put it down.

Emily placed the tray on the table and looked behind her, as if planning a hurried escape. Worse and worse. He should never have begun this, but it was too late.

'Emily, please stay.'

She hesitated, and he started to serve the tea, gesturing for her to sit. He offered her one of the cups, but she looked back at the door.

'I need to get on, sir, if you don't mind.'

'Take the tea, please,' he said, trying to look as unthreatening as possible, and with a pale hint of a smile.

She took the cup reluctantly but stood at a distance.

'You can sit down.'

'It wouldn't be right, sir.'

'It would be. And please call me Richard.'

Emily perched on the very edge of a chair, ready to escape at any second. She held the tea at arm's length, as if it were a bedpan. The thought made him smile, which made her look even more suspicious.

'I'm sorry for intruding downstairs. I was trying to explain in my clumsy way about last night---' She shifted uncomfortably. 'I'm sure I behaved like a wretch. You must hate me.'

'No, sir.'

It was said with conviction, and she looked him in the eye for the first time that day.

'I pledge to lay off the drink from now on. Except tea, obviously.'

She was good enough to smile at his attempt at a joke.

'I hate to see the way my mother treats you. Heaven knows why you've stayed with us for so long. I would have been out that door long ago. Not that I'm encouraging you to do that,' he added quickly.

'It's not so bad, sir.'

'We can do better. The man I was four years ago would have done better. But somewhere along the way, I lost sight of him. There are things I miss about him. It seems to me sometimes I have an "antic disposition", except that there is no pretence in it.'

He had said more than he intended, and sat back in his chair, trying to distance himself from his words. He'd been used to sharing everything with her when he was younger. She had always listened, probably out of politeness. What else could she do?

'I think you know a hawk from a handsaw,' she said slowly, with an encouraging but nervous smile.

It was not the reply he expected, and it took him a moment to realise what she was saying.

'You know Hamlet?'

She nodded again. 'I read it.'

She was looking past him, and he followed the direction of her gaze, across to the books on the shelves. The books that his mother and father had accumulated, for show as much as anything. It was what was expected for a family of their status, or rather, of their pretentions.

'I see. Have you read others?'

She looked sheepish, nodding quickly, as if hoping he wouldn't notice.

'Which ones?'

'All of them.'

'Really?' he said with genuine astonishment.

The thought of her sneaking in, perhaps in the middle of the night, to 'borrow' books, and then return them, unnoticed, for what must have been years, astounded him. The sheer brazenness was remarkable and seemed out of character for the timid person he'd always assumed she was. If she thought he was angry, she couldn't be more wrong. As he looked at her it seemed to him that she was transformed. The girl that he'd been trying to persuade himself was in need of a protector was someone else entirely. It was surprising in the most delightful way. He'd made assumptions about people before. Sergeant Cairns had seemed like no more than a bluff old soldier on first view, but his wisdom was unique. He thought he had learned to avoid easy assumptions, but obviously there was more to learn. And now he was intrigued to discover what else was unexpected about Emily.

'That's more than I have,' he said. 'Any favourites?'

'So many,' she replied, smiling to herself. 'Jane Austen for one. William Blake. And Shakespeare of course. And *Three Men in a Boat*.' She arched an eyebrow at this, just for a moment, with a pointed look, as if testing him. 'You quoted from it last night.'

'I did? What did I quote?'

'"Someone to love and someone to love you"' she replied, with a careful emphasis on the last word.

'What was I thinking?'

He sat forward again. For the first time in days, perhaps longer, he could feel. It was uncertain, like a distant memory of a feeling, but it spread like lifeblood through his body. And then he could imagine what he was thinking, and he grinned involuntarily, a grin that spread across every unused muscle.

'My mother would not approve. She always said it was only a book for "common 'arrys and 'arriets". So, if you won't call me Richard, you can always call me 'arry!'

Emily sniggered. He remembered that laugh. Girlish and unselfconscious. It was the first time he'd heard it since he'd been back, and it brought a wave of nostalgia. Until this point, he hadn't seen anything to enjoy about being back home, but perhaps there was a spark left of his old life. Some ember that could be nurtured back into flame.

'Why such an interest in books?' he asked.

'You can travel anywhere and be anyone,' she replied, her eyes sparkling with conviction. 'I always imagined one day I could pass that on, like my mother did for me. Maybe be a schoolteacher. Silly I know.'

'It's a noble profession. Though I know some would look down on it.'

Emily's face fell and she took a sip of tea. Hansen realised his error. For her it was an ambition not too low, but out of reach.

'That's not what you meant.'

Emily didn't respond, but her expression made it clear he was right. But as he watched her, he began to consider what a waste it was that she had never thought this humble ambition to be realistic. Why shouldn't she be a teacher, just because it was not what was expected for her. Over the last few years, it had been made clear to him that rank was no predictor of someone's value.

'Good tea?' he asked. She nodded her assent. 'I poured it myself.'

Another little laugh. He wanted to make her laugh now, just to hear it.

'I still have my uses.'

Emily looked seriously at him and placed her cup down on the table in a determined gesture. She shifted to the edge of her seat and moved her hand towards his, which was resting on the arm of his chair, but pulled away before touching him, sweeping it back behind her head and smoothing through her hair nervously.

'What are you going to do now, sir? Now you're back?'

'I have no idea. I don't think I could aspire to teach. I don't have the brains! I only know I won't follow my father. Although my writing is enough of a scrawl to be a solicitor.'

The serious expression remained on her face.

'I think you write beautifully. In your letters.'

'You read my letters?'

He studied his teacup, considering what he'd said in those messages home. How much he had disclosed. He'd been circumspect certainly, it couldn't be otherwise, so it was odd that this would bother him so much. He'd hardly described the reality. More like a postcard from a seaside resort – wish you were here – and vivid descriptions of those around him. But if he were to believe that in some sense writing revealed the soul, to borrow from Tolstoy, even writing as bland as in his letters, there was an exposure in that.

Emily looked unsure of how to proceed, conscious of overstepping the bounds of a servant, but there was a relaxed confidence in her now which he was enjoying, and it was clear she wasn't going to let go.

'I'm sorry. I know that was wrong, but I wanted so badly to know how it was for you. What you were seeing and feeling. The papers, the newsreels, they only told some of it, didn't they?'

'War is not the glorious thing my father seems to think it is. But I would never have wanted to share my life there with you.'

'Why not?'

She was in earnest. He knew many at home were curious of the experience they'd had, but what would it serve? With Crosse there was no need to talk about it. With his family there was no wish to talk about it. With her it felt like standing on a precipice. He could easily tell her everything, as he always had, but it would be a burden on her when it was his to carry. And the man it had made him was not the man she had known. The idea of it brought memories crowding to the front of his mind, and he tried to force them down by getting up from his chair and walking to the other side of the room.

'I think you should follow the lead of good Queen Bess. A window into a man's soul can be a tricky thing.'

He sat heavily on the settee in the corner, but he was not alone for long. Emily had made her mind up, and crossed the room to sit next to him, as close as they had been since the evening before.

'I want to know,' she said, eyes fixed on his, determined but kindly. 'To understand.'

'There's a poem,' he said, returning her gaze. 'I'm sure you've read it. "Come away, O human child! To the waters and the wild ---"'

"'With a faery, hand in hand. For the world's more full of weeping than you can understand'" she replied, completing the thought.

'Just so', he said.

They held eye contact, and a tear started to roll down her cheek. He could do no more than gently wipe it away and regret that he had hurt her again.

'Have I missed tea?' said a familiar voice, and Richard turned to find Crosse standing in the open door, his mother by his side.

Chapter Eight

1919

Exeter

'I'll clear away, sir, if there's nothing else?' she said, feeling the full heat of Mrs Hansen's stare.

'Of course,' said Richard, his eyes not leaving her as she got up and began to clear away the tea tray. She cursed herself silently. She had done exactly what she had tried to avoid, and it was folly. She knew there was suspicion growing in Mrs Hansen's mind, and she had done nothing but feed it.

'When did you get back?' asked Richard of his friend, his eyes still following her.

'Not long. I was wanting my lunch,' replied Mr Crosse.

'Is it that late?'

'Thereabouts,' said the padre, consulting his pocket watch.

Mr Crosse wandered the room distractedly, studying paintings and objects on display, while Mrs Hansen remained silent. She was never so quiet and the longer it went on, the more she worried. Finally, she swept her gaze across Emily and flicked her head at Richard.

'Richard, may I have a word?'

He looked in alarm at Emily and then back to his mother, as if she had announced a death in the family. Then she understood.

'Mother, please ---'

'Richard, not here.'

Richard's head fell into his hands, and she could see the colour drain away once more. Mr Crosse, meanwhile, was doing his best to lighten the oppressive atmosphere in the room. He'd loped across to the gong, a Chinese ornament which she would ring to summon everyone for dinner, though she doubted now whether she would ever sound it again. She tried desperately to think clearly, to find some way, any way, to stave off the inevitable. She'd given six years of her life here, and after so many days that were alike, the days ahead might bring an unlooked-for freedom. The freedom to starve on the street was none at all.

'Whenever I see these things, I always have the urge to strike them,' said Mr Crosse, with as much cheerfulness as he could muster. 'I must've been a butler in a former life.'

Then he picked up the mallet and hit the gong several times, delighted with the effect it produced. His delight disappeared as he looked across to Richard.

Richard was looking up now. Still pale, but there was something heightened and urgent in his movements. His eyes were darting around the room and he began to cough. That became a wheezing choke as he struggled to take breaths. They all moved towards him to offer assistance, but as they did so Richard dropped to his knees, drew his revolver and rounded on them, his hand shaking. In his eyes she could see nothing but cold terror.

'Richard, what in God's name are you doing?' demanded Mr Crosse, shepherding Emily out of the line of the gun suddenly aimed towards her. They hid behind a chair while Mrs Hansen screamed and ran for the door.

Looking through the chair legs, Emily could see Richard flailing around, reacting to invisible things, lost in an imagined world. It was doubtful he was even aware of them now. She turned to Mr Crosse in search of some explanation. But Crosse had for the first time lost his insouciant calm. His glasses were fogged, and he removed them with sweaty hands. He tried to smile, but it showed as a grimace.

There was a heavy thump and Emily turned back to see that Richard's revolver had dropped to the floor. He had a hand around his own throat, and he was turning purple, making the most horrible choking sound. All she'd seen since he returned home was a man tearing himself apart, and now she was watching him seemingly about to end his own life. She began to crawl out from behind the chair towards him.

'Don't be foolish' cried out Mr Crosse. 'He doesn't know where he is or what he's doing. He could hurt you.'

She crawled on and was soon on her knees next to him. He was still fighting with himself and his breathing was getting slower and ever more laboured.

'Stop, sir!' she shouted. 'Stop, please!'

'Come away, girl,' called Mrs Hansen from the door.

'He won't hurt me.' She moved closer to him and whispered. 'Richard, please stop.'

Instinctively she grabbed his hands and pulled at them, until finally they came away from his throat, and they both fell back onto the floor. She caught her breath and turned back. He was gasping air now, lying on his back, but as she watched his eyes fell closed and he lost consciousness. She took his hand and searched for a pulse; something that came back to her from a medical book she had once read. She closed her eyes and could feel the steady beat of his heart through her hand. She sighed. Then she felt a hand on her shoulder.

'Well done. I think you saved his life,' said Mr Crosse. He turned to Mrs Hansen, who was still watching from the door. 'I think we should call a doctor.'

She nodded, her face acknowledging a concern that Emily had never seen before. Perhaps there was some human feeling there after all. His mother turned and hurried out of the house.

***

Emily placed the small case on her bed and started to take her few clothes out of the chest of drawers and pack them into it. She picked up the hairbrush that had belonged to her mother and shined the enamel decoration with her sleeve. It shone an opalescent blue as she placed it on the top and slid a book next to it. The only book that truly belonged to her. There was precious little else to pack and when she was sure there was nothing left, she closed the lid and buckled it. 'Let your boat of life be light,' she thought to herself. She weighed the case in her hand and decided it couldn't very well be lighter. Looking around at the little room, she thought again that it had never really felt like home. It was a place to exist, that was all. Then she counted the coins in her purse, which took so little time she did it twice. If she were careful there was enough for a room for a week or two, or food for the same, but not both.

She passed from her tiny room into the kitchen. Everything was in order. She had prided herself on always keeping it immaculate. It was curious to think someone else would use these pots and pans. She smiled for a moment at the thought that Mrs Hansen might have to roll up her own sleeves. Not before time.

Emily ascended the stairs, and, in the hall, Mrs Hansen stood impassively, ready to usher her out. There was no obvious malice, but no regret either. It was just expedient. She must protect her reputation, she'd said. Not Emily's reputation, but the standing of the Hansen family. They could not be associated with someone like her, she'd said, with a degree of disgust. Perhaps, thought Emily, more than a little unkindly, it was the thought of love that was fearful to her. People feared what they did not know, after all.

'How is Mr Richard?' she asked. 'Would I be able to see him?'

Mrs Hansen prickled with indignation. There was to be no goodbye. Then with no ceremony and less courtesy, Emily found herself standing outside on the steps, her little case in her hand, and the door slammed behind her. To make matters worse, a light rain had started to fall. She stepped into the street and started to walk. She was walking without purpose or direction, and her thoughts would not be controlled. It was more a succession of feelings, veering from fear to anger, to regret, and back to fear.

It was a warm day, but the rain chilled her, and she shivered, wiping the water from her hair. She walked on, unable to focus her thoughts. She passed the hospital, and then north again, enjoying the bustle of the High Street and the distraction it provided.

A tram rattled to a stop and people crowded onto it, happy to escape the worsening rain. Others made for the shops or arcade to find shelter. Emily tilted her head up and watched the droplets falling towards her, feeling the water splash onto her eyelids. She stopped under the overhanging canopy of the Guildhall and leaned against a pillar. A newspaper vendor was busy covering his papers to keep them dry. 'Peace treaty signed' she read in the headline. So, it was finally all over. As she watched, a man passed the paper stand, and, as he stepped from the pavement to cross the street, a porcelain mask that had been covering his face came loose. She saw that the bottom part of his jaw was missing, and a jagged scar cut through his cheek, like a ghastly smile. He noticed her watching and hurriedly put the mask back in place, meekly pulling the collar of his coat up to hide it. How could a man with such scars go on about his life so normally?

Without really thinking, she reached the corner of Bedford Street, and stood outside Deller's, looking in at the people enjoying an elegant tea. When she was younger, she had stood here often, imagining what it would be like to be on the other side of the glass. It had been a harmless fancy that made her feel less alone. Watching now, it had the opposite effect. Never had she been further from this life. Tears started to mingle with the rain and stung her eyes. She wiped her face on her sleeve and turned away, back the way she had come. She was angry at her self-pity. Why should she wallow in this, when none of it was her doing? Mrs Hansen had cast her out after years of faithful service for what? Because her son could not control himself! That's what it came down to, and she seethed with bitterness. She hated him, or at least she tried to. And then by turns, when she remembered how he had looked lying unconscious on the carpet, she was desperate with concern.

She came to St Stephens church, and went inside, selecting a pew to one side at the back, out of the way. She had never really believed, despite attending church here every Sunday, but there was some comfort in the act of prayer. She had often treated it like a wish list, asking for the things she most wanted. It hadn't worked of course. But at this moment her dreams were far away from her thoughts, and her prayers were far simpler. She pulled her feet up onto the pew and tucked herself up into a corner. She closed her eyes tight, hoping for some sort of guidance. The church was still and warm, and in time she drifted away into much needed sleep.

***

She woke with a start. Her legs were numb and her back stiff, but a warm sunset was streaming through the stained glass. She let it wash across her face, but as a figure crossed in front of the sunlight and was briefly silhouetted by it, she realised what had woken her. She shielded her eyes and watched him go to the front of the church. As she grew accustomed to the light, she realised it was Richard. She muttered a silent thank you to God that he seemed well enough. She considered going over to him, but before she could decide, the door opened again and a second figure came bustling in, this time making quickly for where Richard was sitting. It was Mr Crosse.

'Richard,' he said, as he reached the front. 'What are you doing? You should be resting.'

There was no answer. Richard simply sat quietly. Crosse's body language slowed, and he sat down on the pew opposite and began to fill his pipe.

'I didn't know you were religious?'

'I can't say that I am,' replied Richard.

'Well, this is the Church of England,' said Crosse, and tilted his head slightly to one side while he lit his pipe. 'Belief is not a prerequisite.'

'Should you be smoking here?' asked Richard.

'Well, I'm sure He doesn't mind,' said Crosse, laconically. 'He is pretty tolerant in the main. He understands what goes on in here.' Crosse was tapping his head with his pipe. 'He's a good listener too I find.'

Mr Crosse arched his back and stretched out his legs, finding a comfortable position, and waited patiently. Emily rested her arms on the pew in front and her chin on her arms. She searched for the anger that had been there before, as much because it was a straightforward feeling as anything else, but it had drained away. As she looked at Richard it was a disappointment that took hold. That he had so easily brushed her away. She had valued so much what she felt to be his friendship, but now she doubted whether he had thought the same. For him it had been convenience. She was there to talk to, and she wouldn't talk back or question him, at least until today. However much she thought she knew him, how much did he actually know about her? And after the last 24 hours, she questioned whether she understood him at all. It was better to walk away now and not look back. Start life again somewhere else and forget all of this.

Now decided in her purpose, she began to slide along the pew, eager to leave without being seen.

'What the hell is happening to me, Ernie?' said Richard suddenly. 'Things should be better here, away from everything that happened, but it's worse. Every moment I'm worried at what I'll do.'

Crosse sat thoughtfully for a moment. Emily stopped still and waited.

'As Doctor Harrison said, it's an illness.'

'An illness where there's no hope of a cure. Where I can't even hear the sound of a bloody gong without it turning me into a raving madman who shoots at anyone who comes near.'

'You didn't shoot anyone.'

'Not this time. But I can't control this, and I'm hurting people. I can't sleep except to have nightmares, and when I'm awake I'm seeing things that aren't there. It scares me.'

Emily looked towards the door. She knew she should leave now, and she would have, but for a part of her which was magnetically fixed on the conversation, and a need to understand.

Crosse pulled a hip flask from his jacket and offered it to Richard, who looked at it like a man in a desert would see a glass of water, before raising his hand in refusal.

'No, thank you.'

'Perhaps you should consider what the doctor said?'

Richard passed his hand through his thick hair and rested it on the back of his head, as if the thought were physically painful to him.

'It would be a safe place,' said Crosse.

'No,' he said firmly.

'You've seen shell shock before,' said Crosse. 'We both have. You will remember Sergeant Cairns? His wife writes to me about his brother, who suffers even now. But people do recover. You heard what the doctor said – these "talking cures" they have been experimenting with. You need to understand what it was that caused this. Something you saw?'

'There are too many things,' said Richard. She saw him turn away, as he always did when evading a question. 'I saw men die every day. So did you. We learned to live with it. So why now?'

'When did it start?'

'I don't remember.'

Crosse got up and started to walk to the crucifix on the wall. He looked up at it and studied it for some time. Eventually he turned back and slowly took off his glasses.

'You said this got worse when you returned home?'

'Yes, I think so.'

'Perhaps that's it?'

'What's it? You're not making sense, Crosse.'

'You came home.'

Richard stared at him with a look of profound realisation.

'I'm responsible,' he said slowly. 'You're right. I wrote letters, do you remember? To the families of men who died under my command. They all died because of what I did, or what I failed to do. I came home, and they didn't.

'My mind is trying to tell me I'm responsible! I was supposed to lead, and I didn't. Time and again I gave away that responsibility to others, and they died in my place. I can't bring them back, but, to borrow from your language, I can atone for it.'

'Meaning what?'

'I don't know. But there must be something I can do to help them.'

As Emily watched, she felt a kinship. He was as powerless as she felt. As one of her favourite writers would have it, there was a cord of communion between them. And if she were to leave, she was afraid that cord of communion would snap, and she would take to bleeding inwardly. But even knowing this she made for the door while the impulse was strong enough. Her exit did not go unnoticed. She knocked a prayer book to the floor as she quit the pew and ran. She heard Richard call her name, but she didn't look back.

As she emerged into the cold evening, her breath clouded the air, and she pulled her poorly fitting coat tighter around her. She turned towards the cathedral, but then Richard stood in her path. She couldn't see how he had got there ahead of her, but she span away.

'Emily, please don't go,' he called out. But she walked on. 'It was my fault. I'm so sorry for what happened.'

She turned. To accept the apology would have been easy enough, but she wouldn't allow that. Not yet.

'I wanted to be your friend,' she told him, 'and for that simple kindness I have lost everything. You promised there was no danger. I don't know if you know how that feels?'

As soon as she said it, she regretted it. She couldn't know what he had lost, but it was honest, and she couldn't completely let go of the anger that still buried itself in her feelings, however much she might wish to.

'You're right,' he replied. 'You are so completely right.'

There seemed little more to be said, and she went on her way again.

'I have a job,' he called after her. 'If you want it.'

She looked back at him. What job could he offer? And surely anything he would offer would be out of pity.

'The doctor said I need a nurse. After this morning's --- after what happened. I would be grateful ---that is, I would like it, if it were you.'

'I would like to help you, sir,' she said, the 'sir' following naturally, from habit. 'But your mother would not approve. And I think it's best I leave. For both of us.'

'I have to make a journey,' he blurted out. 'Perhaps you heard? There are people I need to visit, to make things right. Or to try, at least. I will do it alone if I must, but I would appreciate your company. As a friend?'

Chapter Nine

April 1916
France

'Private Matthews,' said Captain Martin, his pen in his hand, and a form lying in front of him on the upturned box that was serving as a desk.

'12th of April, around 8pm,' replied Hansen, studying the carefully written list of casualties.

'Enemy action?'

'The usual. Unless you'd prefer to write "torn in two by a shell?"' added Hansen darkly.

They took a moment to appreciate the early spring sunshine as they looked across the village marketplace that had been turned into a makeshift cricket pitch. Sergeant Cairns bludgeoned a poor delivery for a 'boundary', the ball finding its way to the feet of a bemused boulanger, who picked it up and studied the odd leather ball. As Corporal Allen remonstrated with the shopkeeper for return of the ball, which the Frenchman seemed to think had damaged his goods, the game was stopped, and the umpire for the day, Reverend Crosse, made his way over to where they were sitting.

'Afternoon, gents.' They nodded in greeting. 'And I should say, congratulations Captain.'

Hansen smiled in acknowledgment and self-consciously straightened his sleeve, with three pips newly sewn on.

'Are you still writing to the families?' asked Martin, of his fellow captain.

'Which families?' said Crosse.

'He's insisting on writing a letter to the family of every --- casualty.'

'You can use the word,' said Hansen. 'What would they have otherwise? Form B104/82. Have you seen it? "Sir, it is my painful duty to inform you that a report has this day been received from the War Office notifying the death of --- / number / rank / name. I am to express to you the sympathy and regret--- blah, blah, blah--- meaningless platitude--- Your obedient servant ---"'

'Compliments of General Haig?' quipped Martin, and they laughed.

Crosse frowned and took a seat next to them, pulling his pipe out of his pocket.

'Would you like me to finish those for you?'

'Thank you, padre, but it has to be done,' said Hansen, looking down the long list of casualties.

'It doesn't do to get too involved,' whispered Crosse, to Hansen.

'You do.'

'Comes with the job,' replied the padre, touching his dog collar.

Hansen took a sip of white wine. It was rough. Almost vinegar. But at least it was cold. He considered the fate of poor Private Matthews. He was within feet of his own lines, returning from scouting the enemy, when a shell had fallen practically on top of him. A stray, the Germans hadn't even been trying to hit their position. The shell cut him in half and then buried itself in the ground. A dud and a stray. He couldn't have been more unlucky. It wasn't clear how long he'd lived. The whimpering seemed to last hours, and more than once Hansen considered bringing things to a close more quickly. His family deserved to know, but not this. They deserved to know the best of him.

'You knew Private Matthews, didn't you Ernie?'

'Ernie knows everyone,' said Martin, holding his cigarette between grinning teeth.

'Yes,' said Crosse. 'His father is a fisherman, I think. His mother died when he was a baby, so his father brought him up. Nice lad. Collected stamps, did you know that?'

Corporal Allen had finally retrieved the cricket ball and stopped at the officers' table, tapping it on the top.

'Fancy a knock Captain?' he asked Hansen.

'Not while Challacombe is bowling,' he replied.

'He's pretty quick, sir, isn't he? And moves it off the seam nice as well.'

'I'll have a bowl though,' said Hansen, getting to his feet. 'Cairns has been there quite long enough.'

Hansen trotted to the middle of the marketplace, where they'd cobbled together some packing crates into makeshift stumps at either end. He scratched a mark into the ground with his boot and threw the ball in the air, spinning it from his hand. Crosse returned to his place as umpire.

'Only another six runs for my half century, sir!' called Cairns from the other end.

Hansen ignored the provocation and skipped up to the wicket, turning the ball out of his hand and landing it where he wanted. Cairns made himself some space and drove it back over Hansen's head, the ball landing in a horse trough. Crosse raised his hands to indicate six runs.

'Bad luck, sir,' said Cairns, striding down the pitch towards his captain.

'Congratulations, Sergeant,' replied Hansen, magnanimously. 'Well played. Though you realise of course that you now owe us all a round of drinks?'

Cairns threw his hands up in mock outrage, while Corporal Allen's slow round of applause suddenly speeded up.

'Mine's a brandy, Sarge!' said Allen, chuckling at the Sergeant's reaction.

***

The April sun was getting low in the sky and the game became impossible to continue. Hansen returned to where Captain Martin was sitting, a straw hat balanced carefully on his nose.

'A good game,' said he, without moving.

'Yes. Young Challacombe might give WG Grace a game. He's got talent.'

As he said it, he realised how odd it was to call him young, when they were probably of a similar age. The months he had been in France could have been years. He sat and took a gulp of the wine, sadly now not even cold. Sergeant Cairns shuffled towards them, his cap in his hands, moving far more uncertainly than his usual purposeful stride.

'Wilf, quite an innings you played,' said Hansen.

'Thank you, sir. I used to play for my local team back in the day.'

'Where was that, in Plymouth?'

'Yes, sir.'

Cairns stood with his head drooping, his hat out in front of him. It reminded Hansen of Oliver Twist in his request for a second helping of gruel, and it was so unlike Cairns that it puzzled him extremely.

'You look like you have something on your mind, Wilf.'

'Yes, sir. Could I ask you a favour?'

'Of course. What is it?'

'In private, sir, if you don't mind?'

Cairns stepped away to one side, indicating that he'd like Hansen to follow him across the square.

'As you like.'

Hansen picked up his weary legs and set off after Cairns, towards the Mairie on the far side, where a French flag flapped in the breeze.

'Look, Wilf, if you're going to tell me you caught something on your adventures the night before last, I'm afraid you've only got yourself to blame. You'll need to see the doc.'

'No, sir, it's not that. Well, not this time anyway. It's my wife, sir ---'

'She found out?'

'No, sir. Can I be serious for a moment?'

'I don't know, can you?'

The look on Cairns' face told him that the usual banter they shared was not welcome at this precise moment, so he returned his cap to his head, as if shifting into an official capacity.

'It's alright, Sergeant. Spit it out.'

'I should like to write to my wife, sir. She's been writing to me regular, and she'll expect it.'

'I don't understand. You know you can write to her. You just need to give me the letter, like the others. Is it a private matter that you wish to write to her about?'

'Not really, sir. I should just like to tell her how I am, and ask about her wellbeing and such, you know.'

Hansen sat down next to the water fountain outside the Mairie and as he did so it dawned on him just what his Sergeant was asking.

'Wilf, are you asking me to write the letter for you?'

Cairns let out a great sigh and nodded his head like a bird pecking at seed.

'If you wouldn't mind, sir?'

'You can't write, can you?' asked Hansen, as kindly as he could.

'No, sir. I never seemed to be able to learn. It was all so many squiggles to me.'

'Of course I'll write it,' said Hansen, pulling out a pen and notepaper. 'Though you might rather Mr Crosse did it for you. I'm sure he has a better turn of phrase than me.'

'Thank you, sir. But I'd rather he not know. I should like to keep it private, and, well, you know how he is. I know I can trust you.'

Hansen smiled. For a clergyman entrusted with everyone's secret thoughts, Crosse did have an unfortunate habit of gossiping at times.

'Very well. You tell me what you'd like to say, and I'll write it down. Just take it slowly so I can keep up.'

They spent the next half hour or so writing the letter together. Cairns was remarkably eloquent, and when he got over his initial nervousness, overcame his reluctance to share his feelings with his Captain, and most tenderly expressed his love for his wife, and his grief at being parted from her. As he wrote, Richard realised that he had written numerous such letters to Madeleine, full of poetic intent but lacking any of the genuine feeling that Wilf was expressing. At the end Cairns closed the letter himself with a carefully practiced signature. He left Cairns to post it and crossed the square again, making a mental note that he must find the words to write to Madeleine soon. It was only fair.

As he reached the table where Martin and Crosse were now tucking into coq au vin, a car pulled up and he noticed a familiar figure bustling towards them, swishing his swagger stick briskly backwards and forwards as he walked.

'Gentlemen, I believe we have company,' whispered Hansen as he sat down.

'Oh, good Lord,' said Crosse, turning to look. 'I shall have indigestion all night now.'

Major Dawes was momentarily lost from view as he became entangled with a crowd of merry soldiers and had to raise his stick to make his presence felt. They made way for him, but as he reached the officers' table his decorum had been temporarily ruffled, and his moustache twitched in irritation.

'Captain Hansen,' he said, paying little attention to the others.

'Good evening, sir.'

'Would you like a glass of wine, Major?' offered Duncan.

'What?' replied the Major, upset at being diverted from his mission, which had clearly been Martin's intention. 'No, thank you, Captain. I'm here on official business.'

'When are you not?' said Crosse, with a butter wouldn't melt innocence. 'You're so dedicated to your job, Major.'

Dawes was unsure how to take the remark and stuttered for a moment, straightening his tie and stretching the leather of his gloves.

'Well, the war won't be won by sitting around,' said Dawes, as the three seated officers looked at each other. 'Captain Hansen, I'm afraid I must recall you and your company to the firing line. I have a very particular job I'd like you to do. I will explain later. Report to me at battalion HQ as soon as you arrive.'

'You'd like us to return tonight, sir?'

'If you please, Captain.'

'Sir, my men have had precious little rest. We were due two weeks.'

'I'm sorry, Captain. Those are the exigencies of the service. You have your orders.'

With a sharp turn Dawes was on his way back to the car, this time giving the crowd of soldiers a wide berth.

'Exigencies?' echoed Crosse.

'Someone must have given him a thesaurus for his birthday,' added Duncan. 'Bad luck, old man.'

Hansen was furious. After an extended spell in the front line, they had spent even longer in support and his men were in dire need of proper rest. What's more, they were waiting for replacements and would be barely two-thirds of full strength. It was pointless to waste time in anger though, and he cast around to find Cairns and Peters. A bunch of half-drunk soldiers would not be easily persuaded to return, but it had to be done.

***

Early the next day Hansen was lying face down in the chill half-light of the morning, studying the German lines through binoculars. He had crawled on his hands and knees to the top of a small hillock, once covered in trees, now in splintered wood, which marked a single high point between the lines, overlooking the Germans at a distance of only some twenty yards. The cover was sparse, and as the sun peeked above the horizon there was every danger of the glare from his binoculars being seen.

He carefully noted the positions of several newly constructed machine gun emplacements, and a dense nest of barbed wire that had been added between them. As he watched, the German working party that had been constructing the new defences began to withdraw from their vulnerable position. He'd been where he was for too long already, and the cover of darkness would last precious little longer. But this was a vital opportunity to note the safe route through the barbed wire in this sector, and he took the chance to watch the retreat and sketch a rough map of their path. It could be critical information.

He blew on his hands to relieve the numbness and opened his eyes wide in an attempt to stave off sleep. A combination of cheap wine and weariness made his head thump. He put the binoculars back in their case and eased his way back down the hill, keeping an eye on the German lines for signs of movement. Steam was rising from one of the trenches to the rear. Breakfast. He had a new jar of strawberry jam stashed in his footlocker and the thought of smearing it onto a croissant and serving it with thick dark coffee was hugely appealing. Of course, the reality was probably a cup of weak tea with the jam on a rock-hard biscuit, but why let that spoil the dream.

As he reached the bottom of the hill he got to his feet and crabbed along, using the hill as cover as much as possible. As he turned back to check once more his foot caught on something and there was a loud rattling from tin cans and other metal objects strung up on the barbed wire. He hadn't noticed them setting this up in the dark, and there followed a chorus of shouting from the German lines.

Then came the flash of a rifle, with an accompanying report, as a shot came in his direction. There was enough light now for him to be visible, and he took to his heels, bounding and leaping across the pitted ground. He heard the crack of a bullet close to his ear and zagged in the other direction. As he clambered up a mound of earth there was a sudden pain in his shoulder, like someone had punched him hard, and then a searing burn which travelled down his whole arm. Like an idiot he stopped still and touched his shoulder, which was wet with blood. He was surprised more than shocked, and quickly gathered his senses and moved on, now realising he was a target for every trigger-happy sniper in the German lines.

He scrambled on and the British line came into view at last. A head appeared in the pale morning light over the trench, aiming a rifle, and he heard the familiar gruff bark of Sergeant Cairns.

'Halt! Who goes there?'

'Friend,' he shouted, his voice hoarse in the cold air.

'If you're a Jerry I'll blow your bloody head off!' shouted Cairns.

'Hansen, Captain, 8th battalion, Devonshire regiment.'

The figure lowered his rifle as Hansen reached the top of the ladder and slid down into the dark safety of the trench.

'Sir? Jesus, we thought you'd, y'know, become a landowner, sir.'

Cairns was beaming, his white teeth visible in the gloom. Hansen clutched his arm, which was aching and throbbing all at once.

'Rumours of my death have been greatly exaggerated,' he replied, with an unexpected calmness. Cairns looked blankly at him.

'Mark Twain.'

'I don't know him, sir, is he new?'

Hansen flopped down onto the fire step and leaned his head back against the wall of the trench. It was surprising how much relief there was in being back in this strange underground world.

'Has anyone ever told you that you're a philistine, Sergeant?'

'Not that I remember, sir. But then I've never had any beef with the Israelites, me. Let me have a look at that arm, sir.'

'I sometimes get the impression you're cleverer than you look, Wilf.'

'Not me sir. But it's better than looking cleverer than you are, sir, isn't it?'

'I'm sure that would make some sort of sense if I weren't so tired.'

Cairns helped him get out of his great coat and unbuttoned his tunic, unhooking the cross strap of his belt and easing it off.

'I'm not ruining my best tunic,' said Hansen. 'I can't afford another at Gieves and Hawkes' prices. But you can rip the shirt.'

Cairns did as instructed and cut the sleeve off. The bullet had made a mess of his shoulder all right. There was a dark bruise forming already and a neat round hole at the front which was bleeding freely. Cairns staunched the blood and began to clean the wound with iodine.

'Where's Corporal Allen?'

'I'll find him for you, sir. I expect he's pawning your kit.'

'If he can find a pawnbroker who will call here, he can have it.'

Cairns completed his work and bound up the wound with a good field dressing.

'As good as new sir.'

'Thank you. My backhand will suffer, that's for sure.'

Hansen's head fell back once more, and he closed his eyes. Food was occupying his disordered thoughts, and he remembered meals with his family. There was a particular lamb dish which Emily made which made his mouth water. It was a favourite of Sebastian as well. Hansen fell into sleep, mumbling incoherently to himself.

***

Hansen awoke later and found that he was lying on his bunk. His arm had been re-dressed and he felt pleasantly light-headed. Lieutenant Peters sat at the table, writing.

'You're awake, sir. How do you feel?'

'A little like I was one over the eight last night to be frank,' he replied.

'That's probably the morphia, sir. The doctor came in to stitch you up.'

Hansen swivelled his legs onto the floor and tried to stand, but a light head made him sit back down again, stars flashing before his eyes.

'I must report.'

'Yes, sir. Major Dawes asked you to see him as soon as you are able.'

'Very well.'

'And we have new orders.'

Peters passed him a stack of new messages and he leafed through them. Mostly run of the mill requests for reports on fighting disposition and supplies and some minor disciplinary infractions. More urgent was an instruction for a supply party to be sent for water. Hansen tried standing again and this time managed it with only modest dizziness.

'There's something else, sir,' said Peters. 'I know it's rotten timing, but I'm being transferred. The 9th battalion need a platoon commander. It means a promotion to 1st.'

'Congratulations, Tom. Richly deserved. I knew I couldn't keep you here forever. When do you leave?'

'Immediately, sir.'

'Goodness. Very well, you'd better pack.'

'Already done, sir.'

'Efficient as ever. Good luck, Tom.'

They shook hands. He might be young, but Peters had become a fine officer. Hansen envied his courage, and he had found a balance between authority and friendliness with the soldiers under his command that had earned him respect and loyalty. It was a balance that he himself never seemed able to find. He went out into the trench and found Sergeant Cairns, busy cleaning his rifle.

'S'ant Cairns.'

Wilf stopped what he was doing and stood to attention.

'Sir. Good to see you on your feet, if I may say that?'

'You just have. Thank you for what you did.'

Hansen stepped closer to Cairns and dropped his voice to a whisper.

'How did I get into the dugout? I can't seem to remember.'

'We carried you, sir. You was done in. I've never been so surprised, sir, when you came back. I really thought I'd lost you.'

Richard noted the use of the pronoun and allowed himself a half-smile. If command was built on trust, he knew he could trust this man absolutely, like an elder brother. Clearly that was the role in which Cairns saw himself too.

'Have you posted the letter to your wife?'

'Yes, sir. I dare say she will be as surprised to receive it as I was when I saw you this morning.'

'I'm sure. It was a good letter.'

Hansen stood back, returning the conversation to official business, and Cairns acknowledged the change by coming back to attention.

'HQ have asked for a ration party to help bring up water supplies. I'd like you to lead it. Take four men.'

'Yes, sir.'

'Wilf. You'll need to go through Crucifix Corner. Don't forget ---'

'Duck my nut. Yes, sir.'

'One other thing. Lieutenant Peters is redeploying to the 9th battalion. They are in reserve at the moment. Could you take him up the lines with you?'

'Of course, sir.'

***

With his debriefing complete, Hansen made his way back from the battalion HQ to his company. Corporal Allen was on watch and reported that everything had been quiet. As Hansen returned to his dugout for some food, there was a commotion further down the trench, and Private Challacombe came sprinting towards him.

'Captain, the ration party has been ambushed.'

He tried to disguise the concern that he felt.

'Where? Show me.'

Challacombe ran back the way he had come, Hansen trailing in his wake. He had shaken off the effects of the morphine, but his arm now ached terribly, and it was making it hard to move smoothly. They wound through the front line and then back into communication trenches before they rounded into a shallower trench where they had to stoop low to avoid being seen. A wooden roadside crucifix, that would once have brought comfort to travellers on the road, loomed above them on the top of the trench wall. A makeshift sign was nailed to the wall nearby and read: 'duck your nut'.

Just ahead there were scattered bodies lying on the ground, with the remnants of wooden handcarts, smashed to pieces, embedded in the mud and strewn around. Water canisters lay around on their sides, their contents seeping into the mud. Medical orderlies were helping one of the wounded.

He saw Lieutenant Peters first. He was on his back, his hand on his revolver, which was still in its holster. A single bullet hole was visible in the middle of his forehead, with a trickle of blood down the side of his face. His eyes were open, and his expression betrayed only the slightest look of surprise. A sniper would target the officer first, and Peters had probably had little time to react or think. Hansen bent down and touched his hand, which was still warm.

'Captain!' called Challacombe. 'Sergeant Cairns is still alive.'

Hansen gave quiet thanks and made his way to where Cairns was lying. Challacombe was propping him up, but if he were still alive, he clearly wouldn't be for very long. Hansen turned his head at the sight of his Sergeant, legs torn off, his ribcage exposed, and with blood turning the mud around him a deep burgundy. Hansen was ashamed of his reaction. Cairns would never let him lie there alone, and he forced himself to turn back and look. He fell to his knees and let Cairns' head rest in his lap. Wilf's grey eyes looked up at him, but as he tried to speak bloody bubbles formed in his mouth. Then the laboured breathing stopped, and his eyes remained fixed. Hansen took a long breath and closed his eyes.

'When did this happen?'

'I don't know, sir,' said Challacombe. 'It's awful quiet out here. No one heard anything. One of the Highlanders was passing and found them.'

'Orderly! Why were you not helping the Sergeant?'

'I'm sorry, he was beyond help, Captain,' replied the orderly with little emotion. It was clearly an answer he had given many times to many people.

Chapter Ten

1919

Plymouth

Emily lay for several minutes looking up at the ceiling. There was a curiously shaped damp spot, and she considered for a moment whether it looked more like the continent of Africa, or a bald man with a big nose. She luxuriated in the soft bed and turned over to find the bedside clock showing 7.30am. She laughed at the absurdity of it. There was never a time, certainly not that she could remember, when she had been able to be so thoroughly slovenly.

She swivelled her legs out of bed and placed them on the carpet. She took a moment to flex her toes in the thick wool and enjoy the feel of it. Then she skipped across to the dresser and poured hot water into the bowl.

As she washed her face, she looked in the mirror. She seldom looked fully at herself. Normally it was a case of simple ablutions and on with her work. But today felt like a new beginning, and she wanted to mark it by resolutely leaving behind the trappings of Emily the maid. She dressed in her Sunday best and applied rouge to her lips, styling her hair in the mode of Mary Pickford. As she looked again at herself in the mirror, a part of her rebelled at the extravagance. She was without a position, and with little money to her name. There might come a time when she was obliged to go back into service and the security it offered. Her mother would have cautioned her against letting her aspirations outstrip her pragmatism, but for now she pushed these doubts aside and enjoyed the moment. Emily the maid was gone. What might this Emily be?

She closed the door to her room and made her way downstairs. Mrs Grant was there tidying away plates and setting down some fresh coffee. Emily had liked her immediately. She had a jolly disposition and called all of her lodgers 'my luvver', in the Devon style.

'Good morning, miss. Would you like a cup of tea?' she asked as Emily reached the bottom of the stairs.

'Thank you, Mrs Grant.' Emily sat down at the table, which was now empty. 'Where are the others?' she asked.

'Oh, most of them have to go early to work, my luvver. You'll see them dreckly.'

'I wanted to tell you I am going away,' said Emily. 'For a day or two at least, I'm not sure. Will you hold my room for me?'

'Of course, my dear. Visiting family?'

'I am going to see a friend.'

'Well, everything will be here for you when you get back.'

***

As Emily reached the railway station, she could see Richard standing beside the entrance. He looked nervous, pacing up and down. Presently Mr Crosse came out from the newsagent and joined Richard. As she approached them, Emily had second thoughts about the trip they were about to embark on. What good would it do Richard, and what exactly was he expecting of her?

Richard smiled when he saw her, and pointed her out to Crosse, who turned to look. It seemed to Emily that he was commenting to Richard about her, perhaps about her appearance, as they both looked her up and down.

'Good morning,' said Richard warmly, as she reached them. 'I asked Ernie to come along as well. For. For ---'

'Spiritual guidance,' cut in Mr Crosse.

'Something like that,' agreed Richard.

They boarded the train and took their seats in a first-class compartment. Although she had occasionally leaned over a bridge to watch trains pass, this was the first time Emily had ever been on one. New experiences were coming fast, one after another, and it was all a little disorienting. The seat was soft and extremely comfortable, and such a size that she felt a little like Alice, at only ten inches high, lost in the middle of it. She craned her neck to look out of the window and let out a little squeak of surprise as the train jolted and started on its way. She looked around sheepishly, slightly embarrassed at her own child-like reaction.

'It always catches me out as well, no matter how many times I travel,' said Mr Crosse, with a kindly smile, carefully cleaning his pipe.

He seemed to be studying her, not in any unpleasant way, but out of simple curiosity. How was it she came to be here? It wasn't a question she could answer easily herself now she came to consider it. She looked across at Richard, lost in his own thoughts, with his eyes closed, and the doubts began to creep in again. With such a tangled mind, it was impossible to be sure of his motivation in inviting her to share this journey, or to predict where it would end. Each moment had been so rich in newness she had not considered what would come next. Her future could be a bleak one if she stopped long enough to think about it, but there was something exciting in just being carried by fate. Structure had dominated her life, and being unbound from that, no matter what came next, was exhilarating.

***

They came to the top of a street of small, terraced houses, poor but well kept, and turned to walk down the hill. From here there was a view across the city, and in the distance a shimmering blue which Emily looked at several times before realising it could only be the sea. It sparkled in the sunlight and the silhouettes of sails passed across it like a Turner painting.

The officers' uniforms attracted attention as they passed shopfronts and outside the local pub men crowded around with drinks in hand. One of them leered at her for some moments, and then sauntered across, beer sloshing out of his glass as he went.

'Hey! Lily,' he called. 'Lily Elsie. Fancy seeing you here. "I'm so very glad I met you"!' Then the man burst into laughter. 'Give us a song!'

There was something in his attentions that she found unsettling. An edge that went beyond friendliness.

'Give us a song or give us a kiss!'

She made to walk on, but Richard turned suddenly, and confronted the man.

'Have a care how you address the lady,' he said, with a chill in his voice. His eyes were hard and cold.

'"Have a care!"' mocked the drunk man. 'I don't have to salute you now, "sir". You can fuck off!'

There was a brief moment of stillness, and then Richard surged forward, grabbing the man by his lapels and almost lifting him off his feet. The man responded with a right hook that caught Richard across the face. In turn Richard dumped him onto the ground and brought his fist down hard on the man's chest, just below his windpipe. He coughed and wheezed, struggling for breath, and Richard raised his fist once more. Rather than anger or hate, his face showed no emotion at all, simply a blank coldness. Before he could punch again, Crosse had intervened, and pulled Richard away, blood streaming from his nose.

As Crosse guided them both away down the street, Richard seemed to snap back from his impassive state, and was in shock or disbelief, as if what he had done, he'd done without conscious thought. Emily pulled out a handkerchief and held it to his nose to staunch the bleeding. A chill passed through her and a reality was made clear. The man whose face she now held gently in her hands was capable of killing. He had been a soldier, and soldiers killed. To think otherwise would be naïve, however much she would wish it. His potential for such explosive violence should have scared her, but somehow it did not. She only cared that a man who had always gone out of his way not to hurt anyone or anything had been forced to it and must now live with those memories every day.

They continued down the hill and found the address they were looking for.

'This is the one,' said Richard.

'Is this sensible, Richard?' asked Crosse. He flashed his eyes back to the pub at the top of the hill.

'Are you thinking I might go on a rampage and beat the people in that house too?' Richard shifted uneasily and rubbed his forehead. 'I'm fine now. There's as much sense in this as anything else.'

He approached the door, and after a brief hesitation, he knocked sharply. There was a voice inside in response to the knock, muffled and indistinct, probably letting them know she was on her way. Then the door opened and a harassed looking woman opened the door, dressed for housework and carrying a basket of laundry. She was still young, but her face was creased with weariness. On sight of the uniform, she took a step back, with a questioning look.

'Mrs. Cairns?' said Richard.

'Yes?' she replied, with a hesitancy in her voice.

'My name is Hansen. Richard Hansen. I wrote to you some time ago.'

The wariness vanished, and a warmth spread across her face, albeit mixed with a tinge of sadness.

'Yes, yes! I remember. Come in, Captain, please. Or I should say Major now I see.'

'Call me Richard.'

They were guided over the threshold and found themselves walking into a small front room. Emily couldn't help but compare it to the Hansen's home. This was far more modest, to be sure, but there was a simple elegance to it, and she could appreciate how scrupulously clean and tidy it was, and the work that had gone into making it so. There was a pride in it, which came from having somewhere of her own.

'Will you sit down, sir?' said Mrs Cairns. Richard frowned good-naturedly and she corrected herself. 'Richard.'

'Thank you.'

Richard and Mr Crosse sat down in chairs by the fire. Emily herself felt awkward at sitting with them and took a chair at the dining table by the window.

'I wanted to come and see you---' began Richard slowly

'Tea!' interrupted Mrs Cairns. 'Will you have some? Stay right there.'

Mrs Cairns bolted for the kitchen next door, scooping up the laundry as she went, and stopping to rearrange a porcelain statue on the mantelpiece. Richard paused and exchanged glances with them both. This would have been a hard conversation to prepare for, she knew, and he looked unsettled by the delay. She tried to offer him a smile of reassurance.

'Well--- this is pleasantly awkward,' said Crosse, not altogether helpfully. Richard shushed him and wrung his hands with impatience.

Emily looked around and noted a photographic portrait hung on the wall next to the fire of an imposing man in army uniform. There was a black sash drooped across it, and medals displayed below, with a small candle burning.

Mrs Cairns returned with a tray and placed it on the table. She began to serve tea, looking nervously from each of them to the others. In the middle of pouring a thought struck her, and she put down the teapot and fished a crumpled letter from her apron.

'I carry your letter, Major - Richard. It was so very kind of you to write ---'

She was unable to continue, and her eyes filled with tears.

'Don't distress yourself. I just wanted to tell you how brave your husband was, how respected he was.'

'Thank you, but I meant the other letter. The one you wrote for him?' Richard looked a little embarrassed. 'I know you must have written it. He'd never write to me and he thought I didn't know why, but I did. I know my husband was a good man, but I'm glad to know others thought so too.'

Mrs Cairns was forced to stop again. She tried to pick up the teapot but was overcome with emotion and she had to sit down, pulling her apron to her face. Emily couldn't leave her like that, and she went across the room and gently took the tea pot from her.

'Let me help, Mrs Cairns.'

'Thank you, dear. You would think after all this time I could, y'know ---'

Emily understood exactly what she meant. The rawness of her mother's passing had never really left her. Perhaps because she had still been so young, so unready for the world and its realities, that she felt it so keenly. But as she reflected now it seemed as if, in so many ways, no time had passed at all.

'I understand,' she told her. 'Years are like days.'

They exchanged a smile of recognition. As Emily looked across to where Richard was sitting, she saw a curious look on his face. She had seen such a look only once before, when they sat together in the parlour and she had talked so freely. She had come to regret that openness and what it had cost her, but at the time it had felt so comfortable. Perhaps he had thought her overemotional and naïve then, and perhaps he was thinking the same now. Mrs Cairns turned to Richard as well.

'Would you tell me what you knew of him? I love to hear my husband talked about.'

'When I joined up, I was 19, a spoiled university man,' said Richard. 'I was handed a section of men to command. Many of them volunteers. I had no idea. Sergeant Cairns – Wilf – he was twice the soldier I could ever be, and I relied on him. If men followed me, it was because he was always by my side. To me he was like an older brother. With bad taste in jokes.'

Richard cleared his throat nervously and took a sip of tea. He tried to make light of it, but Emily could see the vulnerability in his eyes once more, as he fought to hide it.

'He talked about you, sir, when he was last home. He said you was a fair officer. And take no offence, that was high praise.'

Richard waved away the compliment and Emily enjoyed seeing the corners of his mouth turn up once more in pleasurable embarrassment.

'He also likened you to Robert,' added Mrs Cairns.

'His brother?'

'Yes.'

'I'd like to meet Robert, if that's possible?'

'Of course,' she said. 'He's here actually. But will you tell me first about how Wilf died?'

Richard looked immediately uncomfortable, and his face started to turn pale.

'It was in the letter I wrote,' he temporised.

'Yes, but I should like it very much if you would tell me. You were there?'

Richard gulped nervously at his tea, and Emily could see a slight tremor in his hand, much as she had seen at the dinner table before. He looked increasingly unwell, and she was unsure what to do. Then she remembered holding his hand, and how calm he had been in that moment. It might be highly improper, but she felt compelled to do what she could. She sat next to him, and without anyone else noticing she took his hand in hers and held it tight. It was clammy to the touch and she could feel the tremble, but gradually this stopped, and he took a long breath.

'I wasn't there when it happened,' he began. 'We found them later, after the attack. No one knows for sure what happened, but it must have been an ambush. He was killed by a grenade.'

'Did he suffer?'

Richard's hand twisted in hers and he turned away for a moment. Mrs Cairns was listening intently with her eyes closed.

'No,' he said at last. 'No, it was quick.'

'Thank you. It means a lot to know.'

'I'm sorry I wasn't there,' said Richard forcefully. 'I'm so sorry that I ordered him to go.'

'Robert is in the yard if you'd like to meet him?' she replied, choosing to ignore what he had said. She seemed to shake herself back to the moment and led the way through to the kitchen.

Richard gently let go of her hand and followed Mrs Cairns out without a word. Emily went after him and waited in the doorway as he went out into the little enclosed back yard. A burly man, probably in his early twenties, was swinging an axe with huge force and splitting logs with apparently little effort. He was wearing cheap suit trousers with his braces pulled tight over a baggy collarless shirt.

'He followed my husband into the army,' she heard Mrs Cairns whisper to Richard. 'When he came home, he didn't want to be alone so I said he could move in here. He helps me such a lot. But he doesn't like to be indoors. He can't sleep neither.'

Then Robert noticed Richard for the first time, and on seeing the uniform he came sharply to attention, shouldering his axe like a rifle.

'Sir!'

'Stand easy, soldier,' replied Richard, in a commanding tone, and the man relaxed his posture. 'What's your name?'

'Cairns, sir. Private, 2nd battalion, Devonshire regiment.'

'You're a Devon?'

'Yes, sir.'

'I could tell. I'm Major Hansen, 8th battalion – "Buller's Own". I knew your brother.'

Robert smiled broadly at the mention of his older brother.

'He said you were braver than him,' continued Richard. Robert looked sheepish and shook his head vigorously.

'What are you doing, Private?'

'I'm preparing supplies for the quartermaster, sir. He likes them done proper.'

'I'm sure. Take a break, Private. You've done enough. Care for a cigarette?'

Richard offered the open packet to Robert, and he took one, allowing the officer to light it for him. Mrs Cairns turned back towards the door and noticed Emily watching. She gave an exasperated look and shook her head. There was a childlike quality to Robert, lost in a pretend world where he was still a soldier doing menial tasks. Perhaps the physical effort took his mind off other things, as Emily had found herself at times. But that distraction never lasted for long as she knew well, and he would have to face his fears once again.

'You're off duty from now. Get some sleep. I want you at your best.'

'I wouldn't mind a kip, sir,' replied Robert.

Black circles around his eyes spoke to his need for sleep, and he curled up now on a wooden bench, like a child doing as instructed by its parent. The cigarette drooped from his mouth as he closed his eyes, and he was soon asleep. Richard caught the cigarette as it fell and placed it carefully to one side.

'He talks like this sometimes,' said Mrs Cairns. 'Like he's still there. When he does sleep, he wakes screaming. If there's any sudden noise he will hide under the bench and I can't get him out.'

'I want to help,' said Richard. 'If I can.'

'You're kind, sir. But I don't know what we can do.'

Richard stood for some time watching Robert sleep, lost in thought. If there was a cure to be discovered for what afflicted this man, what chance it could cure him as well?

***

Richard had not spoken since they had left the Cairns' house. As they sat in the railway buffet together, she felt she could have been content to be silent in his company at any other time, except that she knew what his thoughts must be in this moment. Mr Crosse had gone to investigate train times, and she was pondering on whether to start some light-hearted and distracting conversation, when Richard broke his silence.

'Thank you for what you did today.'

'What did I do?' she asked, uncomfortable at the mention of the intimate touch they had shared.

'Your support,' he replied, choosing an appropriate euphemism. She searched for a suitable response, and as if he sensed her uneasiness, he changed the subject quickly.

'Can I ask you something? You don't have to tell me. But you were talking about your mother, weren't you? What you said to Mrs Cairns?'

She nodded.

'Can I ask what happened?'

'It was before I worked for your family. She was ill for a long time. I did my best to take care of her. But she died.'

She took a moment, the memory still fresh and vivid.

'I still miss her every day. She used to read to me. We didn't have much, but she always had books. She liked Three Men in a Boat. It made us laugh. I think I heard it ten times. I still read it if I'm a bit sad. When I want to feel her love.'

'You didn't have any other family?'

'It was just us. I never knew my father. Her family disapproved of him I think, so she was alone with me after that.'

'I'm sorry. I'm sorry I never asked.'

He looked sincere, with a softness in his expression. She tried to turn the conversation away from the memories that were in the forefront of her mind.

'I sometimes wished for a brother. Like Sergeant Cairns.'

'I have a picture of him.'

Richard took a photograph out of his tunic pocket and laid it down on the table. It showed him with others in France, holding cricket bats. Mr Crosse was standing at the back, pipe in the mouth as ever, and there were other soldiers too, including another officer and a man with sergeant's stripes with his bat held aloft like a strongman. As she studied the picture, Mr Crosse came back in through the door from the platform.

'There's a train in an hour,' he said, and peered over her shoulder at the photograph. 'What's this? Ah, the whole gang together. That was a good day. Richard took three wickets.'

'Who are the others?' she asked.

'Well,' said Richard, 'apart from myself and this one, there's Sergeant Cairns of course. Captain Martin - surprising we could get him away from his paintbrush. Veale, Challacombe, and this is Corporal Allen. Funny to see them all there.'

There was a wistfulness in the way he said it, like someone remembering times long past. "There is no greater pain than to remember a happy time when one is in misery" she thought, remembering something from Dante.

'You're smiling,' she said, noticing his broad grin in the picture, which she had seen seldom since his return.

'Yes. Not very decorous I know, but it was like a family, not officers and men.'

'Corporal Allen's family are farmers, aren't they?' interjected Mr Crosse. 'In Cornwall?'

'Yes, I believe so. What are you thinking?'

'Only what Mrs Cairns said about Robert being happiest outdoors.'

Richard seemed to see the potential in the thought immediately and began to nod enthusiastically. There was suddenly the old sparkle in his eyes again and it made her smile to see it.

'Well, I do like Cornwall,' said Crosse.

'I haven't ever been to Cornwall,' she added, feeling confident enough to voice her thoughts.

'It's settled then,' said Richard. 'Allen Farm it is.'

'I haven't ever been on a farm either,' she admitted.

'Well, you can't call yourself a proper Devon girl if you've never been on a farm,' said Richard, bubbling with enthusiasm.

'I don't know. I don't suppose a solicitor's son has ever been on a farm either?' she teased. There was a little explosive laugh from Mr Crosse, and Richard shook his head in mock offence.

'True enough. We're both charlatans. I'll have to trade in my smock.'

She laughed out loud, and in meeting his eyes she was surer than ever that the old Richard was still there to be found.

'Shall I find some lunch?' she offered.

'Good idea,' said Crosse. 'And tea.'

'Your capacity for tea is extraordinary,' said Richard.

'Comes with the job,' joked Crosse, tapping his dog collar.

She turned towards the counter with an unexpected lightness of spirit. She relived the conversation in her head once more and couldn't help but look back at him. Richard was watching her too, and she noticed the same expression in the way he looked at her now as she had seen at the Cairns' house, but this time with a captivating smile.

Chapter Eleven

July 1916
Somme, France

Hansen read the paragraph for the third time but still couldn't take in the meaning of the words. His thoughts were elsewhere, and it was hopeless to concentrate on the task in hand. Finally, he laid down the report and paced the dugout restlessly. Crosse put his head in.

'Richard, can I offer you the very latest edition of *The Somme Times*? There's a most excellent article on 100 uses for a dead rat. It really is most instructive. Captain Roberts has outdone himself.'

He chuckled to himself and held out the paper for Richard.

'Thank you, Ernie, but I don't think I'm quite in the mood.'

Crosse took a seat and started to flick through the mound of paperwork that Hansen had left on the table.

'What's this?'

'Major Dawes has asked me to help with getting 'A' company back up to full strength, after --- what happened.'

'I'd swear that man has no heart, or no soul,' tutted Crosse, visibly angry. 'You shouldn't have to do this.'

'It's alright. It's good to be busy.'

Crosse studied the papers while Hansen continued to pace backwards and forwards. There was a clutch of new recruits due any time, straight from basic training into the crucible, and without proper leadership they would be so much cannon fodder tomorrow when they advanced on Delville Wood. But it was becoming impossible to find experienced NCOs or officers.

'You know everyone, Ernie. Where do I find a good Sergeant?'

Crosse leaned back in his chair and tilted it backwards at an alarming angle, so that his head nearly touched the wall. He balanced it thus and took his tobacco tin from his pocket. He began stuffing his pipe with his eyes half-closed in thought.

'Not a sergeant,' he said at last. 'But if you're willing, Corporal Allen would be a fine choice.'

'I must admit I'd thought the same,' he replied. 'Except I'm loathe to lose him. I suppose Private Veale has been angling for a promotion.'

He wanted to see Allen progress, but things had changed so fast lately that it felt almost like keeping a family together, or rather, stopping it breaking up. The last few weeks had been especially torrid, with so many losses, and Hansen had to thank whatever deity, fate or luck that was responsible for leaving him more or less unscathed. Except in this last instance, it was none of those, it was his friend's sacrifice at Mansell Copse.

'You're right,' said Hansen. 'It must be Allen.' He went to the door of the dugout and shouted to the man on duty. 'Pass the word for Corporal Allen.'

A couple of minutes passed, and the Corporal knocked cautiously on the doorframe before poking his head in.

'You asked for me, sir?'

'Yes, Corporal, come in.'

Hansen finished scribbling his notes on the new company disposition and finally tidied the papers and sorted them into a file. He turned back to where Allen stood waiting.

'Albert. I have some news which I think you will welcome. As you know, we are getting 'A' company back up to strength, and we're in need of experienced NCOs. I don't want to lose you from 'C' company, but I'd like you to command a section. It means an uprating to Sergeant. What do you say?'

'Thank you, sir. I'd be pleased to accept,' said Allen, struggling to hold back his very obvious excitement.

'Good. I should think it will only be a hop and a skip from there to Company Sergeant Major. I know you're keen to progress.'

'Yes, sir. I've been meaning to ask you about that, sir.'

'Oh?'

'Well, I might have told you that my father was a soldier too.'

'You did. He was in South Africa, wasn't he?'

'Yes, sir. My family have never been keen on my soldiering, sir, on account of that, but I wanted to follow in his footsteps, so to speak, and there's a long tradition of the army in my family. Mercenary work my grandfather says, us being Cornish and fighting for the British.'

'Ah, I see,' said Hansen, smiling. 'Didn't like you crossing the Tamar?'

'No, sir. But well, I was thinking, we've always been enlisted men. There's never been an officer in my family. Do you think I have a chance?'

He stroked his chin and tried to answer as kindly and directly as he reasonably could.

'Well,' said Hansen. 'You know as well as I do that they will always favour those who have been through an OTC.'

'You mean, gentlemen, sir. Like you?'

'If you like. But there are "temporary gentlemen". Look at Captain Nelson. He was a sergeant.'

'Although he had to win a VC to do it, mind you,' chipped in Crosse, unhelpfully.

Allen visibly deflated and looked at his feet. He was in his late twenties already, and his chances of being commissioned were slim, thought Hansen, privately. Even if he did make it, he knew plenty of so-called gentlemen who scorned the 'TGs' who had been promoted from the ranks, as if they were there because of necessity rather than ability.

'You shouldn't be put off though, Albert. I have no doubt you have all the qualities to be a good officer. Take this promotion, work hard and show the bravery you always have, and they will not be able to ignore you.'

'Yes, sir, thank you.'

'And perhaps you could find an officer you respect and learn from him.'

'Yes, sir. I have, sir.'

'Or perhaps choose another officer of our acquaintance and learn from him how <u>not</u> to do it,' added Crosse, with icy sarcasm. Hansen frowned at him. It was unlike him to cross the line like that, though he might often skirt it.

'Thank you, Albert. I'll push the paperwork through and confirm the promotion in due course, but I want you to remain with 'C' company for tomorrow's show. I will lead 'A' company myself and you'll be in the reserve. Dismiss.'

Allen saluted and then turned sharply and marched out. It was good to see a spring back in his step, but it would be a hard road to be promoted from the ranks.

'Think he'll make it?' said Crosse.

'If there's any justice he will,' replied Hansen.

'Natural justice or army justice?', smiled Crosse, with his head to one side.

***

It was a warm night with a full moon and Hansen could hear the cicadas chirping as he walked his lines. He wondered where they could possibly be finding any shelter or food, with every tree and bush for miles turned to matchwood.

He'd fallen into a routine after so many months, and he couldn't pretend there wasn't now an element of superstition in it too. He would lie on his bunk and fail to sleep for a number of hours before getting up, washing, checking his kit and then walking the trench line talking to his men. When he was finished, he would eat something and then make the walk a second time. He rounded the traverse and came upon a couple of soldiers he didn't recognise. They looked up nervously when they saw him approach.

'Just arrived?' he asked, with the appearance of calm he had perfected.

'Yes, sir,' said one, who looked petrified.

'What are your names?'

'Bovey, sir,' said one.

'Hellier', said the other man.

'And your Christian names?'

'Jack Bovey, sir,' said the first man, with a degree of surprise.

'William Hellier, sir. Bill.' Bovey gave him a dig in the ribs for this and whispered:

'The officer doesn't need to know that you idiot.'

Hansen smiled good-naturedly.

'I do actually,' he said. 'I wouldn't want to call you William if you're a Bill, would I?'

They both looked at him with a mixture of bafflement and wonder, which was what he'd intended. If they were distracted, they wouldn't have time to be afraid.

He continued on his rounds and before long his watch showed 3.25am as he held it up to a flickering lamp. He took his place on the trench ladder and rubbed some mud onto his whistle, both to reduce the shine, and because he always did.

There was a crash of artillery and the bombardment began. As the thunder continued, he counted out the seconds and then blew hard on his whistle to start the attack.

They emerged from the trench to sporadic rifle fire. He'd instructed his company to advance in short bursts, and they made good progress under the cover of darkness, scurrying from shell hole to shell hole.

Hansen stayed close to one of the new recruits carrying a Lewis gun on his shoulder. The artillery barrage stopped as suddenly as it had started, and as the smoke began to clear he prepared himself for the expected reprisals from the German lines; but nothing came.

They closed quickly on the front line and Hansen directed the soldier to set up the Lewis gun on a firebay jutting out across the trench, to give enfilading fire on the whole length. This he did, unmolested by the enemy. But when Hansen surveyed the trench, he realised why – it had been abandoned.

'Forward!' he shouted, as he took a running jump to clear the width of the trench.

As he continued towards the second line, he felt a prickle of instinctive caution, but he pushed his intuition to one side and kept going.

Scanning the ground ahead of him, he came upon a face in the clouded moonlight with what he took to be a rifle aimed in his direction. He took cover amongst some barbed wire and rolled onto his front, aiming his revolver at the figure. He waited, but the figure stayed where it was, and no shot came. Perhaps he hadn't been seen after all? A shot would attract attention, so he maintained his careful watch.

Minutes passed and Hansen began to think about rushing his enemy. He reached one hand down and sought out his dagger as quietly as he could. As his hand grasped the hilt there was a great thud as a landmine detonated in the area ahead. At once firing began from the German lines and he could see the tracers from a machine gun sweep across the ground towards him. He ducked down and could hear the bullets whip past, just above his head.

There was no reason to be quiet now, and he pushed himself up and over the barbed wire towards the figure. As he reached him with his dagger in his hand, he realised that the face was hollowed out with decay and blackened with rot. This man wasn't moving because he hadn't moved in months. He cursed his own stupidity, sliding the dagger back into its sheath. Then he began to run towards the enemy line, keen to make up for time lost in chasing ghosts.

When he reached the second line the trench was already surrounded by Highlanders and his own company, taking heavy casualties as they attempted to enter. As he surveyed the scene, he seemed to see the shadows of the lost 'A' company surrounding them, and this time he wouldn't leave them to their fate. He didn't slow his pace and with reckless abandon he jumped straight into the German trench. As he landed an officer turned towards him in such surprise that he didn't react. Hansen levelled his revolver and shot him in the heart. If he'd stopped to think he would have realised that he was now surrounded by the enemy, but he didn't stop. He fired again at Germans behind the fallen officer and wounded several of them. One of them aimed his rifle at Hansen, but conspired to miss him from five yards, the bullet churning the air just inches from him, and hitting a sandbag behind. The surprise that had accompanied his sudden arrival was gone now, but just as the Germans began to regroup, British soldiers began to arrive, following his lead and charging headlong at the enemy.

The tide was turned. The Germans were climbing out of their own trench and running for safety. An officer and another soldier emerged from a dugout behind him and it was only with difficulty that he prevented himself from shooting them on the spot, when he realised they had their hands in the air. With this the bloodlust that had been filling him began to seep away and he felt ashamed of what he had done.

'It's alright,' he said to the officer at last. 'You are prisoners. You will not be harmed.'

The reserve began to arrive to reinforce their position, including his own 'C' company, and Corporal Allen clambered down into the trench next to him, with Private Veale hard on his heels.

'Allen, I want you to take these two into detention. Treat them well.'

'Yes, sir,' replied Allen, looking at him wide-eyed. 'Are you alright, sir?'

'Yes, fine,' he replied, although the adrenalin had begun to turn his legs to jelly, and his head was swimming.

'I didn't know you spoke Kraut, sir,' continued Allen.

'Was I speaking German?'

Now Allen was looking at him like he was unhinged, and he had to check himself. He'd spoken to the officer without thinking, and without thinking he'd used German. It had been years since he had last spoken it. He could date it to the minute in fact, when he'd stood on his doorstep at home on the eve of war in 1914. He'd thought then it would be the last time.

Major Dawes swung himself over the parapet and began to climb down into the trench.

'Good show, Hansen,' he said. 'We will secure this line. I want you to continue the advance. This could be the breakthrough we've been looking for.'

'Yes, sir. First wave! Follow me!' he shouted and began to climb the trench once again.

Now his lungs were burning with the exertion of tramping through the thick mud. As they went deeper into German territory, the barren mud gave way to corn fields, continuing to grow in this strangest of environments. Hansen waded waist-high through the crop and they began to come under heavy fire from further lines of defence, which they had thought to be merely support trenches.

Hansen crouched down to find some cover amongst the plants. Bullets scythed through the stalks of corn and there were snaps as the stems split. A soldier near Hansen was hit in the leg and stumbled briefly, before being hit again in the neck. He fell forward, dead.

He could see little amongst the corn. It was difficult to know how many of his men had survived, if any at all. As he worked his way forwards, crouching on all fours, he heard the whistle of a shell arching close overhead. He ducked down and covered his head, waiting for the explosion. But the shell seemed to have landed without detonating. He sighed with relief, and having waited a few seconds, started forward again.

He turned back to look at where the shell had landed. As he did so there was a tremendous explosion and an overwhelming force lifted him off his feet and threw him backwards. He felt the corn break around him as he hurtled through the air, out of control. He landed on his shoulder with a crack and rolled forwards several times before coming to rest on his front.

For a moment he lay there. His whole body felt numb, except for his face, which burned with the heat of the explosion. His ears felt blocked and muffled and his head thumped like the worst hangover in history.

He tried to lift himself, but his arm gave way with a searing pain in his shoulder blade. Then he rolled over onto his back and was met with an agonising burning sensation in his leg which made him feel physically sick. His breathing was heavy as he struggled to think of anything else but the extraordinary pain.

He looked down and saw a six-inch piece of jagged metal sticking out of his left leg, just above the knee. There was little blood evident, but that might soon change if he tried to remove it. He'd seen soldiers bleed to death from the most innocuous-looking leg wounds, where the artery had been severed. As he looked more closely, he could see rips in his tunic where smaller fragments of shrapnel were lodged across his chest and side. He counted at least five. His shoulder was likely broken as well.

He tried to raise himself on his remaining good arm and fell back again, panting with pain. A second effort had the same result, and he almost laughed in his misery, to think that perhaps there would be some corner of a foreign corn field which would be forever filled with his bones. Would farmers be ploughing them up for years to come, as they did at Waterloo?

He must have fainted. For when he was conscious again, he could see the sky above him turning grey with the dawn. At first, he was surprised to still be alive, but as he managed to focus his thoughts, he realised there might be a hope. Orderlies may be looking for the wounded in the last minutes before dawn. With a supreme effort he pushed himself up and waved his arm forlornly. He wasn't even certain if it could be seen above the corn, but while there was a chance to live, he wanted to seize it. At that moment he couldn't clearly think of any reason why, except that the war was not yet over, and while it lasted, he must do his duty.

He waved for as long as his ebbing energy would allow, and then he collapsed back onto the ground. As he lay there, he heard voices. Not clear voices, but loud enough to just be distinguishable, and in German. He caught a few words – 'Tommy', the word they used for the British, 'casualties', 'counterattack'. He even thought he heard 'breakfast', but then again, perhaps it was delirium.

There was a kind of silence for a while, and then he heard a scratching sound. A scrambling and a scraping sound. Then, with a final rustle of corn, Private Veale appeared from amongst the plants and came to a stop on his knees next to Hansen.

'Sir!' he said, with relief.

Hansen shushed him and pointed to the German lines. Veale came up close and whispered to him.

'How far, sir?

'Ten yards maybe,' he whispered back, though a whisper was all he could manage anyway.

Veale puffed his cheeks and pulled his field dressings from his tunic. He flinched at the sight of the leg wound.

'Jees, I can't do much with that, sir,' he said in a hoarse whisper.

'Help me up.'

'We're too close, sir. I'm gonna have to drag you.'

Hansen nodded his consent, and Veale grabbed him round the shoulders and began to drag him backwards. The pain was excruciating, and Hansen had to stuff his hand in his own mouth to stifle the noise.

Veale stopped, catching his breath. After a moment he began to pull again. The shrapnel in Hansen's leg caught on the root of one of the corn plants, causing a shiver of nauseating throbbing down his whole leg. It was so intense he felt he might pass out again. Having gone perhaps 20 yards, Veale stopped for a second time, exhausted by the effort.

'I can't do this, sir, I need to get help. And I'll get you some water.'

Hansen could only nod. Veale moved off, half running, half crawling on all fours. There was the crack sound of bullets through the corn as the enemy took pot shots at him, but as he disappeared from view, he was still alive.

'Water, sir?' said Veale, as Hansen opened his eyes again. How much time had passed? The sky was getting brighter all the time, and shafts of sunlight were beginning to flicker through the corn. Veale offered his canteen to Hansen, and he took it and gulped from it gratefully.

'Let's get him on the sheet, lads.'

It was Corporal Allen, who was sitting to one side of him. Challacombe was there too, and another soldier. Private Lord, if he remembered his name correctly.

'You shouldn't all be out here,' he said weakly.

'We just fancied stretching our legs some, sir,' said Allen. 'Quite by chance we ran into you.'

'At least you've got a Blighty, sir,' said Challacombe.

Hansen rolled his eyes at the prospect of returning home. He would feel like a failure to be lying in some comfortable hospital bed while they were here, risking their lives.

They rolled and dragged Hansen in stages onto the canvas sheet, which they had managed to bring out with them. Each manoeuvre caused him intense pain, but he began to think he might make it out of this sodden field after all. Finally, they had it arranged as a kind of stretcher.

'Get a corner each,' ordered Allen. 'With me.'

They started to pull on their hands and knees, keeping below the corn.

'Three men went to mow, went to mow---' began Allen, singing in a whisper. 'Come on, join in.'

'Three men went to mow, went to mow a meadow' they all sang. 'Three men, two men, one man and his dog. Went to mow a meadow---'

'I hope I'm not the dog,' said Hansen, half awake.

'<u>Four</u> men went to mow, went to mow a meadow. Four man, three men, two men, one man and his dog---'

The song was having an effect, and they made good progress, moving quickly and smoothly. They reached an old trench line. It was shallow but crossed by a wooden bridge. Overcoming it would take them above the safety of the corn.

'This won't do,' said Allen.

'Leave me here.'

'Not on your life, sir. At the double, lads, let's do this bloody fast, before the squareheads get a look in.'

They began to drag Hansen across the bridge, and as they did so, their heads came into view above the corn, as much as they tried to duck down. As he looked to one side, Hansen saw German heads pop up from amongst the field, one after the other.

They were nearly across, but Hansen heard a shot ring out. Corporal Allen stopped still and fell to the ground next to him. The others took cover and returned fire, while Hansen lay looking at Allen's face next to him, his eyes staring back, lifeless, with blood trickling down his neck.

Hansen screwed his eyes up tight. For a moment, the pain seemed to recede, and he wanted to cry out in anger and sorrow. Why hadn't they left him out there to die?

'Fuck, I reckon we wait it out till dark,' said Challacombe

Veale looked across at the open ground between them and the safety of the British lines.

'Not getting across there, that's for bloody sure,' he agreed. 'Not with Jerry behind every blade of grass.'

'Get yourselves back,' said Hansen, angry now that they were here with him.

'We'll stick it out with you, sir, if that's alright?' said Veale.

'Can't be more than twelve hours till dark,' said Challacombe, with a wry grin.

'I should have you up for disobeying orders,' said Hansen, unsure of whether he meant it or not.

'Veale, will you do something for me?'

'Sir?'

'Close his eyes.'

Chapter Twelve

1919
Cornwall

'Next station Truro. All change.'

Emily stirred slowly from a deep sleep and found that she had been resting with her head against Richard's shoulder. She moved away slowly, hoping that he hadn't noticed. She caught sight of herself in the door glass and made to tidy her hair, but she was actually looking past her own reflection at Richard. As she looked, she fancied that he was also glancing at her, but when she looked around, he was looking through the window.

The train juddered to a stop with squealing brakes. Richard got to his feet and straightened his lanyard.

'Ready to go?' he asked.

She nodded and followed him out of the compartment onto the station platform. Mr Crosse fell in step beside her as Richard walked ahead to find a cab to take them to the farm.

'It's wonderful to be out in the fresh air again,' he said. 'Enjoying the beautiful English countryside in the Springtime. Don't you agree?'

'Yes,' she agreed, a little unsure of whether he was just offering some innocent small talk, or if there was another intent. She sensed that nothing he said was without purpose.

'I remember a poem I learned by rote when I was a schoolboy,' he continued. 'Many moons ago now. It went something like: "Little boy, Full of joy; Little girl, Sweet and small; Cock does crow, So do you; Merry voice, Infant noise; Merrily, merrily to welcome in the year."'

'William Blake,' she said. 'It's a wonderful poem.'

'Quite so. You'd be good at the quotes game,' he offered, leaving the statement hanging and begging for explanation.

'I don't know that game,' she said, taking the bait.

'Ah, well. Richard and I used to play it. It's very simple. You give a quotation that you can remember, and the other person has to guess who wrote it.'

They walked on through the station and came out onto the road where a pony and trap were waiting, and Richard was talking to the cabbie.

'How does the rest of that poem go?' said Crosse. 'I can't remember.'

"'Little lamb, Here I am; Come and lick, My white neck; Let me pull, Your soft wool; Let me kiss, Your soft face; Merrily, merrily we welcome in the year.'"

As she finished, they came to a stop next to the cab. Crosse took off his glasses and looked at her with a curious half-smile.

'Very nicely done,' he said.

They climbed aboard the trap and soon they were trotting through country lanes. By now it was late afternoon, but the sun was still warm, and Emily enjoyed feeling it on her face, with the smell of the blossoms on the trees drifting through the air. It reminded her of stolen moments on a Sunday afternoon when she had been able to escape the house and enjoy the parks and gardens of the city. But the countryside was something else again, new and enthralling.

The trap let them off at the farm gate, and they walked up the track from there, skirting a field of corn as they made their way towards the farmhouse. Richard looked pensive as he looked across the fields. Something of the spark had gone and his shoulders dropped.

'Are you alright?' she asked.

'I'm well,' he said, but something seemed to be stirring up unpleasant memories.

A farmer leading a horse came into view as they reached the farmyard. He stopped and watched them approach. Old and world-weary, he had short, grizzled hair, a week's growth of stubble and skin hardened by a life outdoors.

'Would you be Mr Allen?' said Richard.

'Whose business if it is?' said the farmer, fixing them with a hard stare.

'My name is Richard Hansen.'

'That would be an English name, would it?'

Richard broke eye contact and looked away.

'It could be,' he replied. 'Though wherever I'm from, I came here to talk with you.'

'Did you now?' said the farmer, with a sneer. 'Well, I'm in no mood to talk to no red tab emmet. You've no business here, boy.'

The farmhouse door opened, and an older woman stepped out. She looked tough, but with a warmth in her countenance. She crossed the yard and stood behind the farmer, curious about the new arrivals.

'Your son---' began Richard.

'My son died nearly 20 year ago, for the English queen, as was then,' said Mr Allen, with bitterness. 'You're a bit late if you're here for ee.'

'Albert, I meant,' said Richard.

'Albert is our grandson,' said the woman, whom Emily took to be the man's wife. '<u>Was</u> our grandson. You were his commanding officer?'

'I had that privilege.'

'Knowing our Bert, not so much a privilege as a pain in the backside I'd warrant.'

'Sometimes.'

She looked at Richard with one eye closed, shielding the other from the sun with her hand. She appeared to be sizing him up. Finally, she nodded her head and turned to go back towards the farmhouse. When no one followed, she turned back.

'Will you be coming in?'

'Will you not listen to what I said?' called her husband.

'I never have for the last 40 years, Will Allen. Like I will start now.'

They all followed Mrs Allen as she crossed the farmyard once again, while Mr Allen muttered to himself and coaxed the horse towards the stables. He kept one eye fixed on Richard as they passed.

The kitchen they entered was the very model of a traditional farmhouse, with a large table on one side, and stove on the other. A butter churn sat on the table with a basket of eggs and a jug of fresh milk. It seemed to Emily to be an idyllic life, to live in such a place, with fresh produce in abundance and no one to answer to.

'Will you have a drink?' said Mrs Allen.

'Tea, if you have any?' said Crosse.

'I don't, but there's beer.'

'Fine,' said Crosse, disappointed.

They sat down at the big table, and Mrs Allen moved the eggs and butter churn onto the side, putting out glasses for each of them, which she then filled with a frothy beer from a large earthenware jug. Emily lifted the glass to her nose cautiously. She had never been allowed alcohol by Mrs Hansen, and the smell was pungent and sour. She tasted some. It was bitter, but pleasantly cool.

'Mrs Allen,' began Richard, turning the glass in his hand.

'Hannah.'

'Hannah,' he continued, with a strange formality. 'I wanted to express my condolences in person. You may know, your grandson saved my life. I could never repay that debt.'

Richard relaxed a little, perhaps glad to have said what he came to say, though she sensed he wasn't saying everything. Mrs Allen sat down next to him and smiled kindly.

'I know he would not wish it repaid. That's not how he was. My husband - he's all bluster, but it hurts him. He blames the army. Our son died in South Africa, and then Bert joined up, a few year before this war. Will wouldn't have it, he went spare, but Bert was set on it, like his father. We've worked all our lives here. It's not an easy living but it's ours. Now, when we go---it will go.'

Richard pushed his beer to one side and steepled his fingers, touching them gently on his bottom lip. He explained the visit they had made to the Cairns' house, and Robert's wish to be in the outdoors.

'He would wish to come here?' said Hannah when he'd finished.

'He might. And I think perhaps he could help you too.'

'We don't need help from you!'

It was William, who had just blown into the room, wiping his hands on a rag. He poured himself a beer and drank it down in one go.

'Oh, be quiet, Will,' said Hannah.

He drank another glass and rounded on Richard, pushing his face in close, so that flecks of spittle landed on him.

'Bloody murdering bastards, you have no care for what you do, any of you. Letting Bert die for you!'

Emily recognised a look she had seen before, in the street in Plymouth, but this time with teeth gritted in anger. In a sudden explosion Richard took hold of his face and pushed the old man backwards. He stumbled and landed in a heap against the wall. Then Richard climbed onto the table, wincing as he pushed off the chair, and swung onto the other side.

'Richard, no!' said Crosse, turning to stop him.

But Richard had stopped short. His hands were clenched tight and he took a deep breath as he turned back, mastering his rage.

'I'm sorry. Forgive me.'

He hurried outside, looking thoroughly ashamed, and Emily moved to follow, but Crosse waved her back and followed himself. A sheepish William gathered himself and what was left of his dignity and sloped off, leaving Emily and Hannah alone at the table.

'My Will. He never knows when to shut up. But I love him, despite all, if you know what I mean?'

She poured Emily some more beer. She realised she had drunk a whole glass rather quickly and she felt strangely giddy.

'Yes. I know what you mean.'

'I'm surprised he would bring his wife with him though, on a visit like this.'

'No, no!' said Emily. 'I'm not---'

'You're not?'

There was no easy way to explain what he was to her, or her to him. Perhaps it was best not to try.

'He suffered I think,' she said, changing the subject.

'In the war?' asked Hannah. Emily nodded. 'I seen it. My son had a bad time with the Boers. And then Bert, what he wrote home, it wasn't the whole picture I know. He didn't want me to worry.'

'I see he's in pain,' said Emily. 'I want to help him, but I don't understand what he's feeling or what it was that has affected him so deeply.'

Her normal caution had deserted her, and she felt a need to confide in this woman. It was peculiarly easy to talk to her.

'I'm sorry,' she said. 'I know I've only just met you.'

'It's alright. I understand. There's all this going on in my Will's head, and in his heart, but will he share it? Will he hell. You have to read them like the weather - storm clouds one minute, sunshine the next.

'Let's take a walk, shall we? I need to feed the pigs.'

Hannah picked up a bucket of scraps and went out into the farmyard. Emily got up to follow but had to steady herself. Her legs had decided not to co-operate, and it took a moment to find her footing. When she got outside, she found Crosse deep in conversation with Richard, who was obviously still rattled.

Crosse smiled broadly as he noticed them, taking his pipe from his pocket and switching on the easy charm that she was accustomed to seeing.

'Richard and I thought it would be a good idea to take a walk down to the village. While we're there we could telegraph Robert Cairns if you would like us to? Perhaps ask him to visit?'

'Yes. Thank you. I think it's a wonderful idea,' said Hannah.

'Good. Well, we'll see you later.'

Richard and Crosse walked off together down the track, continuing the intense conversation that had been interrupted. Meanwhile, Hannah guided her across the yard towards the pig sty.

When they reached the pen, Hannah started throwing kitchen scraps in for them, and Emily peered in at two enormous animals covered in a soft hair, snuffling in the mud for the peelings that they were being thrown. She didn't want to get too near to these strange creatures, which looked like they might bite someone's hand off.

'There you go my darlings,' said Hannah. 'Tuck in!'

'I didn't expect them to be so---big,' said Emily.

'Have you never seen a pig before?'

'Only wrapped in butcher's paper and tied up with string,' she explained. 'I used to cook for Richard and his family.'

She didn't really know why she felt the need to tell her that either. There seemed to be no check on her voicing her mind just now. Hannah's eyebrows rose noticeably, and Emily could easily imagine the thoughts now going through her mind. To her credit, she said nothing, but continued feeding the pigs.

'Ah, well, they're friendly creatures,' she said.

She threw the last of the peelings into the sty and stood back, watching them gorge themselves. Then she turned back to Emily, curiosity having got the better of her.

'You said you used to cook for them. Why did you leave?'

Emily played with her hair nervously. There was no way to answer that honestly without bringing shame on someone, not least herself.

'It's none of my business,' said Hannah, sparing her blushes. 'But you wanted to come here?'

'Yes,' said Emily. 'Being here, outside, travelling, in all this beauty. It's what I've read about. Life. Except until now it has happened to other people. And now I don't think I could bear to lose it - any of it.'

'What might you lose?' said Hannah.

'Well, I mean when the journey ends,' she said.

Hannah smiled kindly and nodded knowingly.

'Let me tell you. When I was your age I wanted, more than anything, to see India.'

'India?'

'Yep. If you can believe it, I had a fancy to ride on an elephant and see tigers, and all that. But it was so far. And my father wanted me married. So, I did. But I still have a picture on my wall, and I look at it now and then, and wish maybe I had been braver. Take it from an old woman who will never ride an elephant, there's nothing worse than settling for what others want you to be.'

***

Some time later, Richard and Crosse returned from their excursion. Emily put down the bowl of vegetables she was peeling for Hannah and skipped across to meet them. She was pleased to see that Richard looked much more relaxed now.

'Good news! Robert Cairns is on his way. He will be here tomorrow,' said Crosse, as Hannah also came outside.

'I'm glad,' she said. 'I will speak to Will. I'm sure he will come around. Eventually.'

'If it's not too much trouble,' said Richard. 'We'd like to stay until he gets here.'

'Of course. But I'm afraid you'll have to work for your supper. The chickens need mucking out and feeding.'

'Oh, well,' said Crosse, coughing politely and edging his way towards the farmhouse. 'I would of course be delighted, but I have a sermon to write, you know. "There is no peace, saith the Lord, unto the wicked."'

'Of course,' said Hannah, with complete sincerity. 'Far be it for me to put a man of the cloth to manual work.'

Crosse made a polite little bow and scurried off quickly into the farmhouse.

'H'ah!' said Richard with mock outrage. Hannah scowled at him with a stare that could melt iron. 'No of course,' said Richard quickly, avoiding her gaze.

'There are shovels and fresh hay in the barn.'

Hannah left them alone, returning to her preparations in the kitchen. Richard turned to Emily and she shrugged.

'Very well. I'll scoop and you can feed,' he said.

They made their way to the chicken coop and found everything they needed. Richard got to work with the smelly task of cleaning out chicken droppings from the coop and putting them into a wheelbarrow. Emily meanwhile scattered corn for them, which the chickens pecked at with great enthusiasm.

'I feel somehow our roles have been reversed,' said Richard, jokingly.

'I don't mind a jot,' she smiled

'No, clearly.'

There was something very companionable as they worked away together in the evening sunshine. They'd found the ease in talking to each other that they'd had before. Or at least it was similar. He wasn't quite as relaxed with her as he had been then, but then he was so changed in every way.

'Don't you think they are funny?' she said.

'Who?'

'Chickens. They have inscrutable expressions. I'd like to know what they're thinking.'

'I suspect they're wondering how they can avoid being put in the pot!' he said, laughing. 'Do you mind all this?'

'Not really,' she replied. 'I'm used to it.'

'I suppose you are,' he said, giving her a sidelong glance. 'But that's not what I meant. I mean, dragging you away on this - whatever it is. You didn't have to come.'

'Would you rather I wasn't here?'

She hadn't intended it to sound as bitter as it did, but he had touched an unexpected nerve. She was surprised at her own reaction when everything had seemed to be so pleasant.

'No, of course not,' he said, clearly stung by her reaction. 'I'm pleased you are. But it can't be very pleasant for you.'

It was curious that he would use the same word that had come to her mind at that moment. Except that she worried that things were too pleasant.

'I wanted to come. I haven't seen much of the world. It's all new for me, and I have enjoyed it.'

'There's a "but" though, isn't there?' he said. 'I'm sorry my temper got the better of me again. If that's what you're worried about?'

'It's true I'm worried,' she said. 'But not in the way I think you mean. I'm worried for you.'

He shuffled around awkwardly.

'You really shouldn't. There's no need,' he said, looking agitated. He started forking the hay more violently.

'Isn't that what friends do?'

He stopped and rested his hands on the handle of the fork, studying her with an intensity that made her a little self-conscious.

'I wanted to help you,' she said, trying to ignore his continuing attention. 'But I don't think you need me. Mr Crosse understands better. He was there, he knows what you ---' she wanted to say 'saw', but it seemed too blunt. 'He knows how it was.'

He dropped his fork and sat down on a fence post near her. He seemed to be contemplating a choice, and then finally he turned to her, although his eyes looked away into the sky.

'When I'm awake,' he began, with a slow determination, 'which is most of the time. I can feel every muscle in my body, taut like a bandage done too tight. My mind surges - one emotion, then another - always thinking, thinking, thinking. Like drowning.' He held his head, deep in concentration.

'But when you held my hand, I felt calm. It's been so long since I knew that feeling. If it helps you to know that?'

He still didn't look at her, but Emily wanted more than anything to reach out and take his hand now.

He stood up, and ran his hand through his hair, laughing a little nervously.

'At least we've both seen a farm now. Although it's ruining your dress.'

As she followed his gaze, she lifted the hem of her skirt and realised it was now covered in mud and muck.

'Oh no! This is my best as well!'

It was a silly thing but seeing her one good dress ruined like that brought all her fears and anxieties gushing to the surface. It was a jolt of reality.

'Now you're a real Devon girl!' he joked, though she wasn't now in the mood for it. 'Come on, let's get cleaned up.'

He picked up the tools and they trudged off back into the farmyard. Now all she could think about was the future. No job, no money, no prospects. It was like being suddenly woken from a pleasant dream and realising that none of it was real.

As they walked, they met William Allen coming in the opposite direction, herding some cows. On sighting them, and especially Richard, he geed up the cows into a trot. The cows spread out and rushed past in such a way that it forced them into a muddy ditch, where they both lost their footing and fell into the muck. William chuckled to himself as he passed.

'Getting stuck in, eh?'

Emily looked down at herself in a shudder of self-pity and felt like weeping. She expected Richard to be angry, but as she looked across, he was quietly shaking, and then burst into roaring, flailing laughter. As he laughed uncontrollably, she couldn't help but join in, and soon they were both caught in a paralysing mirth, struggling to breath or talk. She hadn't laughed like this since she was a child, and it was wonderful.

***

After their evening meal, when everything was tidied away, Emily made her way to the farmhouse door. She breathed in the cool evening air, which was refreshing after the hot kitchen, and she stretched her arms out wide, as if embracing the experience. The moon was out, and it bathed the farmyard in a magical glow. She thought back on the afternoon's events. It was pleasing to think she'd made a difference, and she knew that whatever came next, that must be important. Life had to mean something. There had to be a way of making a contribution, somehow, somewhere, that was more than keeping a house tidy and serving a passable meal. It was surely not prideful to think she was worth more than that, and that she merited being seen at last, after doing what was expected of her for so long. After doing her duty.

Then she noticed William Allen sitting outside on a bench, drinking a mug of coffee. Curls of smoke from his cigarette drifted upwards, white in the moonlight. There was a sadness about him. How many more years did he have, and his life's work would have to be sold and passed to strangers. Richard came around from the side of the house, with his own mug of coffee, and stopped next to him.

'May I sit down?' he asked.

'Do as you please,' said William. 'You will anyway.'

Richard perched near him and took a silver hip flask from his pocket. He unscrewed the cap slowly and then offered it to William. The old man looked at it for a moment, before grabbing it like a child stealing a toy, and pouring some of the contents into his coffee. He handed it back to Richard, who closed it and put it back into his pocket.

'Are you not joining me?' said William.

'No. I made a promise to someone.'

Emily allowed herself a little smile.

'Taken the pledge, have you?'

'In a manner of speaking,' said Richard, drinking his coffee. As he raised his mug, the moonlight glinted off the brass stripes on the sleeve of his tunic. Emily had wondered what they signified. William clearly noticed them too, and then turned back to his own drink.

'You were wounded?' said William. Richard nodded. 'You weren't no staff officer then? How many stripes is that?'

'Three,' said Richard.

William nodded. The gruff expression he had carried all day started to soften and seemed now to show a new respect.

'Any more of that whisky?'

Richard took out the hip flask again and handed it to William, who poured some more into his mug. Richard took a long breath and turned to the farmer.

'Mr Allen, I know you don't like what I am, but I'm only here to try to repay the faith your grandson put in me. You need help here.'

'I can manage.'

'I know you can. But this man who is coming here was a soldier too. I think coming here would help him. He needs space to breathe again, if you understand what I mean?'

He eyed Richard cautiously.

'I reckon I do.'

'Will you help him? Give him a chance?'

The old farmer thought for a moment and then nodded slowly. He handed the hipflask back to Richard, but he put his hand up in refusal.

'You keep it for me now.'

***

Emily lay in bed, wide awake, listening to the hooting of an owl outside. Or two owls, as she reminded herself. A male and female calling to each other. One without the other would leave the familiar call incomplete.

As she listened, she could also hear muffled voices coming from another room. She tried to ignore it at first, but more and more intrigued, she got up to investigate. She put her dressing gown on and opened her door carefully. The voices seemed to be coming from downstairs.

She tip-toed down the hall and reached the top of the stairs. She paused and listened to the voice, which seemed to have a lyrical, musical quality to it. It was someone she didn't recognise, and she edged onto the stairs to be able to look down through the bannisters. She sat on the stair and from where she was, she could see Hannah and William at the table with another woman, who was dressed in a voluminous gown that was difficult to describe. It was a silky black with lace edging, and enormous sleeves. A particularly odd costume compared to the simple style of the Allens.

Their hands were out in front of them, flat against the table, with their fingers touching. The room was very dark, except for a single candle on the table. And their eyes were closed.

'I can feel the presence of Albert very strongly,' said the woman. 'He says your son Thomas is here too. They want to know that you are well and happy.'

'Tell them we think of them every day,' said Hannah, speaking out into the air. 'I miss my boys so much.'

Emily had read about those who put their faith in spiritualism, trying to contact their lost sons, brothers, husbands, fathers. No less than Arthur Conan-Doyle had advocated it and had convinced himself he saw the spirit of his son watching over him in a photograph. She found it unsettling, sad even, but if it brought people comfort, who was she to judge?

'They want me to say that they love you very much, and they are sorry they cannot look after you.'

'Tell my son I'm sorry for what I said,' said William.

'They are worried about the farm.'

William gripped his wife's hand tightly. The man who had showed so little emotion before, the morose watcher of everything they had done since they arrived, was now choked with tears.

'I so wish they were here to take it from me,' he said, bowing his head to the table. 'I would do anything.'

'Albert says he respected the Englishman in life, but you must trust what you feel about him.'

William turned to his wife and she gently stroked his face. She did it with great tenderness, and it was obvious that despite the snappy way she spoke to him, and the fact that the marriage was not her choice, she did love him. At that moment, even in their profound grief, Emily envied them.

She made her way back upstairs. It was too personal a moment, and it felt like intrusion to continue watching. But the feeling remained. No one had loved her like that since her mother. It might be morbid to think it, but who would seek for her spirit if she were to die? And that didn't seem so unlikely when she thought of the future that faced her when this diversion into another life inevitably ended.

She thought to return to her room, when she saw the door to Richard's room was ajar. Her better judgement told her to turn away, to sleep and dream of other things, but curiosity overcame judgement, as it too often had in the last few days.

As she looked in, she could see he was sleeping fitfully, twitching and tense. When he could sleep, he'd said, his dreams were filled with nightmares.

She moved closer and found herself kneeling next to the bed. The night was warm, and he was sleeping without a nightshirt. In the moonlight coming through the window, she could see a deep scar across his arm, and more disfiguring his chest and down his side. She grimaced in sympathy, imagining the injuries that must have left such traces. Such pain, and not just physical. There were so many memories holding him hostage and from which he deserved release.

Without thinking, she reached out and caressed the scars on his chest, as if by the act of touching she could heal them. Seemingly in response to her touch, he relaxed and began to sleep soundly.

"In vain have I struggled," she thought to herself. "It will not do." She rested her head on the mattress next to him, keen for his warmth and his company, desperate not to feel alone.

She closed her eyes and dreamed of fire and storms, and wretchedness beyond reason. And after it there came so long a train of people, that she never would have believed that ever Death so many had undone. And she found herself within a dark woods, where the straight way was lost.

Chapter Thirteen

1919

Cornwall

When Hansen woke, he felt refreshed in a way that he had not done for years. There was light now streaming through the window and he had not woken once during the night. If there had been nightmares, he could not now remember them.

As he turned over, he was shocked to discover Emily lying next to the bed, asleep, with her head lying uncomfortably on the edge of the mattress. Instinctively he shuffled away to the other edge of the bed and pulled the blanket up to cover his nakedness.

This time his memory of the previous night was clear, and he was sure she had not been there. She had, as far as he knew, gone to her own room. So how was it she was here now? He dared not move in case he woke her.

Awkward though her position was, in more ways than one, she nevertheless looked peaceful. He was compelled to watch, though she might wake at any moment and find him out. Her dark hair had come loose and there was a long strand hanging across her face, making her eye twitch a little in her sleep. He thought about sweeping it gently away, but that only made him think further about caressing her beautiful face.

For a moment he allowed his desires free reign over him and imagined how it would be to wake up to find her lying next to him every day. He had always felt comfortable in her company, always able to share his thoughts, but more than anything else he could sense that she saw the world as he once had. With an optimism and a passion that was intoxicating. He found himself wondering if what he felt was really all for her or if there was a part that was simply reaching for what he had lost in himself.

He slipped out of the bed and tip toed as quietly as he could manage with his wretched, misfunctioning leg, to the chair where his clothes hung. Every time he looked down at the angry red scar around his knee, he thought of the process of learning to walk again. It had taken him months, and at times he'd wished he had died there in the field of corn. And perhaps a piece of him had.

He turned back to look at Emily as he buttoned his shirt. He wondered if she would know the quote that had come to his mind as he watched her. He was sure she would. "I cannot fix on the hour, or the spot, or the look or the words, which laid the foundation" he thought. "I was in the middle before I knew that I had begun."

His thoughts continued in this vein as he finished dressing, but by the time he reached the door he was decided on an altogether different course. He could not dishonour her again when she was so obviously repelled before. And more than that, he was the cause of her dismissal and it was incumbent on him to make amends. She deserved to be fulfilled in her life, and that would not happen if she were tied to such a man as him. Her contentment and security would be his aim now. It was his duty, whatever his feelings.

***

Crosse sat at the kitchen table, breakfasting on ham and eggs. Hansen wondered at how the little man was not as big as a house, such was his appetite. He himself stood over the kettle, watching it fail to boil. Mrs Allen and her husband were early risers and were already busy at work on the farm, leaving them to fend for themselves.

As he continued to await the kettle, he heard footsteps on the stairs. The moment had arrived. She would surely know that he had seen her, but there was nothing to do but brazen it out as if it had never happened.

'I'm sorry, I didn't realise what time it was,' she said in a fluster, as she came down into the kitchen. She didn't look in his direction. As he had thought, she was mortified. In all likelihood she had simply felt pity for him and had been there to offer some solace, as a nurse would, when she had fallen asleep.

'Good morning!' he cried, acting the confident, carefree commander as he so often had for his men. 'Sit, sit. Would you like some tea?'

'Our host got that especially for me,' said Crosse.

'Yes, I think she has a soft spot for our reverend,' he replied, with a surreptitious wink at Emily.

She joined him at the stove.

'I can do that, sir.' He noted the return to the formal address with disappointment.

'No need. Pouring tea is one of my specialities if you remember? There are eggs and ham too, and toast. A real spread.'

He poured a cup for her, and she accepted it guiltily.

'You're not a servant here,' he whispered.

She went to sit down at the table opposite Crosse, and he could see in the reflection of the window that she was smiling a little to herself, in all probability out of relief that he had chosen not to make anything of it. He joined them at the table as Emily started to help herself to the food on offer.

'Robert Cairns is here already,' said Hansen.

'He must have got an early train?' said Crosse.

'Yes. The milk train he said. He must have been up before dawn. It's good to see. I really think it might help him.'

When he had spent time rehabilitating after his injuries, he'd seen patients struggling in the same way, and the doctors had sent them to work on local farms. Others were taught to sew or knit. It seemed to have worked, at least for a time. Except that the war department's motivation for helping them seemed to be to put a rifle back in their hands as soon as possible. He saw men who were still clearly unwell being returned to duty because they were deemed capable of fighting. Some had to be returned in short order, whilst others found a way to continue at the front. But it was difficult to say what the effect would be on them in the long term.

'I was thinking, how do you fancy a trip to Newlyn?' he continued.

'Capital idea!' said Crosse. 'It's a pretty place.'

'Why Newlyn?' said Emily.

Hansen took out the photograph once again and laid it on the table in front of her. He pointed to the languid captain seated, in customary fashion, with a glass of wine.

'Captain Martin. Duncan. He lived there before the war. And he went back every time he had leave.'

'Did he paint there?' she replied.

He was a little surprised, but only a little this time, now that he was beginning to appreciate her remarkable perception. Or had she read about him in his letters? He tried to remember.

'Yes, he did. How did you know?'

'You sort of mentioned it before. And there are many artists in Newlyn.'

'Well, I hope we shall see some of his paintings. Not that I ever understood them. I want to speak to Robert, and then we can be off. I have a new energy! Must be the country air or something.'

He realised as he said it that it was possibly an inappropriate thing to say, but he rather enjoyed the idea of the secret that they now shared. Was it too provocative? He couldn't tell from Emily's expression, although she herself was watching Crosse carefully, as if to read his reaction. Of which there seemed to be none. He went on chewing noisily on his toast.

Hansen finished his breakfast and went out into the yard. The air was warm already and dusty. It would likely be a hot day. He enjoyed the sun on his face as he placed his cap on his head and carefully adjusted it.

Walking around the farmhouse, he took a dusty track towards where Robert had been working earlier. If he could persuade him to stay, and the Allens to accept him, it might create a future for both of them. But he struggled to order his thoughts on what he might say, with other feelings about that morning's events vying for attention.

He found Robert looking over a fence at the sheep in the field. As he noticed Hansen arriving, he came immediately to attention.

'Sir!'

'Stand easy, Robert. You're not in the army now you know?'

'I know, sir.'

He looked disappointed, as if the idea of being out of the army was an unsettling and confusing experience. It was a feeling with which Hansen could identify.

'You miss it, don't you?'

'Sometimes. I mean it were awful, but I knew we was making a difference when I were out there. We looked after each other, didn't we?'

Hansen nodded in empathy. He couldn't have said it better. It seemed odd to think of such an experience as in any way positive, and he hesitated even now to admit his own feelings. But he knew he was far from alone, and like him, Robert needed to find a purpose again in life.

'What do you think of the place?'

'It's beautiful here, sir.'

'It is that.'

'I feel safe, you know. Inside I feel like I can't breathe sometimes. I feel trapped, like I can't escape.'

Hearing him speak in this way triggered a memory for Hansen. He recalled reading that the second battalion had fought a determined rear guard in the face of overwhelming odds during the German spring offensive the previous year. The Germans had thrown everything at them – tanks, aeroplanes, infantry, artillery. Only about 40 made it back to British lines, from over 600. To allow others to retreat and regroup they had stood and died in their hundreds. There had been no escape for them.

'Were you at Bois de Buttes last year?' he asked.

Robert nodded, though he flinched as he said it, and his lips tightened.

'I kept fighting, sir,' he said, agitated. 'I kept fighting. I did. I kept on till I had no ammunition left. I never ran. I never. I tried to swim the river, with a few others, but they caught me.'

'The Germans?'

He nodded again.

'I kept fighting, sir.'

'I know you did. You all did.'

They stood together and looked out across the landscape in silence. Not an awkward silence, but a silence that acknowledged that there was nothing more that need be said.

'Will you stay?' said Hansen at last. 'They need you. You could make a difference here.'

'I'd like that, sir. But I can't leave Sybil. She doesn't have anyone else to look after her now my brother is gone.'

'It's a big farm, you know.'

'Do you think they'd let her live here as well?'

'I'm sure Mrs Allen would. Mr Allen might take some convincing mind you---'

'I like him. He's been kind to me.'

'He and I haven't exactly hit it off. Well, perhaps you should mention it then.'

'Yes, sir. Thank you, sir.'

There was a straightforwardness to Robert that Hansen envied. Perhaps he had misjudged William too. What he had said the day before had pricked his own guilt, but what was there that was not true? Had he not as good as killed his grandson? Robert had stood and faced his enemy in reality. For Hansen it had been all too easy to walk away from his own responsibilities.

They walked back together down the track and into the farmyard. William was there with the horses and signalled for Robert to join him.

'Perhaps I can visit you again here, Robert?' said Hansen.

'I hope so, sir,' he replied, and they shook hands.

Robert went across to William and began helping him tack the horse. William actually seemed to be smiling as he showed the young man the ropes.

Emily and Crosse joined him in the yard, carrying their cases, and Emily handed him his own. William noticed them gathering and came across.

'You're off?' he said.

'Yes.'

'He's a good lad. He'll do well.'

He wiped his hand on his trousers and offered it to Hansen. He took it willingly.

'Good day to you,' said William, and with a slight nod of the head he returned to Robert with little more ceremony.

'Do you think that was an apology?' asked Crosse, sidling up to him.

Hansen shrugged. He caught Robert's eye once more, and the young man gave him a sharp salute. He was pleased to return the courtesy.

At the same time Hannah had bustled out from the house carrying some food wrapped up in paper. She went over to Emily, who was taking a last look around.

'Some of them porkers for your journey. More how you're used to seeing them,' she said, handing her the food packages. 'Take care. Remember what I told 'ee. Don't settle.'

She gave Emily a big hug. There seemed to be a real warmth between them. Hansen wondered how they had developed such a connection in such a short time, though it didn't surprise him that Emily could earn her affection so quickly. He had wondered whether losing her mother when she was so young had affected Emily. He himself could be considered fortunate in that regard, though it frequently didn't feel like it.

They took their leave and walked down the track way. It was another gloriously warm day that signalled the start of summer. He stopped to take in the view as they reached the gate again. From where they were, they could see across the Carrick Roads where the Helford river widened out towards the sea. Emily joined him in looking out, while Crosse was busy lighting his pipe again.

'Not bad, eh?' he said.

'Magnificent,' she agreed.

'Not that I want to break into your reverie,' said Crosse. 'But we'll miss our train.'

'"There never was any poetry about Harris,"' he said, raising an eye towards Emily.

She smiled in recognition of the reference.

As he turned to go his sleeve caught on the fence, and he was forced to unhook himself from the barbed wire. He caught his breath and, as he looked up again, his eyes fell onto a scarecrow standing in the field nearby. His stomach tightened and his breathing grew shallower. He couldn't understand his own reaction, except that there was something grotesque in the scarecrow, with its grain sack for a head and hollowed out holes for eyes. His head span and as he tried to pull away from looking at the thing, in his mind's eye he could only see the rotating chamber of his revolver, cold and metallic. He felt like vomiting and had to force his head down between his legs. He wanted to stop it, but the turning seemed inexorable, and then with the gun firing he saw the scarecrow's head explode.

Chapter Fourteen

July 1914
Exeter

Emily placed her prayer book back on the shelf and made her way to the door. The vicar's sermon had for once stayed with her. 'Blessed are the peacemakers.' They may be, she thought, but the newspapers seemed to disagree. She had struggled to understand the complexities of the situation, but it was clear that war was imminent. She'd read enough history to know that the wars against Napoleon had seen millions in uniform across Europe, and that had been a century ago, when killing was less refined. She nodded to the vicar and thanked him on her way out, turning towards home.

As she rounded the corner, she noticed Richard, Sebastian and Madeleine walking a short way ahead. She tried to keep a respectful distance, but their voices were raised such that it was impossible not to hear what they were saying.

'It's surely not likely,' Richard was saying. 'I can't believe the government would allow us to sleepwalk into a European war.'

'It's inevitable,' said Sebastian. 'And when it comes to it, we will be required to make a choice, Richard.'

'You can make a choice?'

'Certainly I can.'

'What choice?' asked Madeleine, standing between the two of them and holding tight to Richard's arm.

'The choice to fight,' said Sebastian. 'It will be a matter of duty; you can't deny it.'

'I deny there will be any need.'

Sebastian walked around in front of Richard and stopped him by holding his hand up.

'You are fooling yourself, cousin. You need to think about this, seriously. What you will do. I have.'

'You would fight?'

Sebastian looked irritated and threw his arms up in the air in frustration. He paced a wide circle around and came back to Richard, grabbing him by the shoulders.

'I am fighting! I've already decided on joining up. My father wants me home, and as soon as I get there, I'm volunteering.'

Richard simply stared at him in shocked silence.

'Have you nothing to say to that?'

Sebastian cursed and turned his back, striding away from the others, kicking the ground. Richard watched him go. Madeleine turned to him and tried to touch his face, but he backed away.

'You're not afraid are you, Richard? To fight?'

'You don't understand, Madeleine,' he said, with some irritation.

'Stop treating me as some sort of dunce,' she snapped back. 'I may not have my nose in books the whole time, as you do, but I'm not a fool.'

'I didn't say that you were.'

'You don't have to. Just as you don't have to tell me you love me, when I say it.'

They walked on in silence, and Emily decided to walk home another way, letting them have the street to themselves.

She wandered back towards the house through the gardens in Southernhay and sat down on her usual bench under the ash tree. Sunday afternoons were precious, but after the busy week she often just spent them reading under the tree. Today she didn't have a book with her, so she just enjoyed the summer sunshine and the birds flitting around in the trees. She let her mind drift as it would, and strange thoughts began to occur to her. In war, she thought, there were always those who followed the army, like Becky Sharp. It was a way to see the world, if nothing else. Not that she approved of her behaviour, but there was something compelling in the way Becky would pursue what she wanted. Nothing held her back.

She was so lost in thought that she hadn't noticed Sebastian, and only now saw that he was pacing the lawn, with his chin to his chest. She watched him for a moment, and then, as if sensing her eyes on him, he looked up and saw her. She turned away, but now he wandered over to where she was. They had never really talked, even though he spent much time at the house. He had always seemed to her to be a bit reserved. Not cold, just distant, except when he was with Richard. They were as close as brothers. Their argument was obviously on his mind.

'Emily, I did not see you here,' he said.

She smiled and hoped that he would decide to leave her to her thoughts.

'I must look a strange sight, pacing around as you see?'

'No, sir,' she said.

'I have a lot on my mind just now.'

She didn't like to say that she'd seen the argument, so she just stayed quiet.

'Richard and I had something of a disagreement. A falling out.'

'I'm sorry, sir,' she said. It seemed the right thing to say.

'Not over a girl or anything,' he laughed nervously. 'That might be easier.'

He seemed to decide that he was going to make her a confidante. Maybe he had no one else to share it with?

'My father wants me to return home you see. Even though I like it here, it is not my home, is it? And with the war coming, well, we all need to make sacrifices I suppose.'

'I'm sure Mr Richard understands that,' she ventured.

'Perhaps. But he thinks it's too soon to make that choice.'

'There might not be a war.'

'That is what he said. But I should not want to wait for a choice to be forced on me. I can see my duty, even if he cannot. I know there is a risk I may never see any of you again, but that is not in our hands, is it?'

'I suppose not.'

'No.' He wandered away distractedly. 'No.'

He walked off with no more consideration, as if he had just been voicing his thoughts out loud, and she were a convenient sounding board. It was the strangest of encounters, out of the blue, but it left her feeling disquieted. She hadn't considered before that people she knew might be called to fight. To fight and to die.

***

The following week, Emily was going about her usual afternoon tasks, sweeping the hall and polishing, when the evening paper dropped onto the mat. She stopped what she was doing and went to pick it up. The headline stood out immediately: 'Austria declares war'. The discussions that had been taking place had clearly come to nothing, and the continent was moving inexorably towards war.

She took the paper through to the study as she had been asked to do, to leave it for Mr Hansen. As she got to the door, she was surprised to discover that he was at home, and what's more, he was not alone in the study.

'You agree with him?'

It was Richard, and he sounded incredulous.

'That's not what I said. But I can't disagree that this is his choice to make.'

'And would you wish me to make the same choice, if it came to that?'

His father sighed heavily, and she heard the sound of the desk chair creaking as he sat down in it.

'I think you should fight for your country if you are needed, as any patriotic man would.'

'Do you hear yourself?'

His father banged the table, suddenly angrier than she had ever heard him before.

'Don't you dare question my love of this country. I couldn't have made my way to where I am now anywhere else in the world. That's what this country is, and that deserves our loyalty. If I were of an age to serve, I would take up arms for my king and my country tomorrow. I thought I had raised you to feel the same sense of duty?'

'I know my duty!' shouted Richard.

There was a silence, and then the half-open door which she had been sheltering behind suddenly opened wide, and Mr Hansen was holding it. He pointed the way out to Richard.

'I think you should leave.'

They both noticed Emily at the same moment, and she awkwardly held out the paper to Mr Hansen.

'I'm sorry to interrupt. I was only bringing you the evening paper, sir,' she said.

He took the paper from her without a word, while Richard stormed past into the hall. She bobbed a curtsy awkwardly and made her way back downstairs, partly to make a start on dinner, but mainly to just make herself scarce.

She reached the kitchen, and as she started to prepare the joint for the oven, she reflected on the intense exchange upstairs. It was unlike both of them, normally so good natured. They had never exchanged a cross word before. The talk of war seemed to have everyone on edge, and ever since the sermon the previous Sunday, she had found it difficult to think of anything else herself.

It had put an idea in her head that perhaps Richard was afraid to fight, but she didn't like to think that he could ever be a coward. She tried to sweep the idea out of her head, but it concerned her. Although less than the idea of him having to fight at all. She felt for Sebastian and hoped he would not be hurt, if war were to come. It was a concern she would have for anyone going into danger. But with Richard it was different. It was a visceral fear, almost as if she were in danger herself. She tried to tell herself that it was unlikely, that any war must be short anyway, but the feeling wouldn't leave her.

She put the meat into the oven, and as she started to chop vegetables, Richard came down the stairs, as he so often did, and leapt up onto the counter by the window, where he usually perched. He just sat there for a moment, while she waited for him to say something.

'You're probably wondering what that was all about?' he said at last.

'It's none of my business, sir,' she replied.

'Sebastian thinks there is going to be a war,' he said in a rush, ignoring what she said. 'And he's going to volunteer to fight. But you see I happen to think he's only doing it because his father is pressuring him, and I don't think he's thinking this through. The consequences of that. And my father, well, we disagree, as you saw.

'I would fight,' he continued. 'I would. I would do my duty. But I can't understand the rush to it, as if it were something glorious. It's not that I'm afraid.'

'No, sir,' she said, trying to disguise her doubts.

'It's all a game anyway, isn't it? Not so long ago the Prussians were our allies, and we fought the French. Now, it's the other way. But who's to say it won't change again?'

He seemed to be thinking as he talked, much as Sebastian had, trying to comprehend what war might mean. She could understand it, and for him, with a promising career ahead, after his first year at Oxford, it must be far more disconcerting.

'Perhaps there won't be a war any way,' he said. 'And none of us will have to fight.'

'I hope not,' she said, with more strength of feeling than she had intended. He smiled kindly in response.

'I didn't mean to worry you,' he said. 'Perhaps I'm concerned about something that will never happen.'

He said it as if he were trying to persuade himself as well, but to little effect. He swung off the counter again and trotted away upstairs. It seemed like a selfish thought on her part, but if he did go, she would desperately miss his little visits to the kitchen. It had already been difficult when he was away at university, leaving her alone, but at least she could look forward to a resumption of their conversations. The idea of those conversations being ended forever was worse. She could feel a tightening in her chest when she thought of it. It was certainly because the idea of feeling alone and friendless again frightened her, but there was more than that.

***

She had just finished putting away the breakfast things, when the doorbell jangled, and Emily made her way to answer it. She pulled the heavy door open, and found Sebastian waiting on the step. She stood to one side, ready for him to barrel past her, as he usually did. His visits were so common and so informal, that no one stood on ceremony anymore. But he didn't move. Then she noticed a cab on the street behind him, with luggage piled on the front platform.

'Emily, would you mind letting Richard know I am here? I should like to speak to him before I leave.'

'Yes, sir.'

She was about to turn to find him, when the inner door opened, and Richard joined her on the step.

'It's alright, I heard,' said Richard.

She backed away into the hall to give them space, but having moved that far, she decided that the coat rack needed to be tidied at this precise moment, keeping her handily within earshot.

'I thought you might reconsider,' said Richard.

'I have,' replied his cousin. 'I have considered and reconsidered a thousand times. But duty is duty, as you have always said. None of us is entirely free.'

'No.'

'Will you shake my hand and say goodbye?'

'I will shake your hand,' said Richard.

'Then if not goodbye, then perhaps I will simply say wiedersehen,' said Sebastian.

'Wiedersehen,' said Richard. 'Until we meet again.'

There was a long pause, and then the front door closed. She turned back to look, as Richard came back inside. Their eyes met and he offered simply a sad smile and made his way slowly upstairs.

As she returned to her work, she wondered how many other goodbyes there would be before this was all over.

Chapter Fifteen

June 1916
Somme, France

The rain was coming down hard as Richard made his way back down the communication trench. The soldiers on duty all had their heads hunched down close into their capes, like a row of tall mushrooms, their faces hidden by their steel helmets. For a continental summer it was feeling particularly British just at the moment.

As he entered the dugout, he took off his coat and sprayed droplets of water across the table where Captain Martin was busy sketching in a notebook.

'Do you mind, Richard?' said Duncan.

'Sorry, old chap. It's not easy to keep the weather out.'

Richard hung up his things and poured himself some coffee. Without much thought he poured a good measure of cheap brandy into the mug and took a swig. It was warm and tasted strongly of alcohol, but that was about all it had going for it. He peered over Duncan's shoulder at the sketch he was making. It seemed to be roughly a human form, but he couldn't really discern much else.

'What are you drawing?'

'It's a portrait.'

'I'll take your word for it.'

Duncan did his impression of a Gallic shrug with a comic splutter of contempt.

'You Eeeenglish, you 'ave no, 'ow you say, coolture?' he said, with a pencil in his mouth to mimic a Gauloise.

'You great dolt,' said Richard, laughing. 'If you could make your doodles look like something I could identify, I wouldn't have such problems.'

'I speak not ze Eeeeenglish. Napoo! Napoo! No beer 'ere!'

'I see I'm not getting any sense out of you this evening,' said Hansen, slumping down onto his bunk.

'I will give you this much sense,' said Duncan, turning towards him as he continued sketching. 'We have been summoned to see the boss tomorrow.'

'Oh, good Lord.'

'Forfeit!' shouted Duncan.

'What?'

'You swore upon mention of the Major's name – you must pay a forfeit; you know the rules.'

'Good Lord is not swearing.'

'I think the padre would disagree with you.'

He sighed and pulled a shilling out of his pocket and posted it into the little tin box that was already rattling with previous payments. He swivelled back onto his bed and reached for the newspaper from the previous week.

'Are we to be told why we are being summoned?' he asked.

'Of course not. Where would be the fun in that? Though I suspect it has something to do with the big push.'

Martin was holding his pencil up to Richard and squinting.

'Who are you drawing anyway, as if I couldn't tell.'

'There aren't many models to be had around here, you know. Stay still can't you?'

'I'm not taking my clothes off.'

He struck an exaggerated pose as Martin continued scratching away at the paper.

'What do you do with all these daubs?'

'Daubs?' He shook his head. 'I send it all back home to my dear friend in Cornwall. I've left instructions that in the event of my death she must make a great pyre and burn it all. And she can then throw herself upon it if she wishes to make a great artistic statement, but that part is optional.'

'I'm sure that's a relief for her.'

They sat in silence for some minutes as he watched Duncan draw, his hand flicking from one side to the other, shading, rubbing with his thumb, concentrating intensely.

'Why do you paint?' he asked.

'You're getting philosophical this evening. That's rather like asking a bird why it flies, or a lion why it hunts,' he said, smiling. 'It's what I've always done. I suppose---

He stopped for a moment and looked thoughtful.

'I suppose I need it. You have to have something to stop you going mad, don't you?'

There was a knock on the wooden doorway and a very soggy Corporal Allen poked his head in.

'Captain?'

'Yes, what is it Corporal?'

'I'm sorry to interrupt, sir,' he said, looking at them with a considerable degree of curiosity.

'It's alright, I'm just having my portrait taken,' said Hansen.

'Yes, sir. Could you come? We have another two cases of fever, sir.'

'No rest for the wicked,' said Duncan.

'In which case how are you looking so well?' said Hansen, with a smile, pulling his oilskins back on.

'I'm just going outside,' he said, with mock seriousness. 'I may be some time.'

'Bring me back a penguin.'

***

The sun rose over the trench after the overnight rain, and it sparkled an orangey-red off the droplets hanging on the beams. It looked strangely beautiful, as if there could be a splendour in the fires of hell. Somewhere a bird was singing. A blackbird he thought, but it had been so long since he'd heard a bird sing, he couldn't be sure. Soldiers were beginning the morning ritual of 'standing to', fixing bayonets and taking up their positions on the firing step.

Hansen ran his eye over everything as he walked, looking for anything out of place. He carried on down the trench until he reached battalion HQ. He turned into the dugout to find Major Dawes, Captain Martin and other officers of the battalion milling around the briefing table. A clay model had pride of place in front of Martin, depicting a landscape with trenches and roads carved carefully into it.

'Duncan.'

'Morning Richard.'

'You must have been up with the lark? What's this?'

'This is Mansell Copse. I had to finish it.'

'It's shrunk since I last saw it.'

Martin put his arm around Hansen's shoulder and then gave him a pat on the head.

'You just don't appreciate art, old chap.'

Major Dawes brought a map across and unfolded it with some considerable difficulty, laying it across the table and placing wooden tokens down onto it to show deployments.

'Pay attention. These are your instructions for the show this morning. We're to advance through Mansell Copse towards Mametz, as seen here on Captain Martin's excellent model.'

Hansen mockingly tipped his cap to Martin.

'A barrage will prepare the way, so we expect little resistance, and we should again have the element of surprise. Hansen, your company will take the firing line. Martin, yours will form a reserve line. Kick-off is at 0725. Questions?'

'Sir, I've been considering this,' said Martin. 'We know there is a machine gun emplacement here at Shrine Valley.'

He pointed out a position on the model.

'If it's not destroyed, they will have a clear line on our advance. This will be the danger spot.'

Dawes looked somewhat irritated, and flexed up and down on his ankles, clearing his throat.

'Captain, thank you for your contribution, but the point of the barrage is to destroy their positions. Surprise is on our side, gentlemen.'

'It could be an ambush,' continued Martin, not giving up, despite the clear signals he was getting from Dawes.

'Nonsense. Better minds than yours and mine have planned every inch of this, Martin. We will go as planned.'

'Then may I respectfully request sir, that my company lead? My seniority should give me this right.'

There was a deep sigh from Dawes, and he puffed out his cheeks.

'As you wish.'

'Sir!' interjected Hansen.

'Thank you, gentlemen, that's enough. Martin will lead the firing line. Hansen, you will form up behind and provide support. Very good. If there are no more questions, you're dismissed. Good hunting, gentlemen.'

Martin left the dug out at pace, and Hansen ran to catch up with him. He was furious. Despite the danger, there was still an honour in leading the charge and he struggled to see why Duncan would want to deny him it.

Duncan strode off down the trench, and Hansen followed, slipping and sliding on the wet duckboards. Eventually he caught up and pulled him back.

'What do you mean by this Duncan? I never thought you in pursuit of medals and glory. That was not on and you know it.'

'You always said my painting was too avant garde for you,' said his friend, trying make light of things. 'Well, it's only right that I should be in the advance guard, isn't it?'

'It's not a joke. I don't understand. Do you care so little for our friendship?'

Martin's expression changed to one of total seriousness, and he took Richard by the shoulders.

'Very much the reverse, old boy. Very much.' Martin checked his watch. 'Now, it's nearly time. I must away. Just remember. Where I lead, you need not follow.'

Hansen had never seen his friend like this. He was hiding it behind his usual humour, but he could see there was a genuine concern in his face. Fear even.

'The machine gun will be destroyed,' he said, trying to reassure him.

'We must hope so. Good luck Richard.'

Hansen watched him walk away, and a shiver went through him, a feeling he had had once before, when he worried that he would not see that person again.

***

Hansen led his men from the support trench into the front line, as Martin's men disappeared from view. He studied the scene through his periscope, looking across at their objective at the top of the hill. A line of German trenches. The artillery had only just died away, and there were still streams of smoke rising. They would have to charge down the bank and then up again, along a track that was overlooked by a machine gun emplacement, with a tangle of barbed wire on either side. The danger spot that Duncan had identified. There was nothing to do but wait, and hope that he was wrong.

He waited for Duncan to begin the climb up the hill before ordering his own men to follow him up the ladder and out into the open. The firing from the German lines was sporadic at first, a shot here or there.

They reached the bottom of the hill and he looked up. Captain Martin was leading his party up the track, in a long thin line. He saw Martin signal his men to wait for a moment. He was watching the emplacement carefully. Hansen squinted to see if he could detect any movement, but all seemed quiet. Perhaps Dawes had been right after all.

Hansen held his men too and they waited, crouching where they could. The wait seemed endless but was probably no more than seconds. Hansen realised he was holding his breath and forced himself to breathe normally, in and out, concentrating on each breath.

Then he saw Martin signal again, and his men continued the advance up the hill. Bit by bit they got close to the emplacement, and Hansen prayed that they might take it with no shots fired.

Then, when they were just yards away, he saw German heads suddenly pop up from above the banks of the emplacement. They manoeuvred a machine gun around, and there was a shout in German.

'Run', thought Hansen, 'run, you bloody fools.' But they stood, frozen. There was nowhere to go in any case. No cover. Barbed wire all around them. Time seemed to slow down. Duncan stood calmly as Hansen watched the shots rip into him. He felt himself screaming at the top of his voice, but there was no sound. Nothing at all.

'A' company turned and scrambled to run, their leader gone, but they too were trapped, falling on top of each other, tangled in barbed wire, shot down where they stood or where they fell. There was a ghastly, gut-churning inevitability to it all, and all he could do was watch.

***

Hansen watched as Crosse dug out the ground. He was mucking in with the rest. They all dug except him. He stood and stared, unable to move himself, or think, or feel.

There were so many holes in the ground, so many men lying lifeless because of an act of stupidity. It should make him angry, but it didn't.

Each hole they dug had first to be cleared of stones and roots, and other things. Men who had been buried before and would have to be buried again. It should have made him sick, but it didn't.

Crosse spoke the words over each and said something personal about each. He knew them all, as he always did. It should have moved him, but it didn't.

The padre came up to him and touched him on the arm.

'Richard, would you like to say something?'

He shook his head and couldn't speak.

'Is there anything you need?'

He shook his head again. There was only one thing he could think now, and he turned and walked away.

'Where are you going?' said Crosse.

'I'm on duty,' he said.

He took one look back as he walked away. Crosse had erected a wooden sign on the hill. He would read it later. It said:

> 'THE DEVONSHIRES HELD THIS TRENCH.
> THE DEVONSHIRES HOLD IT STILL.'

Chapter Sixteen

1919

Cornwall

Richard stared ahead, a look of complete terror on his face. He seemed to be fixed on the field, where a shabby scarecrow hung from a wooden frame.

'Richard?' said Crosse.

'I'm fine,' he said, wiping sweat from his face.

As Crosse looked out across the field, trying to understand what had provoked the reaction, Emily went to him and offered her hand. He looked down, and for a moment reached out his fingers, as if to take it. But then his fist clenched tight, and he turned away, hiding his face from her.

'Just a funny turn,' he said. 'Let's get on, shall we?'

He set off, and they followed slowly behind.

***

They reached Newlyn in the early afternoon, taking a cab for the last part of the journey from Penzance. Having seen the sea at a distance in Plymouth, Emily was delighted at being so close now. The water stretched away from the little fishing village, and at the horizon seemed to merge with the blue sky, such that it was difficult to tell one from the other, or where each ended and the other began. White gulls wheeled about over the colourful fishing boats, pulled up on the beach and the slipway. There was a tang of salt in her throat, and the smell was so rich she wanted to take great gulps of air.

They walked up the narrow streets from the harbour to the top of the village, and in short order they reached a pretty row of houses, set back from the road, with views out across the sea. A woman in her middle years, dressed in a loose, free-flowing dress in bold patterns was standing in front of one of the cottages with an easel and a brush in her hand. A silk scarf was tied around her hair, which was itself cut short in a fashionable style. She reminded Emily of the stars of the moving pictures she'd seen in magazines. She transferred the brush to her mouth as she used her fingers on the canvas.

'Good morning!' she said, the brush still clenched in her teeth, and her eyes intently focused on the painting. 'A glorious day, don't you think?'

'Yes indeed,' said Richard.

'If I'm not mistaken, that's a crown on your uniform, which would make you Major Hansen? I received your wire.'

She was still working away at her painting, and had apparently not looked once in their direction, so it was a mystery how she knew who they were. She took the brush from her mouth and held it lightly as she squinted at what she had done.

'Mrs Harvey?'

'Oh, Gertrude, please. Formality is so tiresome.'

'I'm Richard. This is Emily and Reverend Crosse - Ernest.'

Crosse raised an eyebrow and took his glasses off to clean them once again.

'Not even my mother calls me Ernest.'

Gertrude put her brush down finally and stood back from her painting, examining it carefully.

'Sometimes one just has to stop tinkering. I thought I had it a moment ago, but it's gone. Never mind.'

She wiped her hands on a rag and turned to face them for the first time.

'You knew Duncan?'

Richard nodded.

'So sad. Perhaps he told you, I modelled for him before the war. Before I met Harold, my husband. He had the most perfect blue eyes. I don't mind admitting I set my cap at him at one time. But of course, that was never going to happen. You said you wanted to see some of his work?'

'Yes, if you have any?'

'Do I have any? Well, yes. One or two. Come inside and I'll show you.'

Gertrude led them inside, into a house simply whitewashed and painted a pale blue. There were books piled high in one room, and then as they went into a larger room, with French doors opening to a garden, it was full of paintings. They covered every wall, stacked in every available space, and there were even some scattered on the floor.

'If you think this is one or two,' said Crosse, 'then your head for mathematics is as bad as mine.'

'He has a sister I understand, in Sussex?' said Richard. '<u>Had</u> a sister, that is.'

'Yes,' she replied. 'I never know which tense I'm in either. "Was" doesn't seem right when there is so much of him still here. I wrote to his sister. She took a couple of his paintings, but she doesn't have room for more. So here they stay.'

She stepped across a canvas on the floor and pulled out a small painting from the cupboard. She turned it towards them and revealed a landscape. To Emily's eyes, much though she wanted to like it, it was simply lifeless. Boring.

'This is one of his.'

Richard nodded approvingly, but she could tell he was as unconvinced as she was herself. Gertrude held it for a moment, appreciating it, but then her expression broke, and she smiled.

'Dreadful, isn't it? When he first came here, this was what he was producing.' She put the painting away again.

'But my goodness he had talent. It just needed breaking open, and he started painting like this---'

She swept around the room, pointing to a succession of paintings, and pulling more out to show them. They followed a progression from an impressionistic style, echoing Monet, to fearlessly abstract. He had experimented with every idea, and there was a boldness and vivacity to them.

Emily moved close to see the brushstrokes on one painting in particular: a dazzling abstract portrait.

'You like it?' said Gertrude, noticing her excitement.

'There's such passion in it,' said Emily, unable to stop herself from conveying what she was feeling. 'It's so delicate. Loving even.'

Gertrude tilted her head to one side and stood beside Emily in studying it.

'Oh yes. It's a portrait of love all right. You're very perceptive.'

Emily turned to look at her and she had a warm smile across her face, coupled with an expression of longing.

'Is it of you?' said Richard, clearly puzzled by it.

'Goodness no. He wouldn't have painted me like this. He would never tell me who it was.'

She shook her head sadly and moved on to a striking abstract of reds and golds.

'This is the last one he did. He called it "sunrise and birdsong". They sent it to me, with his other possessions. He'd always said I should burn his work. I never knew if he was in earnest, but I made my mind up to take it otherwise and preserve everything.'

Richard was clearly struck by the painting and crossed the room to look deeply into the image. Emily stood beside him. She looked too, but what she saw must have been utterly different to his experience, for a cold sweat was now forming on his face, and all at once he swung around and dashed out into the garden.

They all followed him outside, where Richard had his head down between his knees.

'Are you quite well Richard?' asked Gertrude.

'Forgive me. It's the heat I think,' he said, pulling at his collar and struggling for air. Perspiration was running down his face, and he pulled out a handkerchief to wipe it away.

'Would you like some water?'

'I shall be fine.'

'If you're quite sure?'

'Perfectly.'

He stood up, showing a brave face, but his ashen pallor told a different story. Emily wished they might be alone, so she could hold his hand and comfort him.

'How many of Duncan's paintings do you have?' said Richard.

'I should say a few dozen at least. As you saw.'

'It would be appropriate, don't you think, to have some sort of an exhibition?'

'I've often thought so, but I have never had the funds for properly presenting them all.'

'Then I shall help. I will reimburse any expense.'

'That's very kind. Thank you.'

'It's the least I can do.'

He smiled weakly, but he still looked a deathly white.

'Well, I think I shall get some refreshments after all,' said Gertrude. 'We have something to celebrate.'

She went back inside and left the three of them alone. Richard slumped onto a garden bench and Emily went across immediately to sit next to him.

Crosse cleared his throat. 'I think I'll go for a walk,' he said, and tactfully left them alone. Emily nodded in thanks to him as he turned away and headed off across the garden.

She took his hand, and they sat together in silence for a moment. A bird sang loudly in the trees above them.

'You know I never noticed birdsong before,' he said. 'It was just in the background of life. Always there. Until it wasn't. Until all you can hear is artillery, and worse. As soon as the guns stopped, the birds came back. Strange how nature will always survive our attempts to obliterate it.'

He turned to her and smiled suddenly, a strange smile of innocence and embarrassment.

'Not like you,' he said. 'You notice things. And you notice people. You've listened to me so much. All the nonsense I wanted to tell you. I should listen to you for a change. That's what friends do, isn't it? Except I didn't listen to him.'

He looked up and she wondered for a moment if there might be tears in his eyes. They were glassy and shined with the afternoon sunlight.

'You really like his paintings?' he said at last.

'Yes,' she said. 'I do. They're so full of life and imagination. You can see it in every brush stroke. An energy, a brightness.'

'You speak as if you knew him.'

'I feel I do in a way. I think you can know someone through what they paint. To see the world through their eyes.'

It was the way in which she had learned to understand all the people in her life – the artists, the writers, the poets. The people she would never meet, except in her imagination, but who were no less real for that. She had learned to notice the small details, which were somehow most revealing. She only regretted that she could never meet those people to understand if what she saw were their truth.

'I think,' she continued, 'he's not painting what he sees, but what he feels when he sees.'

She closed her eyes.

'The warmth of the sunset when you close your eyes and feel the gentle sun on your eyelids, and you draw in the moment around you. The birdsong, the peace. Being alone and at the same time wanting to share it with the people you love.'

'You see your mother,' he said.

She opened her eyes and turned to him, and then she realised he was just inches from her. There was that expression again. The one she had seen before. But now she thought she knew what it meant.

'Not only her,' she said.

'He would have liked you,' he said, now looking away. 'You have the same passion, the same love of life. I envy you.'

He looked sad suddenly, and just as quickly seemed to strike it away, making light of things again.

'I can't see how you could ever accept life below stairs!' he joked.

The situation had made her impulsive suddenly. This was a time for honesty.

'There aren't many options for an orphan,' she said. 'All I knew how to do was look after people. I must work to live, until I marry; if I marry.'

'You don't think that you will?'

'Who could I meet? In any case, sweethearts were not allowed. You were the only person who ever really talked to me.

'My grandmother never liked how my mother was with me. She always said I would get ideas above my station. That any man who would look twice at me wouldn't want a girl who thinks too much.'

She waited for his reply. He was quiet in his thoughts. She would have given worlds to know his mind then, and to know whether there was a chance of what she hoped, or whether she had been mistaken in what she had sensed. She had left herself so exposed, she shook with nerves, as if the air around her had become chill.

'"Men of sense, whatever you may choose to say, do not want silly wives,"' he said at last. It wasn't quite what she had expected.

'I'm not Jane Austen,' she replied. 'I'm not a lady. I have to be practical.'

'We're all more than what we do,' he said. 'Someone will see that. I can't see that class matters any longer if you really care for someone.'

He turned back to her and took both her hands in his, looking her straight in the eye.

'You deserve someone that's worthy of you, and to have a life like this where you can be all the person that you are. No one should hold you back from that.'

As he said it, his voice seemed to choke a little, and he turned away, as she knew he always did when avoiding a question.

'I will do everything I can to help,' he said. 'That's what friends do, isn't it?'

He patted her hand gently and got to his feet.

'Now, I must see about these paintings.'

He went inside and left her sitting there, alone. She had wanted to know, and now she did. She felt hollowed out and empty. Her eyes stung and she could feel tears forming. She covered her mouth to stop anyone hearing.

Then Crosse was beside her and offering her his handkerchief.

'How long did you work for the Hansens?' he asked.

'Since I was thirteen,' she said, dabbing her eyes.

'It's very young to be on your own. To spend your life watching and caring for others. No one thinking of you. I know how it feels.' He touched his dog collar once again.

'It comes with the job. It came with his too. "Trapped within a dark wood where the straight way is lost."'

'And maybe I should just abandon all hope,' she snarled.

She threw the handkerchief back at him and walked off into the garden. She knew he was only trying to help, but she couldn't bear to hear it. When she thought back on the expectation he had given her, it was true that there had not been anything certain. Perhaps it had been a product of her own desires, and nothing more. But however it had been, she was chastened again. She'd known this trip was a suspension of reality, and now reality was hitting hard. It was clear now she needed to wake up from the dream and focus on her own survival. No job, little money. But she would fight not to go back. Whatever the future was, she was determined that she would be all she could be.

She wandered for some time among the plants, enjoying the coolness of the shade, but repeating the conversation endlessly, much though she tried to stop herself.

At length she saw Gertrude approach down the path towards her. There was a gracefulness in the way she moved, a confidence she admired.

'Richard was looking for you,' she said.

Her expression must have given away her thoughts at once, and Gertrude gave a rueful smile.

'Or you can continue to lose yourself here for a while if you'd like? I won't say anything.'

'Thank you.'

Gertrude walked beside her, and they came to a pond, where there were enormous fish swimming.

'I often paint these carp,' she said. 'The way they move, the way the light plays on their scales, it's a challenge and a joy. Do you paint?'

'No, ma'am,' she replied. Her distractedness brought the habit back.

'Gertrude,' she corrected. 'I'd recommend it.'

She fed the fish some crumbs and stood with her hands on her hips.

'Forgive my curiosity. But it seems to me you have a story that's worth hearing. If you wish to tell it?'

'The only stories I have to tell are other people's,' she said. It felt true enough, or perhaps, she might have said, the only stories worth telling.

'Now you have piqued my interest. I'm not sure I believe you, but I'll go along with it. So, then I will tell you a story of my own, if you will indulge me?'

Emily sat beside the pond, with one hand in the water, and nodded her agreement.

'Some years ago now I lived here on my own. I didn't have any of this. I had an idea that I wanted to be an artist, but no notion of how that might be accomplished. My parents disapproved, as parents are wont to do. Few people believed in me, or even took the trouble to make my acquaintance. But I persisted. Then some years before the war I met a man who embodied everything one could want. Duncan Martin. He was kind and decent, and devilishly handsome to boot. Like in a penny novella I fell for him. For years I gave more emotional energy to that than anything else.

'It seemed to me that he offered that which I was missing, although I could never tell you what it was. Affection perhaps, or companionship, or a dozen other things. But for reasons of his own, he never wanted me. Not unkindly. I think he knew, and he did all he could to soften it, but that was just not for him. It was little solace when I felt as I did, and I kept forlorn hopes of something changing. Not, of course, that it ever would.

'The feeling never left. It's still here.' She put her hand across her heart. 'But I changed myself around it. I put it aside and opened myself to other things. Not because it didn't matter, but because my life mattered more, and I could see it passing before me. So, I looked about me, and I found all this – my husband, my work, and a cause worth fighting for.

'What did you think of my story?'

'How long did it take?' she asked. 'To put it aside?'

'Oh, not so long as you'd think. Now we have the vote, it's all there for us, you know. Things are changing. You must just decide what it is you wish to do or to be.'

'I don't know,' said Emily. 'I'd wish to make a difference somewhere, that's all.'

The more she thought about it, the clearer it had become in her own mind that above all else she cared about preventing what had happened to her from happening to others. A life wasted by circumstance and an unkind bureaucracy.

'The workhouse,' she said. 'I would change that. If I could. And it's wrong that I should have had to work so many hours for so little.' She began to warm to her subject.

'Why should I have been barred from marrying? And be dismissed for nothing. Or be denied a proper education?'

'Bravo!' said Gertrude. 'So, go to it.'

'How?' said Emily. It seemed fantastical to think that she could change any of those things in any way, and she knew so little of the world, who was she to even consider it?

'I don't know either,' said Gertrude, 'but isn't that exciting? What I do have is perhaps a starting point. I have something in the house that I think you might be interested in.'

***

Emily watched the steam billow past outside the window of the train compartment. It seemed an appropriate metaphor for the cloudiness of her mind at that moment. She had chosen to sit on the opposite side of the compartment to Richard, even though it had meant moving away from him, and now he was shooting cautious glances towards her. She had hurt him. But it was impossible not to feel it was in some way deserved, even if he had never given her any expectation of more than friendship.

The train pulled to a stop, and a few moments later the compartment door slid open. A short, stout man with a carefully waxed moustache entered.

'Excuse me,' he said, glancing around the compartment. He saw her briefly and then turned back to her with a longer look. Then when he saw Richard his eyes narrowed.

'Goodness me. Is that you Hansen?'

'Sir.'

They shook hands.

'It's good to see you. Well, you made it through the show, eh? I'm glad.'

Richard smiled uncomfortably, then he stood and gestured across towards her and Crosse.

'You remember Reverend Crosse?'

'Oh, yes. Nice to see you padre.'

'Colonel Dawes, how lovely,' said Crosse. 'I never thought I'd see you again.'

Dawes nodded briefly to Crosse and then looked back across at her.

'Will you introduce your companion?' he said.

'Of course. My pleasure. Colonel, this is Miss Emily Portinari. Emily, Colonel Dawes.'

'I'm delighted to make your acquaintance Miss... Portinari?' He took her hand and kissed it. 'Is that Italian?'

'Yes, sir. My family is from Italy. Or my father at least.'

'Hansen was in Italy - you didn't bring Miss Portinari back with you, did you Hansen?'

She could tell that the Colonel's presence was irritating Richard. He was grinding his teeth.

'No, sir. I have known Emily for some years.'

'I see,' said Dawes.

He sat down next to Richard and smiled across at her. Richard was straightening his tie and continued to look discomforted.

In a moment of peevishness, she smiled back exaggeratedly at the Colonel, and then flicked her eyes across to Richard, noting his reaction. He turned away and looked out of the window.

Chapter Seventeen

September 1917
Passchendaele, Belgium

'Captain Roper wanted to know if you would join them for dinner, sir? He said to say they have some half decent claret.'

Corporal Veale busied himself with tidying up some empty mugs and half-eaten plates of food. He tutted to himself as he noticed the toast he had made earlier, which Hansen had hardly touched.

'Please give him my apologies,' said Hansen. 'I have too much to do this evening.'

'Yes, sir. Can I get you something else to eat, sir?'

'No. I'm not hungry, thank you, Veale.'

Veale left him alone again. He shuffled through the papers once more and then gave it up, his eyes sore from scrutinising the indecipherable writing by the feeble oil lamp. He stood up to stretch and a sharp pain shot down his leg. He slapped his knee in frustration, as if somehow that would return it to full working order. It was remarkable how much trouble a piece of shrapnel could cause. When the doctors had got hold of him, they were amazed that he hadn't bled out. As it was the metal had shattered his femur, broken the patella and left ligaments shredded. There had been doubt that he'd walk again, but after months of effort he had reached a point where he had been passed fit.

He'd returned to the front after nine months away to find things altered, yet also unchanged. In the space of that two weeks in July the year before, the heart had been torn out of the regiment he knew. A two weeks that had begun with the death of his friend and ended in that field of corn. On that first morning back, he had struggled to put names to faces, recognising perhaps 1 in 20 of the men now under his command. Before he would have learned their names, but now he didn't ask. He told himself that if he didn't know them, there were would be less reason to feel their absence when they were gone.

He put the gramophone on again. He had other records, but he found himself playing the same one again and again. Schubert, symphony number four. It did little for his mood, and the memories it evoked were painful, but he needed to hear it.

'Knock, knock,' said Crosse, as he swung round the doorframe. 'How's the knee?' he said, noticing how Hansen was clutching it.

'Still attached to my leg,' he replied, sardonically.

'Can't you listen to something else?' he said, frowning at the gramophone. 'I have a recording of Lily Elsie you would like.'

'Not that I wish to be uncivil, Ernie, but I am very busy.'

'No, you're not,' said Crosse, looking over his spectacles. 'You have the appearance of being busy, and that is not the same thing at all.'

'I don't like your tone, padre,' he said, knowing there was truth in what the clergyman said.

'Like it or don't like it, but why don't you join your fellow officers for a drink, hmm?'

'Perhaps later.'

'As you wish. But they would value it. Young Prescott. Harper. They look as lost as you did two years ago.'

'As bad as that? Was that only two years ago?'

Crosse tapped his pipe out on the table and blew into it, before turning it around to inspect the bowl.

'I always say I must get a new pipe. I've had this one since I got here. It's cracked and blackened. But you know, it does the job, and where would I find another one as good?'

'Subtle as ever,' smiled Hansen.

Crosse shuffled out in his singular way, and Hansen was left again with his own thoughts. He had battled through months of rehabilitation to return to duty, and above all that word must carry him through now.

***

The rain had not let up for what seemed like days, and now mud was in everything. Boots, clothes, food. It had become as ubiquitous as the bully beef they were given to eat.

'S'ant-Major Mills,' he called down the trench.

Mills pulled his boot from the sticky mud, and nearly lost it in the process, before squelching his way towards him. He did his best to come to attention without slipping over.

'S'ant-Major, are you clear on how we are to proceed tomorrow?'

'Yes, sir. We're to follow the Wipers road?'

'As much as we can. There's precious little cover, so I want them spread out, using whatever is available. I want respirators at the ready position. I'm not taking any chances.'

'Captain!'

He looked around to locate the voice and saw Corporal Veale tearing around the corner.

'That's all S'ant-Major.'

Mills saluted and made his way gingerly down the trench. Hansen signalled to Veale that he was going into the dugout and then went inside to find Lieutenants Prescott, Harper and Treuren waiting for him. Prescott and Harper were young, students like himself when they were called up. Treuren was older, a staff officer who had got bored of pushing paper and asked to be transferred. He hadn't had the heart to tell him that paperwork was still 90 per cent of the job, but just with the added challenge of keeping the mud off it. He was about to run through the plan for the second time when Veale slid up to the doorway, panting heavily.

'Captain! Can you come, sir?'

Hansen wheeled around.

'Corporal Veale, do you always make a report in this fashion?'

'No, sir.'

'Take a breath.'

He gathered his breath and thoughts in equal measure and came to attention.

'Captain. The MO's compliments and can you attend the clearing station immediately.'

'Very well. Treuren, would you be so good as to run through things once more? Carry on, gentlemen.'

Hansen followed Veale back out and then off into a communication trench. He was in a hurry and kept looking back at his officer, eager for him to speed up, but unable to tell him so. Hansen's knee clicked with every step. He could no longer just walk but every step now was conscious. Every twinge and pain noticed.

'It's Challers, sir,' said Veale. 'Private Challacombe I mean.'

'I'm well aware of who he is. Is he injured?'

'I don't rightly know, sir. He just keeps asking for the orderlies.'

After a few minutes they reached the casualty clearing station. There was a smell of iodine in the air, and there were rows of stretchers and bandages laid out. With the attack scheduled for the following day it was a sensible, if macabre, precaution.

The Medical Officer came striding over, carrying a clipboard in one hand. His coat was more grey than white, and he had a sour expression, enhanced by the cigarette in the corner of his mouth which he was sucking on ferociously.

The MO blocked his path, but behind him he could see Challacombe shouting and screaming, with orderlies trying to move him away. He was bent over, with his hands over his ears, and in obvious distress.

'Captain, can you do something about your man, he shouldn't be here. I have the genuinely injured to deal with.'

'What's wrong with him?'

'Nothing that I can see. Just got the wind up and I won't have it.'

Hansen looked over his shoulder. This man had walked out into No Man's Land to bring him back. He'd stood shoulder to shoulder and fought off waves of enemy attacks. This was no coward.

'Thank you, doctor.'

He moved the MO firmly out of his way and went across to where Challacombe was now sitting, rocking backwards and forwards. His hands were still clamped hard to his ears, and he seemed to be whispering to himself.

'Challacombe, what's going on here?'

The soldier looked up him for a moment, before resuming his motion.

'Sir, it's the noise, sir,' he said, or rather, shouted. 'I can't take it. They won't help me.'

'There's nothing wrong with you, soldier,' said the doctor, standing close by, his hands on his hips.

'I just need to get away,' said Challacombe. 'Some rest.'

'You're due for leave next week, aren't you?' said Hansen.

'No, sir. Now! I can't wait a week, I need fucking help now! Now! Bloody now! Not next week!'

'Steady!' said Hansen.

He was getting more and more agitated, with tears running down his face.

'Look, Arthur, you know that can't happen. We have a job to do and I need you.'

There was no answer. He just sobbed and clutched his ears, his face now in his own lap.

'I promise I'll get you some leave. You can get some rest, a proper civvy kip. You can see your new wife. Betty, isn't it? But for now, we need to go. Veale will look after you. You two together, you've been through worse.'

He seemed a little calmer, and the desperate sobbing was easing a little.

'Come on,' said Hansen. 'Alley at the toot!'

He tried to coax him to stand up, gently tugging him by the arm. But he wouldn't move. Then, with little warning, Challacombe swung about, more out of instinct and irritation than anger, and hit him full in the face. Hansen felt the impact sting his cheek and he staggered back, falling to the ground, surprised by the weight of the punch.

'Right!' said the MO. 'Orderly, fetch the MPs. I want this man placed under arrest.'

Hansen licked his lips and tasted blood. He gathered himself and got back to his feet. It took him a moment to process what had happened, but then he felt a desperate sadness and pity. He knew what would happen now, and there seemed little he could do to stop it.

'It's alright,' he said. 'There's no need for that.'

'Captain, this man is a coward. Malingering, disobeying orders, and now he has struck an officer. There's only one course.'

He was right, according to the book, but he would be damned if he'd let the doctor know it.

'I'm sure Private Challacombe will resume his duties and we can say no more of this.

'You know the consequences if you don't, Challacombe. I'm ordering you to return with me now.'

He stared at the stricken Challacombe, as if he could, by sheer force of will, shake him out of his despair and into his right mind. But he just curled up, taking no notice of anything.

Veale had stood back and let his officer act, but at last he couldn't stand idle any longer.

'Challers, do as he says you silly sod.'

Three military policemen arrived.

'Sergeant,' said the doctor. 'Take this man away.'

Veale was on his knees now, begging his friend.

'Challers, come with us!'

'Charge him with cowardice,' said the MO, 'refusing orders and striking an officer.'

The MPs picked up a now docile Challacombe, handcuffed him, and began to lead him away.

'Challers!' shouted Veale. He turned to Hansen. 'He's not a coward, sir! You know that.'

'I know, Veale. I know.'

Veale turned, full of frustration, and kicked out at the wall, before running back towards the front line. The MO clucked and went back to his clipboard.

'You might keep better control of your men, Captain.'

At that moment he could have easily taken the man apart. He was white with rage, all the more because he blamed himself for not seeing this before. How could he have failed to notice one of his own men and have allowed him to reach this stage without acting?

'What happened to "do no harm", doctor?' he spat back, and pulled himself away before he did harm himself.

***

He looked up from his notes to the three officers sitting in judgement on the bench, raised above the rest of the court. Dawes sat in the middle, now a Lieutenant-Colonel, flanked by two officers who Hansen did not know. Challacombe stood calmly in the dock, looking straight ahead. It wasn't clear whether he knew what was happening, or understood the consequences if things went against him.

'Captain Hansen,' said Dawes. 'Do you wish to make any further remarks on behalf of Private Challacombe?'

Hansen got to his feet.

'Thank you, sir, yes, I would. I would like the court to note that of the numerous acts of bravery I have witnessed on the part of Private Challacombe, his most notable was a rescue he effected alongside Corporal Veale and others when I was injured, at great risk to himself. It would not be inaccurate to say he saved my life---'

'---Captain,' interrupted the Colonel. 'Commendable though that is, we are interested in his most recent actions. You yourself told us under oath that this man struck you, did you not?'

'There were mitigating circumstances, Colonel, I---'

'---I can't agree. If we are to allow such things there will be no discipline, would you not agree?'

'Yes, sir, but---'

'---we also have sworn medical testimony that Private Challacombe was not in any way injured or unwell at this time, and yet refused all orders to return to duty when an action was planned for that day. Are any of these facts untrue?'

It was impossible to argue otherwise. He knew that what Challacombe was suffering was real, and whatever it was, it was not cowardice. But it was useless to argue when the case was seemingly so clear cut, at least in the eyes of people who didn't know him.

'No, sir.'

The Colonel stroked his moustache and drummed his fingers on the desk in front of him.

'Very well. I see no reason to delay any further. We three are here agreed. Private Challacombe is guilty on all counts. In the instance of cowardice there is only one sentence we can hand down.'

He turned to the defendant, registering his presence for perhaps the first time, or at least that was how it seemed.

'Private Challacombe, you will be taken from here to a place of detention. The sentence of death to be carried out by firing squad tomorrow morning at dawn. Court dismissed.'

The three officers stood and made their way out, while Hansen watched as Challacombe was removed, powerless to help. He looked down at his papers and wondered if there was some argument, some legal trick that he might have found. It was a disgrace in any case that he had been forced to act on his behalf. He had felt utterly unprepared, and it was to cost Challacombe his life.

Colonel Dawes made his way across to where Hansen stood, unmoving.

'You did your best, Hansen,' he said. 'You played the game well. But there was nothing you could do. It was cut and dried. Nevertheless, I respect your stance. We need officers who can earn the respect of their men. To that end, I'm delighted to say your promotion is confirmed.'

He was holding out an envelope and a small box, waiting for Hansen to take them from him. Hansen looked from the box to Dawes and back again, but otherwise remained still. After a moment the colonel placed them on the desk and cleared his throat nervously.

'Well, congratulations, Major. You will take command of the 8th battalion, which is being deployed to the Italian front. Report to me tomorrow at 0800 for orders.'

'Yes, sir,' he said at last, forcing the words out.

'Very well. Chin up, Hansen.'

Dawes strode out. There was something comical in his walk. Pompous and self-regarding. It was easy to despise him.

He picked up the box which Dawes had left, and inside were two crown insignia. In disgust he threw them across the room.

***

He forced himself to watch. He stood alone as the firing squad made their way into the yard. A grey stone square to the rear of the school building which had been requisitioned to function as an army prison. It was a cold morning, and the sky matched the grey stone. A chill drizzle made the air misty.

Challacombe stood against the wall, his hands tied behind his back, and he refused the hood that was offered to him. He seemed almost preternaturally calm. A stark contrast to the man who had screamed and wept to be allowed to return home. Now he never would go home.

'Ready,' said the Sergeant-Major.

He wished, hoped and prayed that this would be quick.

'Aim.'

Challacombe looked across at him and smiled.

'Fire.'

Chapter Eighteen

1919

Exeter

She watched him sleep. Except she wasn't convinced that he was really asleep. Richard had his eyes closed and his head back against the seat cushion, but otherwise there were no signs of sleep. She had reflected on what Gertrude had said for every mile of their journey home, and she knew there was sense in it. And yet…

The train jolted and Richard sat bolt upright. He looked around him, as if reminding himself of where he was. There was a look of distain as his eyes fell upon Dawes. Then they flicked to her and he turned quickly to look out of the window.

'Where are we?' he asked of the compartment.

'Nearly back in Exeter,' said Crosse.

'Good.'

He leaned forward towards the padre.

'Ernie, do you have the address for Private Challacombe's widow?'

'I daresay I do.'

'Challacombe?' said Dawes, interrupting with a splutter of surprise. 'Not that wretched coward?

'I know you stood up for him at the time, but he brought it on himself. Why are you still thinking on it? You really should let it go, Major. We did what was required.'

'Did we?' said Richard, with a calmness that spoke of suppressed fury.

'My conscience is clear,' said Dawes 'Let's talk no more about it.'

Richard looked like he was about to respond, but then a look from Crosse made him think better of it and he sat back in his seat again.

The train began to draw into the station, and she saw the signs indicating Exeter move past the window.

'Miss Portinari,' said the Colonel. 'Do you live nearby?'

'Yes, sir,' she answered hesitantly.

'Excellent. Perhaps I can renew your acquaintance? Might I call on you?'

'Well---' she began. She hardly wanted to cultivate such an acquaintance, and in any case, he had no idea of her background. Richard had been careful to avoid mentioning what their association had been before.

Richard got up now and took his bag down from the rack. He cast a heated glance at Dawes, who failed to notice, and indignantly went out into the corridor. Dawes turned as he heard the door close, and then looked back in surprise.

'I always said the mark of a weak officer was to feel too much.'

'Not something one could say of you, Colonel,' said Crosse, with a heavy sarcasm that Dawes appeared to miss entirely.

'Indeed. I was tough but fair, always.'

The train came to a stop, and Dawes insisted on carrying her bag out to the platform, where Richard was already waiting, standing a few feet away.

'A very pleasant journey,' said the Colonel. 'I do hope I shall see you again Miss Portinari. If I may give you my card, perhaps you will write?'

She didn't like to refuse and accepted the thick ivory-coloured calling card from him. One glance at the address told her he was wealthy, and the name read:

LT. COLONEL SIR ANTHONY DAWES, BT. DSO

'Goodbye,' he said, tipping his hat courteously.

They watched him stride off down the platform, and Crosse shook his head.

'Well, it's nice to see some people don't change.'

Richard re-joined them, and his good temper seemed to return with the departure of the Colonel.

'I've decided to make a visit to Mrs Challacombe. Will you come with me, Ernie?'

'I will,' said Crosse, hesitating. 'Though I think Colonel "Bores" was right.'

'Let's not mention him again,' he said abruptly. 'Emily, will you come?'

She'd been considering what she might say for the last hour. Not to this particular question, but to take her leave with as little fuss as possible.

'Thank you,' she said. 'I've enjoyed the journey. But I should start searching for a new position, if you don't mind?'

'No, of course,' he said.

'I'll go and find a cab,' said Crosse, hurrying away with unwelcome tact.

She went to pick up her case, but Richard got to it first.

'Let me.'

She started to walk away from him quickly, knowing he would struggle to keep up. Nevertheless, he picked up speed and limped beside her. It felt cruel, but to be alone with him again was too uncomfortable.

'Slow down a bit, will you?' he said, with an affected nonchalance, but she could tell he was struggling.

She stopped but did not look at him. He took the hint.

'You're obviously in a hurry to get home,' he said, lightly. But then more seriously:

'Are we not friends, Emily?'

He said it in a tone that pained her to hear.

'I don't think that would be appropriate,' she said, and took her luggage from him without once looking him in the eye.

She left him there and walked home alone, despite his objection that it was getting dark. It was clear that she had been unkind, and she felt badly for it. She had always thought, like Mr Knightley, that he was the last man in the world who would intentionally give any woman the idea of his feeling for her more than he really did. But what he had said was one thing, what she had interpreted was another, and she was sure she had not been wrong. Or she had been sure.

Now doubt filled every thought. She doubted that she could do any of the things that Gertrude had inspired her to think of. Or that she could even secure a job that had more reward.

At length she reached the boarding house and found Mrs Grant clearing away the dinner. She offered her something, but Emily politely declined and made her way upstairs. She wanted to sleep, and most of all she wanted to stop thinking. Perhaps it was memories of the journey, but she pictured her thoughts like a train at full speed with no one at the plate to stop it.

***

She had awoken early the next morning. Over breakfast, while the other guests chattered, she had worked out a plan. Working through a mental list of potential positions, she had decided to begin with what she wanted most. To that end she had set out in optimistic spirit to visit the schools in the area. She had been ready to prove her knowledge, but as the day had worn on it had become clear that without a university degree and without experience, the answer would be the same.

By the afternoon she had adjusted her expectations and visited secretarial bureaux. An office job would at least hold some interest. But here too the answer was the same. Without experience or skills in shorthand or typing, the door was closed.

Now, as she sat at the table in the dining room, writing forlorn letters to potential employers, the morning's optimism had all but vanished.

Mrs Grant came into the room carrying a vase of flowers, which she placed in the middle of the table.

'Makes things look a little brighter, doesn't it?' she said. 'Oh, don't you write beautifully!' she added, peering at the letters. 'What beautiful penmanship.'

'Thank you,' she said. 'My mother taught me, but I don't often write letters.'

'No? I thought perhaps you were a secretary.'

'No. Not a secretary.'

'What do you do for work then?'

This was the conversation she had hoped to avoid, but now she was asking, it seemed best to be honest. She explained her circumstances and that she was searching for work, although she stopped short of going into detail about her meagre prospects.

'Well, I shall look out for you,' said Mrs Grant kindly.

'Thank you.'

'Especially as it seems you and I have something in common,' she said, looking down at the pamphlets that Gertrude had given her, which were mixed with the letters on the table. Amongst them was one entitled 'What is socialism?'.

'Oh, these,' she said. 'Someone gave them to me. I'm not sure about politics, I just want to feel that I'm doing something useful. To change things for people. People like me.

'I mean, I would have stayed in school if I could, to get a proper education, but instead I was given no choice.'

Mrs Grant nodded appreciatively.

'And what would you have wanted to do if you'd had a choice?'

'I think I should have liked to have been a schoolteacher.'

She shrugged as if to say, 'what an idea', and smiled nervously.

'Now there, perhaps I can help,' said Mrs Grant. 'At least, after a fashion.'

For a moment she wasn't sure if she had heard correctly and she held back the excitement that began to flicker in her.

'What do you mean?'

'I do what I can to help poorer people in the city. I run a soup kitchen. And there is a group for needy children and adults as well, who need to learn their three Rs. Our teacher has just moved away.'

'You'd let me teach them?'

'Well, perhaps on a trial basis? I mean, you might not like it, my luvver! We can't pay you anything, but you would be making a difference, that's for definite.'

'That's very kind, Mrs Grant. 'But if I can't find a job, I won't be able to---'

'Pay the rent?' she said. 'Well, I'm sure we can manage. There is supposed to be a class tomorrow actually. If you would be willing?'

'Yes, absolutely!'

Mrs Grant winked and made her way back to the kitchen to continue preparing the evening meal. As others in the house began to return home, Emily cleared away the letters and went out to post them. She was excited again, albeit terrified too, and this was a chance she couldn't turn down. But just where to start?

***

The following afternoon she left the parish hall where the classes were held and found herself bidding everyone she met a cheery good day. Each step was easy, and she was giddy with a sense of accomplishment. It had been a strange day in some ways. The lessons had not gone as she had intended, but nevertheless the progress she had seen in only a few hours, and the idea that this was because of what she, she personally, had said and done, was enthralling. They had even thanked her. One girl had run after her and given her a drawing she had done, showing the two of them reading books with big smiles. She had even asked if there was a book she could take home to read. Would that she'd had one to give her.

Emily smiled to herself as she walked, such that several passers-by gave her strange looks. But she didn't care. She had seldom known a day of such satisfaction. No. More even than that. There had never been a day where she had felt so proud, even if things weren't perfect. And that in itself was a wonderful thing, to know she could do better. There were already ideas bubbling in her mind.

So it was that she found herself by chance walking back by way of Barnfield Road, close to the Hansen house. If it had been chance. She had chosen this route when there were others. This cord of communion between them would not be so easy to cut. But she walked on, making the decided choice to ignore it.

As she reached the curb and waited to cross, she had to step back as a motor car roared around the corner. She recognised it at once as belonging to Doctor Harrison. And when it stopped outside the house her stomach turned over. Almost as if she were being pulled by a rope in two directions, she was drawn away by everything rational, and drawn to it by everything feeling. When she saw Richard being helped from the car by the doctor the choice was made, and she started along the pavement towards them.

When she arrived outside, they had gone inside, but Mr Crosse was stepping out of the motor car.

'What happened?' she asked.

Crosse sighed heavily.

'It's been the most frightful day,' he said. Then he looked at the door and gestured to her to come across the road. 'You'd better not be seen here.'

They sat on a bench under the trees and he took out his pipe. For the first time he seemed not to want to light it, but simply rested it in his hand.

'We went to find Mrs Challacombe, as you know. The poor young widow. Barely older than you I would think. She'd moved from the address I had, and it took some time. We finally found her in a somewhat disreputable place near the river. The kind of place that would make the trenches look enticing.

'Inside there was a shabby woman with a bottle of gin who didn't seem to care whether her tenants were at home or not. She looked askance at me when she noticed my dog collar. When we went to Mrs Challacombe's room, I understood why. She was clearly used to visitors of all descriptions, if you understand me, on very accommodating financial terms. Richard made clear our intentions, but she had little time for us, and I should have seen she wasn't well.

'She had a baby, no more than about a month old. And even with my head for arithmetic I could work out it has been a year and a half since her husband… died. There was almost no furniture in the room, except for the cradle, which was immaculate. Richard told her he knew her husband and she said: "So, you've come to see what the widow of a coward looks like?" Richard said she was wrong, he was never a coward, and she said: "Tell that to the war office. Not just content to murder my husband, they leave me with nothing. I'm not even worth a widow's pension."

'We tried to give her some money, for her son, but she wouldn't accept it. I asked what work she had done before, and she said she was a typist. She'd tried to find respectable work, but no one had given her a job. All because of her husband and his supposed dishonour. It's wrong. So wrong.

'So, Richard told her he would find her something. I didn't give much for his chances. But he was determined, and we spent the rest of the day talking to everyone we could think of, and more today. I lost count of the number of doors we knocked on. Eventually he found an old school friend who was willing to offer her a position on a trial basis. So, we went back to find her and to tell her the good news---'

He stopped and took his glasses off, wiping them carefully. Normally so calm and assured, he looked unsettled, shocked even.

'Richard was so delighted, you know, to think that he might be able to help her out of that awful place. He felt a duty to Arthur, and I can understand why. He knew him and the man he was, when those who judged him did not.

'He was running to get there, even with his leg. But when we did---' he stopped again.

'When we got there, we met Dr Harrison. In a mask. He stopped us going in. There had been an outbreak of the Spanish 'flu. And it had taken her. Within a day. A day too late.'

He looked angry now, his hand gripping his pipe so tightly that his knuckles were white.

'And her baby?' she asked.

He shook his head sadly.

'As if that weren't enough,' he continued. 'Richard took it badly. We were watching them bringing bodies out, these figures in masks. It was sickening. And then he seemed to be somewhere else again. I tried to help, but he backed away, as if he were afraid of me, and the next thing I knew he'd passed out and fallen backwards down some steps. Fortunately, the doctor was there to assist.'

She got to her feet and went towards the house.

'Don't blame yourself,' said Crosse.

She turned back to him, angry at first, but in the unerring way he had, she realised he was right. It was exactly what she was thinking, though she only half knew it herself.

'It would have turned out the same, had you been there.'

'But I would have been there,' she said, and went on towards the house.

She rang the doorbell, and as she did so, it occurred to her that it was the first time she ever had. Mrs Hansen answered the door and was about to close it in her face when Emily darted through and past her towards the stairs.

'Where do you think you're going, girl?'

'I'd like to help.'

'You have done quite enough.'

'I only want---'

'--- Oh, I know full well what you want. I turned a blind eye because I thought it was just a harmless infatuation. But all this is because you've turned his mind away from his family, propriety and duty. This is what happens. He knew who he was before, what he needed to do, and now he's just thrown it all in because of a skivvy like you? I saw you, disgracing yourself in his room. You're nothing but a whore!'

Emily bit her tongue, as she so often had, stifling frustration and anger. But this time she didn't want to be obedient or demure, or any of the things expected of her.

'You don't know me!' she exploded. 'And you certainly don't know your son. He never touched me, just like you never touched him.

'The war broke him; can't you see that? I was a child when I came here, scared, and lonely, and you never saw. And you've never seen Richard for the kind and good man he is. He's treated me like a friend, no more. And yes, I wanted more, so much more, but if friendship is all there is, then I'm not going to let him down when he needs someone to show him the love you never could.'

Mrs Hansen stood frozen for a moment, but her façade of indifference slowly started to crack. Her face fell in upon itself and emotion seemed to empty across every pore.

'How dare you!' she shouted, shaking with feeling. 'I have done all I can to protect him. Always. Because of you, now he could be condemned, like my father was, to half a life, merely existing in an institution. You foolish girl, you really have no idea what you've done.'

She was in tears now, distraught in a way that Emily had never seen before. All pretence gone. She seemed genuinely frightened.

'I don't understand, what institution?'

'Just go,' she sobbed.

'Please,' said Emily. 'What do you mean?'

She gathered herself for a moment and shot Emily with a look of pure fear and loathing. She grabbed her by the wrists and pushed her face close.

'When this happened the first time the doctor said we should commit him to an insane asylum. That it would be the only way to treat him. I told him no, and he agreed then, but he said if it happened again his hand might be forced, for Richard's own protection.'

Her face was wet with tears now, and she was almost pleading.

'My father was in one of those places for 30 years! Half his life. He died there. I never saw him again. I can't let that happen a second time. I can't. Now do you see? The best thing you can do for all of us is to leave!'

She pushed Emily away and wiped the tears from her face, trying desperately to recreate the mask of calm, but with little success. She sat down on the stairs and created a physical barrier, and Emily turned and went back out of the door, not saying a word more.

Outside she found Crosse waiting. He looked quizzically at her, but she kept her face blank.

'Mrs Hansen won't let me see Richard. Will you give him something from me?'

'Of course'.

She reached into her bag, took out a book and handed it to him.

'He'll understand,' she said.

Chapter Nineteen

1919
Exeter

Hansen lay curled up on the bed. The room seemed dark, although the sun shone brightly. The feeling was returning, creeping its way across his soul. Almost as if the last few days were the aberration, and the same aimless, crushing weariness he felt before were now normal.

He uncurled himself and went over to his dressing table. He looked out of the window and could see Emily walking away down the street. He wanted to open the window and shout her name. He mouthed it, and reached for the latch, but stayed his hand. It was better that she should walk away.

He turned to the mirror and studied the man there.

'What does she see that I do not?' he said out loud.

He pulled open his drawer and took out his service revolver. He felt the weight of it in his hand.

'I'm going to assume you're cleaning that,' said Crosse, who had entered the room unnoticed.

'"Dirty gun, dead soldier," as Cairns used to say' he replied.

He slid the gun back into the drawer, but it was still there in his hand. No matter which way he looked or even if he closed his eyes, it was still in his hand.

Crosse put a book down on the dresser in front of him.

'Emily left this for you. She said you would understand.'

He picked it up and read the cover: *Three Men in a Boat*. 'Someone to love, and someone to love you' he remembered.

'Where did that world go?' he wondered aloud. Now it made him think only of pre-war days when life had seemed endless with possibility. 'So many things were buried in France.'

'We must have faith,' said Crosse.

'Faith?' he said bitterly. It seemed an extreme kind of naivety on Crosse's part, and it made him angry. 'How can you still wear that cross, after all we've seen? What we saw again today?

'How can you believe in heaven and hell? When hell is here, on Earth. A good man can't survive in hell, so what are we left with?'

'You did.'

Hansen laughed cynically and lay back on the bed, his eyes closed. If he knew the full truth, he wouldn't dare say it.

'You're a self-pitying bastard sometimes,' said Crosse, suddenly passionately angry. It was no longer the Crosse he knew.

'Do you know that? You think you're the only one who lives with memories? With guilt? I was there too. I buried hundreds.

Men I knew. I comforted people who I knew would die, but I had to tell them everything would be alright. I had to cheer others when all I could think of was how bloody scared I was!'

Hansen sat up and looked him in the eye.

'My belief is all that saw me through. That and my trust in good people, like you, to do their best. Now you would rob me of that little I have? Good and evil, it's a choice, and sometimes we choose evil. All of us. But do you know what makes you a good person? Because you know that choice is wrong, and you choose to make it right. You care. Not like Colonels who will throw men to the fire as easily as a lump of coal. All the choices you made; they were the right choices. Not easy, but right.'

'Not all.'

'You're human. This purgatory you've created, it's of your own making.'

'I thought we agreed this was hell?'

'There is at least hope of escape from purgatory, with the right guide. Dante had his Beatrice.'

'And where would she guide me?'

'Somewhere else. Somewhere where you can start again and leave the war behind. You know what will happen now if you stay here. The doctor is preparing the paperwork as we speak.'

'It may be for the best. I wouldn't hurt anyone there.'

'Is that all the life you want? Because the Richard Hansen I know would never accept it.'

Crosse went out and slammed the door behind him. It would be easy to give in, to be taken to a safe place, where there would be three meals a day and walks outside on sunny days. Where there would be no responsibilities. But as he thought about it, he began to feel again. He felt shame. His duty was not so easily shifted.

He went downstairs and found his father in his study, staring at papers on his desk, although from his eyes, it did not seem that he was reading so much as thinking.

'Papa. Could I speak to you?'

His father looked up, a little surprised and pleased in equal measure.

'Of course, Richard. Come and sit down, my boy. Eventful day, eh?'

'You could say so.'

His father shifted uneasily. It was clear he knew the score. Hansen was faintly embarrassed, feeling he had somehow let his father down by being too weak.

'Will you help me?' he said.

'Of course. You know you don't have to ask,' said his father, his expression one of seriousness. 'If we can find another doctor, perhaps---'

'No, not about that.'

'Then what?'

'I need to go away. To leave here.'

'I was thinking the same,' said his father. 'It's better than going to –

He stopped short of naming the place.

'It's better.'

His father went to the safe and took out a roll of banknotes. He flicked through them and then pushed them across the desk towards him.

'There is 500 pounds here. All I can do, I'm afraid, at present at least. I want you to take it. What will you do, go abroad?'

'Yes,' he said. 'That's what I was planning.'

'Good, good. Where?'

'Germany.'

His father's face fell, and his brows furrowed, before he seemed to reconsider, and he looked at him as if perhaps he really were mad.

'Have you seen what's happening there? Demobbed soldiers enforcing order, insurrections. It's not safe.'

'I should be used to that.'

'I don't understand. Why on Earth would you want to go there now?'

He said it though he knew the reason. They both knew it.

'It should be obvious.'

'No!' his father shouted suddenly. 'No!'

'I have to,' said Hansen. 'I have to leave, and I have to know what happened to our family. Don't you want to know how your brother is?'

'No!' shouted his father again. 'We are not---'

'German?'

'Schämst du dich? Are you ashamed to say it?'

His father's head fell onto the desk, and when he finally raised his head again, there were tears in his eyes.

'Am I ashamed? How could you understand? I left because there was nothing for me there. And here – just a foreigner. To be more English than the English, that was the only way to be accepted, though I know they laughed at me. Well, they don't laugh when you're rich.

'Then when all this started, I saw people's windows broken, just because they had a German name. The royal family changed theirs for God's sake. So, I said nothing. I was the loyal patriot. But I can assure you, I felt everything.'

'Then you can see,' said Richard, 'why now is the time to go, now it's all over.'

'Perhaps,' he said slowly. He studied Richard for some moments, the anger subsiding.

'You know I never thought. When you went to fight. I assumed. I assumed because you were born here---'

'I did my duty,' he replied.

His father nodded.

'You must go.'

Hansen picked up the money and was about to take his leave, when his father called out.

'When you see him, will you give my brother my love?'

'Of course.'

'And write and tell me about Sebastian.'

'What about Sebastian?'

'Whether he is – you know – in good health? I'm sure you want to know too. He was your friend.'

'Yes.'

He went back out into the hall and his mother was there. She turned away quickly and made a pretence of arranging some flowers.

'You don't have to pretend you didn't hear,' he said. 'I will leave tonight. No one need know. You can tell people whatever you wish.'

'Don't go yet,' she said quietly. 'I mean to say there's no need. I spoke to the doctor. I persuaded him to return at the weekend. You have time enough to take your leave.'

'Thank you,' he said, though he couldn't see what purpose it would serve to prolong things.

'I'm sure you have much to do,' she said. 'Don't leave without saying goodbye.'

***

He tapped the little box on the table in front of him, and then felt the soft leather case in his other hand. He held them, one in the palm of each hand, as if measuring their weight and balancing their worth. Then he placed them onto the crisp white tablecloth and looked down at them. He picked up the case again and opened it, thumbing idly through the five-pound notes rolled up inside. Then he put it away and flicked open the little box, studying the silver ring that nestled in a little pocket of silk.

He looked up at the ceiling, an elegant oval shape painted in pale blue like the sky and trimmed with intricate white plasterwork. Crystal chandeliers twinkled, lit by electric bulbs, and he could hear the gentle hubbub around him of people enjoying their pleasant conversations. A string quartet played a soothing and gentle accompaniment.

All in all, it should have been the most agreeable of ambiences, except for the choice before him, literal and figurative. In the corner of his eye he noticed the door open and he looked across. Emily stood in the entrance, looking uneasily around. She was wearing the dress, a rich sea green, which matched her dark hair perfectly. His was not the only head to turn to look, and for a moment his resolution wavered. He held more tightly to the small box in his left hand.

She looked up and saw him, raising one hand diffidently to acknowledge him, and smiling. He swept the objects into his pockets and let them drop from his fingers. He stood up as she reached the table.

'I'm so glad you came. I was worried you wouldn't.'

'I had to thank you for the dress,' she said.

'Well, it was the least I could do, to replace the one that was so tarnished in Cornwall!' he smiled.

'You look beautiful.'

'Thank you,' she said, blushing.

'Won't you sit down?'

She took a seat and gazed wide-eyed at the room.

'It's like I imagined,' she said.

'You've never been here before?'

'No. Why would I? Though I remember you asked me if I had on the day we met, and I thought it was a strange thing to ask. Nice, but strange. I dreamed maybe one day I would come here, in a beautiful dress, for an elegant tea, with---'

'With?'

'Oh, anyone. It was just a dream.'

A waiter in a starched white jacket and bow tie glided up to the table and set down a tower of dainty cakes and tiny, perfectly cut sandwiches. Then he brought across a tea pot and hovered.

'Shall I pour, sir?'

'No, no. I have a talent for pouring tea,' he said.

Emily smiled. He poured a cup and passed it to her. She took some cake and started to delicately nibble on it, mimicking others in the restaurant as she took side long glances at them.

'How is it where you are staying now?'

'I have a room in a house. It's comfortable. The landlady is very kind.

'Actually, it's because of her that I have started teaching some needy children. It's voluntary, but I so enjoy it!'

'That's wonderful,' he said. 'It's what you always wanted. The children are fortunate to have such a teacher. I'm pleased for you.'

He meant it too. He was completely happy to see her delight, and he would have enjoyed it for longer, except that there was a decision to make.

They fell into silence, and his hands went back to his pockets, instinctively gripping the objects inside.

'Richard---'

Her face was serious now. She had never called him by his first name before.

'I wanted to apologise. For leaving the way I did. It was unkind.'

'Nothing, I suspect, that I did not deserve. It's why I asked you to come.'

'Oh?'

He stopped for a moment and picked up his knife to spread some butter. As he did so the light glinted off it, and unwelcome images burned themselves across his mind like hot metal. The memories were almost tangibly painful. His hand was shaking now, and he dropped the knife, screwing his eyes up to drive them from his mind.

'Damn. I'm sorry.'

Emily reached an arm across the table and took his hand. His mind cleared again, and he took some deep breaths.

'I have to go away,' he said.

She blanched at this and her hand tightened.

'Where?'

'Germany.'

Her nose wrinkled with confusion and she took a moment to work it through in her mind, before clearly deciding that there was no good explanation.

'Surely the war is over?' she asked finally.

'I wish I could explain it all,' he said. 'I have a duty. To my family.'

She nodded and smiled, as if he had confirmed something she was thinking.

'I think I understand,' she said. Then her expression turned sorrowful. 'It must have been so difficult for you. When your cousin left. To know who you were fighting there.'

He let go of her hand and shrank away.

'I'm sorry,' she said. 'I didn't mean to offend you.'

'It's alright.'

He tried to conceal his shock. He felt revealed; vulnerable. But also, as he looked across the table, somehow relieved.

'I could come with you?' she ventured, after a few moments of awkwardness.

'No, not this time. But before I go, my family are not the only people to whom I have an obligation. I have something I'd like to give you.'

He put his hand into his left pocket. Emily was watching him expectantly, a slight smile creeping onto her face. Then he stopped. However much he might wish it, what he proposed was unfair. Impossible even. Instead, he went to his right pocket, and pulled out the leather wallet, placing it on the table in front of Emily.

She looked confused, not unsurprisingly, and cautiously opened the package to peek inside. Then she sat back quickly.

'What is this?' she said, sternly.

'It's why I asked you to come. I threw your life into disarray I know. This is to help you in whatever you want to do. What you've already started to do. There's no one now to stop you being who you should be.'

She leaned closer to him and dropped her voice to a taught whisper.

'I can't take money from you. There's a word for women who take money from men.'

'You know that's not what I think of you.'

'Oh, I know,' she snarled. Now she was red with anger and struggling to keep her voice down. 'You have to bring me here like this and humiliate me by giving me money! What am I to you? Because that's not what you do for a friend.'

He allowed her anger to flood across him, knowing that he deserved it. It was transitory, he told himself. She would hate him, but that was for the best.

'I wanted to make sure you are taken care of.'

'I take care of myself,' she said. 'I always have. I only thought we could be equals.'

'I was just trying to help you.'

'I know. I don't know what I was thinking. I'm a fool.'

'That's the last thing you are.'

He got to his feet unsteadily, his knee stiff from sitting down for too long, and gathered his hat.

'You're leaving. Just like that?'

'I've offended you and I won't compound it.'

He offered her his hand, but she turned away.

'Will you not say goodbye?'

Emily remained silent. He dropped some money on the table to pay the bill and started to walk away, then turned back.

'We were always equals,' he said, and left her.

***

Hansen drew the string across the brown paper wrapping and tied it loosely. Then he set the package down and stood back. He wasn't sure how it would be received, but it would, perhaps, go some way to repairing how she felt about him.

He turned back to his case on the dresser and checked through what he had packed. Satisfied that he had everything, he closed the lid and noticed Emily's copy of *Three Men in a Boat* lying on the side. He picked it up and studied it. In the same way that the story now seemed from another era, the sentiment in Emily leaving it was now lost to him as well. He put it down and pushed it away.

He pulled open the drawer where his revolver lay. He put his hand out to touch it, but he pulled back, as it were hot to touch.

It might be sensible to take it, but what did sense have to do with this trip?

As he closed the case there was a knock at the door, and Crosse bounded in.

'All set?' he said, keeping the mood light.

'More or less. Would you do something for me?'

'If I can.'

He leant over his desk and scribbled a note. He could sense Crosse peering over his shoulder as he did so. He blotted the paper, folded it carefully and slid it into an envelope.

'Will you take this to Emily? And the parcel.'

'Can't you take it yourself?'

'This afternoon if you can,' he replied, deliberately evading the question. Crosse put his pipe into his mouth and began chewing on it, pushing his glasses up his nose.

'You made your choice, Richard. This could be considered unkind. Leave her be.'

'Please.'

'If that's what you would like.'

He shook his hand warmly.

'Thank you, Ernie. Take care in New Zealand. I hear there are more sheep than people there.'

'A different kind of flock for a priest! If you should find yourself in that part of the world---'

'I will look you up. Perhaps I'll listen to what you teach for once.'

'Unlikely. Take good care.'

Crosse picked up the parcel and nodded a final farewell. Hansen turned back to pick up his case and was about to leave when he paused. He went back to the table and picked up Emily's book again. This time he opened his case and put it inside.

Chapter Twenty

1919

Exeter

'Mrs Hansen won't let me see Richard,' she said. 'Will you give him something from me?'

'Of course,' said Crosse.

She reached into her bag, took out her copy of *Three Men in a Boat* and handed it to him.

'He'll understand,' she said.

She turned away and walked back the way she had come. She had meant what she had said to Mrs Hansen. The friendship meant too much to her to abandon him. Though it needs must be at a distance.

She understood the fear that she had seen in his mother's eyes. It was the same fear that ran through her every day, the spectre of the workhouse shadowing her every step. But there was little help she could give, and her words stayed with her: what she had done? Was any of it because of what she had done? Or failed to do?

She had still reached no firm conclusions as she reached her lodgings once again. Much of the bounce that had been in her step on leaving her pupils had gone now, and she was more troubled when she saw Mrs Grant tussling on the doorstep with a couple of men in overalls who were carrying the dresser from the kitchen out into the street.

'I've written explaining my circumstances,' she was saying. 'You might leave it here until I can straighten this out.'

'We're just doing our job, missus' said the older of the two.

'You're doing a heartless job!'

'If you can't pay, you can't keep it,' he said, with a shake of the head as they took the furniture to a cart waiting on the road.

'Mrs Grant,' said Emily, 'what's going on?'

'Oh, nothing for you to worry about my dear,' she replied. 'Why don't you come in off the street.'

They went inside and Emily pulled the door shut behind her, hoping that the privacy would lead her to explain.

'Bailiffs,' said Mrs Grant, practically spitting out the word in contempt. 'My late husband was better with money than I, and I'm afraid I haven't kept up with payments as I should have.

'Still, nothing to do. We carry on, don't we, as always?'

Emily followed her through to the kitchen, where she helped her to pick up the bowls, plates and other crockery that was scattered on the floor, hurriedly removed from the now missing dresser.

'Are things difficult?' said Emily, cautiously.

'Oh, well. It's not an easy time for anyone.'

Mrs Grant continued to pack the objects into other cupboards, though there was little room for it all. Emily thought back to their previous conversation.

'I know you said we might make an arrangement about the rent,' she said nervously, 'but if you need the money, I will find it.'

'Don't you worry my luvver,' she said, smiling. 'Let me think about that. Now, how went your first day with the children?'

Emily was pleased to share her day, and in telling it again her mood returned to something of what it had been. There was something comfortable about talking with Mrs Grant. She seemed genuinely interested. Oftentimes over the years she had had thoughts, sometimes serious, sometimes silly, but no one to tell.

Except, as she walked upstairs, she no longer felt so secure. Could she afford to continue with this work, however much it meant to her, if it cost others? And what if Mrs Grant's business were at risk? There was still a need to secure a paying job soon, so she could feel easy in her own mind.

As she tried to fall asleep that night, she considered the new life that she had so eagerly embarked upon only a few days before. The world as she looked at it now had lost something of its lustre. It was a little darker, and a little more tangled than she had seen in it before.

***

Emily sat under the tree where she had sat so many times before. There was something in feeling the green around her, and the birdsong, that made her feel safe. The day had been one of contrasts. The children were a delight to teach, and those hours were a precious interlude in the rest of the day, which had been a frustrating one. She had continued her search for paid employment, but at every turn her life, as it had been, held her back. It felt like shackles around her feet, and no matter what she might do, it would drag her down. She looked up through the leaves into the blue sky and wanted to cry out in frustration. The money was almost gone, and she could no longer trespass on Mrs Grant's goodwill. The more she turned it over in her mind, the more there seemed to be only one outcome.

    She stood up and started to walk aimlessly, much as she had that first day in the rain. The weather had matched her mood then, but now the warm sunshine seemed to tease her, just as things were turning for the better, she would be returned to the beginning. 'I don't want to have to come back for you,' the man had said when he had brought her to the house. And she had lived in fear that it would happen, for months, years even. Now there was no need for him to return, because she would be forced to go back of her own volition.

'Miss Portinari?' said a voice, interrupting her thoughts.

She looked up and saw Colonel Dawes walking in the opposite direction. He stopped and smiled at her.

'I was hoping to run into you,' he said, looking at his feet. His nervousness was endearing in a strange way.

'Forgive me, Colonel, I didn't see you.'

'You seemed lost in thought. A little sad, if I may say?'

They fell into step together and by the time they reached her lodgings, she had told him at least part of the truth. Perhaps it was a weak moment, or a need to confide in someone, but she was surprised that he didn't turn away. Moreover, he invited her to walk out with him the next day. In the heat of the moment, she had agreed, though it was difficult to say why.

The next day they walked in the gardens, and he was kind and considerate. Then they walked by the river and he was agreeable and amiable company. For several days they spent time together, and she agreed to everything he suggested, except when he invited her to tea at Deller's. She was too occupied with preparations for her lessons, she said, to accept this particular suggestion. Instead, she proposed that they visit the museum.

She had often visited before on her few days off, studying the fossils and the strange specimens in jars. but it was much more pleasant to have company.

'I want to get the children to write their own stories,' she was telling Colonel Dawes, or Anthony, as he now pressed her to call him, though it did not feel comfortable. There were few people she had ever called by their first name, and it did not come naturally.

'Hmm' he responded, idly examining a bird in a glass case.

'"Tell me and I forget, teach me and I may remember, involve me and I learn,"' she said, waiting for him to react.

'That's very clever', he said, looking at her in admiration, 'how did you come up with that?'

'Well, it's nothing really,' she said, not liking to correct him. 'I'm sure others have had the same idea.'

He hummed again and wandered off towards the fine art galleries. To be thought clever was something she had always wished, and yet it seemed too easy; there was no challenge in it.

She meandered along the gallery, fascinated by the paintings. There were several in a style she recognised as pre-Raphaelite. Dawes studied the exhibition programme and blew out his cheeks.

'Are there many rooms in this exhibition?'

She ignored the comment and read the description of the painting, which, although a little fanciful for her taste, had a grandeur to it that was appealing.

'Dante and his Beatrice,' she read. 'I've always loved this story. Did you know she had the same name as me? The real

Beatrice I mean. My mother used to say that perhaps we were related. I love the intense colours and the detail, don't you?'

'Yes,' he said, though his attention was focused squarely on his pocket watch. She sucked her teeth and tried to be patient.

'Would you rather go somewhere else?' she said.

'Oh no! I'm sorry,' he said, putting the watch away and returning his attention to her. 'I know you enjoy all this. I'm a man of simple tastes, that's all. Hunting, fishing, you know.'

'Perhaps we could talk about something else?' she said. 'Do you read?'

'Now and then,' he replied, distracted again. He came closer and took her by the arm. 'Look, Miss Portinari - Emily - I know we haven't known each other very long, but I admire you a great deal. Would you come over here for a moment?'

He led her to a quiet corner of the gallery and motioned for her to sit on the bench.

'I'm not one for fancy words I'm afraid, but I believe I can offer you a great deal, and well---'

He took a small box from his waistcoat pocket and opened it. He turned it slowly towards her and revealed a diamond ring, which shimmered blue in the dim light.

'What do you say?'

***

She lay on the bed, thinking. Her mother had always taught her to list out everything on one side and then the other in any decision. As she had always said, it was the only way to make a properly informed choice. To follow instinct was the surest way to fail she had said, learned from the bitterest of experience.

Emily made the lists now, in her mind, and there was one sure conclusion. The path she was on would lead to poverty and destitution. And she might lead Mrs Grant with her. All sense suggested, for security and for stability, she must accept. And yet, she could hear the voice of Jane Bennet addressing her sister, as clearly as if she were in the room, speaking: 'do anything rather than marry without affection'.

As she lay considering, there was a knock at the door, and she got up to answer it. Mrs Grant stood outside, trying to stifle an enormous grin, and holding something behind her back.

'Well, miss, I think you've been holding out on me.'

Emily's face must have shown her perplexity, for Mrs Grant laughed amiably and brought from behind her back a smart-looking cardboard box bearing the name of a couturier she recognised.

'You didn't say you had a gentleman admirer,' said Mrs Grant, 'though I'm not surprised.'

'Oh,' she said, trying not to sound disappointed, but failing. 'It must be from Colonel Dawes.'

He had promised not to press her on the matter, and she was disappointed that he now saw fit to send her expensive gifts, as if her affection could be bought.

'No, not a Colonel,' said Mrs Grant, laying the box on the bed. 'I should know my army ranks by now, with the war and all, and this man was a Major.'

'A Major?' said Emily, turning suddenly.

'Yes. Blonde hair and blue eyes. Rather dashing, if you don't mind my saying.'

Emily tore the lid off the box as if it were about to catch fire. The dress inside was a beautiful dark green silk gown. Fashionably cut, and short enough to be considered racy, it was exactly what she would have picked herself.

As she lifted it a note dropped onto the covers. She opened it eagerly and read:

I WOULD SUGGEST NOT WEARING THIS ONE FOR AGRICULTURAL LABOUR. PERHAPS INSTEAD YOU MIGHT WISH TO DEBUT IT FOR TEA TOMORROW, IF YOU WOULD HONOUR ME WITH YOUR COMPANY? I HAVE SOMETHING I WISH TO GIVE YOU.

I WILL BE AT DELLER'S AT 4PM IF THAT IS CONVENIENT?

R.

'I take it this gift is not so unwelcome after all?' said Mrs Grant, 'seeing your face!' and she laughed heartily.

***

As he walked away from the table, she looked at the leather wallet on the table in front of her. She felt sick, as if the roll of notes inside somehow represented her life's value. There was a prickle on her neck, like all the eyes in the room were boring into her, a feeling that only became more pronounced as she stood up. She almost left the money where it was, disgusted to touch it again, but her mother's voice still rang in her mind. It would pay the rent. She took it, hiding it in the folds of her dress, ashamed to be holding it.

She began to walk towards the door, and the room that had been at first so startling and wondrous on entering now seemed too dazzling. She felt conspicuous and out of place. And there was a shame in remembering her dream now. It was supposed to end very differently, with tears of a different kind. It was the innocent fancy of a girl who knew no better.

Reaching the door, it was held open for her by a doorman in a top hat and tails, who touched the brim as she passed. She stood aside to allow another woman to enter, who was in a party with several other well-dressed ladies. Emily recognised her at once and the woman smiled briefly at her, before turning back, apparently recognising her in turn.

'Excuse me,' she said. 'But do we know each other? I'm usually so good at remembering faces, this is very embarrassing.'

'We have met,' said Emily, uncertainly. There was no way to explain it easily, so she said the first thing that came into her head. 'I'm a friend of Richard.'

'Oh,' said the woman. 'Of course. I'm Madeleine. Montgomery. Or rather, Giles now. I should be used to it by now.'

'Emily. Emily Portinari.'

Madeleine seemed still to be frantically trying to place her face, but eventually gave in and simply smiled.

'I'm sure Richard has mentioned me?'

'In passing,' said Emily, with a little spite, at which Madeleine's face fell.

She had never had much time for Madeleine when she had been a frequent visitor, though she couldn't put her finger on quite why. She had never really acknowledged Emily's existence before, but it wasn't that. After all, that was not unusual. However, there was something of a pleasure in having her at a disadvantage now.

'You're married, Mrs Giles?'

'Yes. Just last week. Hence the name confusion.' She smiled again, nervously now. 'And how is Richard?'

'He's well,' she said, as succinctly as she could.

'Good. I'm very pleased to hear it,' said Madeleine. 'He is back in Exeter?'

'Yes. For now.'

'For now?'

'He's going abroad.'

Emily longed to end this conversation and leave. To have to talk politely about him, and especially to her, was unendurable.

'I see,' said Madeleine. 'Well, give him my best, Miss Portinari, when you see him again.'

'I shall,' she said. 'If I do.'

Emily nodded in acknowledgement as Madeleine's friends steered her towards the dining room. As Emily went to go, she felt a hand on her arm. Madeleine bent towards her in a whisper.

'It's none of my concern,' she began. 'But if you are waiting for him to propose---' she carefully noted Emily's reaction. 'I see that you are. Well, have a care. I understand the wish for the attachment. I felt it myself. But there is a cruelty in being too kind you know, and he was too kind to me for too long before he revealed his true feelings.

'Now I am married and well matched to a man who was never unclear in his intentions. I wish you similar happiness.'

She patted Emily on the arm and then re-joined her friends.

***

'Are you sure, my luvver?' said Mrs Grant.

'Yes,' she replied. 'Perhaps you can sell it or find someone who wants it.'

'It's such a beautiful dress though.'

She didn't press the point and took it from Emily. She laid it across her arm and rocked on her feet, lingering in the room.

'It's one thing to give away a dress,' she said. 'But what you were saying about the school, you didn't mean that surely?'

'I would continue if I could,' said Emily. 'You know how much it means to me.'

'And that's why I mention it,' said Mrs Grant. 'But you know your own mind. If it is your mind, and not your heart?'

'Why should it be my heart?' said Emily sternly.

'I think you answer your own question,' she said, and made her way, frowning, back to the scullery.

The irony was that it had been a choice made with little regard to her heart, or at least that was what she tried to believe. The pragmatic, sensible choice that would secure her future.

There was a knock at the front door and Mrs Grant came steaming back as Emily reached the hall.

'I'll see to it, dear,' she said, wiping her hands on her apron.

She threw the door open to find Mr Crosse standing on the step, carrying a large flat parcel. Mrs Grant looked shocked.

'Well, you don't hang around, do you?'

'I beg your pardon?' said Crosse, pushing the glasses up his nose in characteristic fashion. Emily interrupted.

'Mr Crosse! How lovely to see you. Please come in.'

'Why don't you show him into the parlour, Emily?'

'Thank you, Mrs Grant. Come this way, Mr Crosse.'

She led the way into the more formal sitting room, which she had not yet been allowed to enter, and showed Crosse to a chair. Then she perched herself on the edge of the settee.

'Would you and your guest like some tea, my dear?' said Mrs Grant.

'Thank you, Mrs Grant,' she said. 'Mr Crosse has a great fondness for tea.'

'No, thank you, he replied. 'For once I have had my fill.'

'Oh well, perhaps later?' said Mrs Grant. 'I'll leave you alone, I'm sure you've much to discuss.'

She went out, raising her eyebrows as she looked at Emily, and closed the door behind her. There was a steady ticking of the clock on the mantelpiece as Crosse studied the room around him and pulled his pipe from his pocket. He seemed unsure whether he could light it, and he eventually opted to place it on the arm of the chair.

'I'm glad you're here,' said Emily, keen to break the silence. 'I have some news.'

She angled the ring on her finger towards him so that the light glinted off it and dazzled him.

'How did you get that?' he asked.

He looked confused more than shocked, and the question bemused and rather offended her.

'What do you mean? Is that all you can say?'

'Forgive me,' he said, recovering his sangfroid. 'I was just a little surprised. Congratulations my dear.'

'Thank you.'

He smiled benevolently, but there was something in his face which marked disappointment as well, a reflection which underscored her own feelings.

'What's his name?'

'It's Colonel Dawes. Anthony.'

'I see.'

He instinctively went to pick up his pipe but knocked it to the floor and self-consciously bent to pick it up. He wiped it with his handkerchief and thrust it into his mouth.

'There's no need to say anything,' she said. 'I know you don't like him.'

'What I think really is of the slightest of importance.'

Several times he took his pipe out and then returned it to his mouth again, as if distracted by a thought.

'It's just he is so--- conventional. Does he know?' He nodded towards her, not wishing to complete the sentence. 'Does he know that you were---'

'A skivvy? Yes, he knows. And he deems it to be of not the slightest importance,' she said, with something of a sneer.

'I'm glad.'

Crosse got up and started to pace around the room.

'May I smoke?' he asked, and she nodded.

He lit his pipe and waved the match to blow it out before throwing it into the fireplace. He puffed away for some moments and paced backwards and forwards. It was clear that he had more to say.

'You're sure about this?' he said at last.

'What kind of a question is that to ask?' she said, getting angry now. 'Of course I'm sure!'

But of course, it was a lie. She had not been sure of anything since the day before when she had walked into the tearoom.

'And you love him?'

'It's a good match. He's kind, and I know he loves me. I have to think of the future.'

Crosse paced once more, and then returned to his seat, putting a hand absently to the parcel he had brought with him.

'What have you there?' she asked.

He looked down at the package and gave her an odd half-smile.

'This is why I was here. It's for you.'

'For me? What is it? It can't be an engagement present – you didn't know.'

'There's a tried and tested way to find out,' he said, with a slight tilt of the head.

She took it from him and started to examine it.

'It's from Richard.'

The name was bitter to her like the homemade beer she had tasted in Cornwall, and the effect was similar. She pushed the parcel back to him.

'Can you take it away please.'

He held it for a moment, and then slowly removed his spectacles and cleaned them.

'I really think you should open it'.

Her façade of composure was beginning to crumble, and she could feel the torrent of emotions that had occupied her mind for the last day returning. The certainty of the decision she had made that morning was swept away and she furiously tried to govern a confusion of thoughts.

'Did he tell you what he did?' she said quietly.

'He mentioned it. But I don't think you understand---'

'I don't understand, because I'm a simple servant? You know what happened in Cornwall. I came to terms with that. But then he just left me there with this envelope of money, like a--- and everyone looking at me!'

'Please open it.'

As much as she wanted him to leave with it, she wanted to know what was inside, and in the end, she gave in and began tearing the paper from the package. It was a painting, and when she turned it towards her, she realised it was Captain Martin's depiction of the sunset, now beautifully framed.

'Oh my.'

'There is a note too.'

She took the note which Crosse was holding out to her and ripped open the envelope. She unfolded the letter and read:

> BECAUSE YOU SAW WHAT HE FELT WHEN HE PAINTED IT.
> THAT YOU MIGHT SEE WHAT I FEEL WHEN I WRITE THIS.
> LIVE WELL. R.

She sobbed and smiled all at once. Her stomach tightened and she turned the ring on her finger repeatedly.

'What does this mean?' she asked.

'I don't think you need me to interpret for you.'

The meaning was clear, albeit now she doubted her own perception. But there was a finality to it as well that frightened her. Now it was her turn to pace the room, as she restlessly went from one end to the other. Crosse watched her. She searched her memory and gradually remembered why the words were familiar. In his letters he had always ended them in a conventional way, except when a battle was imminent, when he had been able to say little. In those cases, he had always used those words: 'live well'.

'Did he tell you why he was going to Germany?' she asked.

'Yes,' said Crosse. 'He wanted to see his family.'

'And what else?'

'I don't know. I do know he plans to settle somewhere else. His father told me he gave him the means. Some five hundred pounds I understand. Enough to start a new life.'

'Five hundred pounds?' she exclaimed.

'Yes. Why?'

She ran to her room, where the money was hidden, and pulled it out. She took it back downstairs and handed it to Crosse.

'I haven't counted it, I didn't want to touch it, but there must be five hundred pounds here. Why would he give me all his money?'

The conclusion struck both of them at the same time. She looked down at the ring on her finger once more and she had a sudden clarity of mind. In her life she had been shackled by circumstance, shackled by poverty, or the fear of poverty, and even shackled by her feelings for Richard. In that moment she took a hammer to them. She delighted in the certainty of her uncertainty, and she knew what she needed to do to be seen finally. Or rather, what she wanted to do.

She took off her ring and placed it on the table, then she walked towards the door.

'Where are you going?' asked Crosse.

'Germany,' she replied, simply. 'Are you coming?'

Chapter Twenty-One

1919

Germany

Hansen stood at the rail looking out to sea. There was a nausea in the depths of his stomach, but he couldn't be sure if it were down to the sea journey, or his anxiety.

The sea air was cold, and he plunged his hands deep into the pockets of his tweed jacket. He felt an object in the corner of one pocket and pulled it out. He had automatically transferred the contents of his uniform tunic when he had left it behind, and unthinkingly had carried this small box with him. He squeezed it open with his thumb and gazed on the ring inside, which had once belonged to his grandmother, his father's mother.

He took a long breath and snapped the box shut. He made to fling it over the side but stopped at the last moment and returned it to his pocket. It was an heirloom, and it might someday find a use again.

Sweat trickled down his face, despite the chilly weather, and he took out a handkerchief to wipe his lip. His hand shook and he clasped it in his other hand to stop it. One of the ship's officers came over to him.

'Are you quite well, sir? You look awfully pale.'

'A touch of seasickness,' he replied.

'Well, it's not uncommon,' said the officer. 'Perhaps you should lie down in your cabin?'

'Thank you. Perhaps I shall.'

He went with the roll of the ship and eased his way down a passageway to his cabin. Once he was inside, he threw himself down on to the bed.

He didn't want to sleep. Ever since Cornwall he had been tormented by dreams that had become progressively more grotesque. The latest had found him in a dark forest, surrounded by mists and watched by eyes from the darkness. When he tried to run the trees had caught him in their branches and bound him tight, before forcing him towards a sharp stump jutting up from the ground. Just as he had been about to be impaled through the neck, he had woken, shaking and frozen. He would not sleep again now until this was all over.

He turned on to his back and lay looking up at the steel bulkheads. Just for a moment he fancied he heard Emily's voice, and he sat up, listening intently. There was nothing. Just the creaking of the ship and the whistling of the wind. He went to the door and opened it, but there was no one outside. He lay back down on the bed. Scholars had debated for decades whether Hamlet was actually mad, or just feigning it. Perhaps, he began to wonder darkly, he himself was fit for an asylum after all.

He had done what he could to provide for Emily, to make right the wrong he had done her, but still she had been on his mind since he had left her. He couldn't forget the look on her face when he had presented her with the money. It was an expression of profound sadness, betrayal and devastation. Without the war, perhaps he would have chosen differently, but without the war he might never have realised who she was.

***

He walked across the cobbled square, past the Frauenkirche, and everywhere around him there was evidence of fighting. Carts were pulled across the street, ammunition rounds scattered on the ground, and several buildings still smoked, blackened around their windows, with roof tiles fallen in.

As he walked on further a squad of Freikorps marched towards him and then spread out, entering shops and buildings. He skirted around the square, trying to give them a wide berth, and headed towards a café. As he reached the tables, he realised that chairs were thrown to the ground, and the windows of the café were broken. A soldier came out, forcing a man ahead of him. It appeared to be the café owner. The soldier handed his charge to an officer, who had just arrived, and he sent them off towards a group that was gathering in the centre of the square. Then the officer saw Hansen and shouted to him. He feigned innocence, holding his hands out to the sides and shrugging.

'Papers please,' said the officer, who looked young enough to still be in school.

'I'm sorry,' said Hansen, patting his pockets. 'I've only just arrived, and I seem to have left the hotel without them.'

The officer looked him up and down suspiciously.

'You are visiting our city?'

'Yes.'

'Where are you from? I don't recognise your accent.'

'I am from Saxony,' he said. 'Meissen.'

'What are you doing here?'

'I'm on business. I sell porcelain.'

The officer squinted at him, looking him in the eye. Then he grinned and rocked back on his heels.

'You chose a good time! Plenty of porcelain has been broken here, and much else, by the damn Communists. You will do well!'

He laughed, taking some half-eaten rolls from a table. He meandered off, chewing on the stale bread and chuckling to himself. Hansen let out a long breath and continued on his way, now carefully keeping away from any crowds. There were no trains running at the station, so he hired a cab to take him out of the city.

At length he arrived at Peterhausen and walked from there along dusty tracks to the family farm. He stopped at the gate and saw the farmhouse where his father had grown up. It was at the end of a long driveway, surrounded by tall cypress trees, and as he got closer, he could see that it was built of a warm yellowish stone. It had more in common with the houses he had seen in Italy than with anything archetypically German. There was something welcoming and homely about it that appealed to him, though the reaction to his arrival was likely to be anything but friendly. He searched in his bag for the book Emily had given him and held it to his chest as he walked.

He rounded some trees and reached a small garden outside the house, with a table and chairs set up on the lawn. He paused for a moment and took in his surroundings, and as he did so, a woman came out of the house carrying a bottle of wine and some glasses. She was in her fifties, quite short and round, with a ready smile and silver hair plaited around her head in the Bavarian style.

'I thought you were coming later?' she said without looking at him. Then she stopped still when she realised it was not the person she had expected.

'Oh, forgive me,' she said. 'I thought you were Johan, our land agent.'

Her eyes narrowed and she looked pale, almost shocked.

'Are you alright?' he asked.

'Yes,' she said. 'It's just you look so very much like my son. I was a little taken aback for a moment.'

'It's not so surprising,' he said, and waited.

'You don't recognise me, do you?'

She put down the wine and looked back at him.

'Richard?'

He nodded. She stood silently for a moment, her hands to her mouth, shaking her head and smiling.

'Oh, what must you think!' she said suddenly. 'I am Gerda. When I last saw you, you were so tiny. Will you sit down and have a drink? I will fetch your uncle.'

She went towards the house, unsure of what to do first, and then turned back with a questioning look.

'You recognised me?'

'Only from your photograph' he said.

'Ah. Of course. This is so wonderful! Have some wine.'

'No, thank you,' he said.

'No? Very well.' Then she remembered her previous mission. 'Your uncle!' she exclaimed and hurried off back into the house.

Hansen sat down at the table and put the book down, stretching out his leg, which was sore with all the walking he had done.

Presently Gerda returned, with her husband following. He was tall and heavily built, with a small green hat perched incongruously on his head. A full white beard brushed his chest as he peered at Hansen. There was a noticeable similarity to his father, but this face was sterner and harder.

'My husband – your uncle – Leopold,' said Gerda, introducing them. 'Isn't it wonderful that your nephew is here?'

'Yes,' grunted Leopold, unsmiling. 'Why are you here?'

'Leopold!'

Hansen dropped his head, not wanting to look at either of them in the eye, but particularly his uncle.

'I wanted to come to see you,' he began. 'I wanted to talk to you about Sebastian.'

Gerda smiled sadly.

'You heard?'

He nodded.

'I was saying, Leopold, how much Richard looks like him?'

His uncle nodded and studied him all the more. Hansen picked up his bag and put it onto the table.

'I have some things I wanted to return to you.'

In turn he slowly took from the bag some dog tags, an iron cross and finally a pistol, and placed them on the table. Gerda picked up the tags and the iron cross and kissed them tenderly, tears beginning to form in her eyes.

'Thank you for bringing these. It is very kind.'

His uncle eyed him with some suspicion.

'How do you have these things?' He pulled the dogtags from his wife and read the name. 'They are his. Were you there?'

Hansen's heart felt heavy in his chest and his throat constricted. His hands began to tremor once more, and he stifled it by clutching them together tightly.

'I was,' he began. His mouth was dry now, and his voice began to crack. 'I saw him die. I---

He felt faint, but he forced himself to continue.

'I didn't know it was him. Believe me, I didn't know. I couldn't know. Until I saw what I had done.'

Gerda's face looked blank, but pale.

'I don't understand,' she said. 'Perhaps it is his German, Leopold, but I don't know what he is saying.'

His uncle had become totally still, his eyes like pin pricks. Gerda turned from one to the other and began to allow herself to understand a truth that was too horrible for any of them to speak.

Hansen picked up Emily's book and stood up, walking a few paces away from the table. He could feel the heat of his uncle's rage and instinctively he backed away from it.

Then Gerda started to scream manically, completely lost to grief and despair, covering her face, tears streaming.

'How could you come here and tell me this? Tell us this? How could you!'

'I'm sorry,' he said, feebly. 'I'm so sorry.'

Gerda opened her mouth to reply, but no words came. She took hold of the cross hanging around her neck, mouthing a prayer. Hansen watched her and time became an irrelevance. He was trapped in the torment that had not left him for over three years. There was only satisfaction in having finally confessed his guilt. So many times he had told himself it was an accident, that there had been no way to know, but it didn't change anything.

'I think you must go,' said Gerda at last. 'Go! Go now!'

He bowed his head in acknowledgement and made to go. As he turned, he heard the metal click of the pistol being cocked.

'No,' said his uncle, in a chilling whisper.

He turned back to face him. His body was calm now, ready, willing to accept his fate.

Leopold's hand shook as he pointed the pistol at Hansen.

'No!' said Gerda suddenly, touching her husband on his outstretched arm. 'This is not right. You who stood against the war?'

'It's alright,' said Hansen, calmer now than ever. He let go of the book and it fell from his hand and landed on the ground beside him.

He stood as Challacombe had done. He had died bravely as an innocent man. He could surely do the same as a guilty one.

Hansen closed his eyes, and a shot rang out.

Chapter Twenty-Two

1919

Germany

She drank in the salty sea air and felt the cold on her face, starting to become accustomed to the strange swaying of the ship under her feet. Even though Crosse hopped around next to her, rubbing his hands together, and her own coat was still inadequate, she would have stood there all day. The heady mixture of sensations produced a pleasurable overload.

'Shall we go below?' asked Crosse, his nose chilled red.

'If you wish,' she said.

They made their way unsteadily down some stairs and passed cabins along the deck.

'Is that better, Mr Crosse?' she asked. 'You were turning a little blue up there.'

'I've never been a good sailor,' he said, with a little tilt of the head. 'When I was a child, I got seasick on the Serpentine.'

They went inside and found some seats in the lounge. Crosse ordered himself a brandy and cradled it in his hands as he tried to warm up. He looked over his glass at her and seemed to be studying her again, much as he had on the train the first time. Curious, a little perplexed, but kindly.

'Forgive me being blunt,' he said after a moment or two. 'But why exactly are we here?'

She wrinkled her nose.

'We, or me?' she said.

He grinned unexpectedly, not something he was given to.

'A good answer. I suppose I mean, you seemed set for a new life. No one would have blamed you for staying with that.'

'I would,' she said. 'Not because of Richard. I realised that I was giving in. Choosing the same my mother would have chosen.'

He raised an eyebrow.

'I don't mean any disrespect,' she said. 'My mother meant everything to me. I didn't have anyone else. But I've come to realise her choices in life weren't always the right ones. Because she chose my father, and it ruined her, she didn't risk anything for the rest of her life, and she didn't want me to either.

'Colonel Dawes was very pleasant to me, and I would have had everything materially I could wish – I would be a Lady, have fine clothes, servants, money. But he is---'

'You don't have to tell me,' said Crosse, smirking.

'It's not even that I don't love him. My life as a maid was monotonous, grey, like a prison. When you showed me the painting, I could see the colour in it, the life in it, and then I realised what I would be missing. I would be giving up all the things I loved. It would be another kind of prison where I would be comfortable, but never challenged, never excited. Never alive.'

Crosse took out his pipe and started filling it meticulously.

'If that is why you didn't stay, then why,' and he prodded towards her with his pipe, 'why are we <u>here</u>?'

'Because he needs me,' was her short answer. It was the truth. There was no expectation this time, despite his message. No new beginnings, only a wish to prevent an ending.

'And it's what a friend does,' she added.

Crosse lit his pipe and sat back, puffing contentedly.

'I will tell you a secret,' he said after a minute or two. 'When I met Richard, I didn't think he would make it. He felt everything to such a degree, tried to be the gentleman at every turn. He wouldn't even let his men use derogatory language about the enemy. Colonel "Bores" may be a prize chump, but he was right about one thing. Officers who feel too much fall by the wayside. You harden to war, or you don't survive.

'There was a moment for Richard, when he killed a German officer during a gas attack. It hit him hard. I don't know whether it was the first man he'd killed, but he nearly went over the edge. When he came back, he wasn't the same man, but he was the man he needed to be.

'Captain Martin and he were great friends, as you know, probably more on one side than the other in truth, but great friends. Having that friendship helped him through. But when we lost Captain Martin, he didn't make any others.'

'He had you,' she said.

'Yes,' he said. 'But your friendship has given him back something – that which he had put aside because he needed to. But which he needs now. If I say that I am the Virgil to his Dante, you'll understand me when I say: Virgil cannot go with him on the final part of his journey.'

***

Emily was drawn to look out of the window of the train as it passed across a viaduct, high above a landscape that was bereft of life. As far as she could see it was grey or brown, pitted and cratered, with the ghosts of what had once been trees, bowing as if in grief.

She turned to Crosse, wanting to speak, but no words came to her lips. They watched together in silence for some minutes, then Crosse closed his eyes, and she could see him mouthing a silent prayer.

'It's difficult to think that anything will grow here again,' he said at last.

'Maybe it will take time,' she said. 'Maybe it won't be like it was. But with the right nurturing---'

'Yes,' he said, looking at her with a smile, 'with the right nurturing, there is hope.'

As she studied the blasted landscape, she wondered at how they could have lived; buried into the ground, hiding from the devastation all around. Was it so surprising that someone like Richard might struggle to see a future for himself after that?

If, she thought, if she were to share that future with him, it would not, could not, be a conventional one. But the cord of communion that connected them was strong. She needed him and now he needed her. He had reached out a hand to her when she had been at her lowest point and had never really let go. He had protected her as much as he could, even when she had hated him for it. He had, it seemed, even tried to protect her from himself. Now, she was determined, she had no need of that.

There had been something in what Crosse had said though that had stayed with her. The moment of change for Richard when he had killed an enemy officer. He had not talked about it in his letters, but she too had sensed a difference. There had been a gap of several weeks when there had been no letters at all. When he began to write again, they seemed shallow somehow, as if he were going through the motions. He had often written about his life at home, the people and the places, but after this they had been all about the war or people there, except for the usual pleasantries. Then something occurred to her. She put the idea aside, but it wouldn't leave her mind, and she kept mulling on it as they travelled. At last, she had to relieve herself of the troubling idea, and she shared her thoughts with Crosse.

'The officer Richard killed,' she asked him. 'Can you remember him?'

Crosse looked thoughtful and tapped his pipe on his knee as he worked through his memories.

'I'm not sure,' he said. 'I can't say that I took particular notice of enemy soldiers, though I'm ashamed to say so now. Though---' He seemed to be reaching for a hidden memory. 'I do remember one thing. It was very odd. I think I remarked upon it at the time, that perhaps Richard took such fright because the chap could have been his doppelganger. To kill oneself as it were.'

He seemed more than a little disturbed by the memory and his thoughts and retreated into silence. Emily turned the idea over and over and it made her nauseous. Could this be possible? Then she remembered the wretched hollowness in his eyes that she had seen that first night, and she started to weep silently for him.

At length they reached Munich and were glad to escape from a city which seemed to have descended into chaos. They bought transport at great cost and some hours later they got down from the wagon that had brought them deep into the countryside and stood at a gate which read 'Hansen Hof'.

A long track ran up to a pretty farmhouse surrounded by trees, and they both lingered there, unsure whether they should go on.

Then came the echoing crack of a distant gunshot.

'Dear God!' exclaimed Crosse.

Her heart froze in her chest and she was rooted to the spot, unable to breathe. She fought through the shock and pushed herself on, beginning to run up the track towards the sound.

'Emily, stop! It could be anything.'

But she knew in herself that it could only be one thing, and she ran, faster and faster. In despair, she prayed that she was wrong.

Chapter Twenty-Three

1919

Germany

Hansen opened his eyes. There was no pain. But as he looked down, he realised there was no wound either. The shot had missed, either accidentally or by choice.

There were tears now in his uncle's eyes. With an explosion of anger and grief, he threw down the gun and dropped to his knees, and his wife embraced him, holding him close as they both wept.

'Pick it up,' said Hansen, slowly. Then with sudden urgency, as if the moment might slip away and he would lose the courage to face it: 'Please, pick it up!'

As Emily ran, her heart pounded, and each breath became sore to take. She couldn't bear the idea that they might have come so far and yet there may be no hope. No way to reach out her hand and bring him back to her. And selfishly, that she would never say the words to him that she now longed to have a chance to say.

Gerda let go of her husband and moved closer to Hansen. She picked up the pistol from the ground and cradled it in her hands. He stayed still, willing himself not to feel fear.

'You want to die?' she asked.

'It's justice.'

She looked down at the gun and ran her fingers across its edges. Then she turned back to him and though her eyes were wet, the kindness shone back again, and she let her eyelids droop. She sighed and then lifted the gun.

Emily reached the trees and heard voices speaking German. She slowed to a walk and edged around to see who was talking. Her heart leapt as she saw Richard standing there, alive and well, but with a woman standing close by holding a gun. Another man was on his knees, holding onto a chair, tears streaming down his face.

Gerda held the gun up, but rather than firing she ejected the magazine and the round in the chamber and threw everything away in disgust.

'No,' she said to him with certainty. 'It's not justice. Sebastian did not tell me much about the war. I tried to imagine. But whatever I imagined; it didn't seem enough. How can you picture hell?

'He talked about you often. He felt so badly that he left England in the way he did. He felt as you do – torn between two countries. Two families. He told me when he had to kill it was like he was killing his brothers. But he did his duty.

'I wished that I could take his guilt from him and bear it myself. If he were here, I would only tell him that he is loved, because what more can I say? And I would embrace him.'

She stepped towards Hansen and pulled him in, enfolding him in her arms.

'And if he wished it,' she whispered in his ear. 'I would tell him that he is forgiven. That I forgive him.'

Emily watched as Richard's legs seemed to give way, and he dropped to the ground, the woman with him. He heaved a great sob and then dissolved into uncontrollable tears. All at once she understood, and she began to tear up in sympathy.

The woman glanced across at her, first with a look of concern, but then, as she discerned Emily's expression, she smiled and beckoned to her.

Hansen clung to his aunt. His guilt, unquenchable, but no longer burning so bright. He felt Gerda pull back, and as he watched, saw her looking away to one side. She beckoned to someone, and he turned to see where she was looking.

Then in a moment of pure joy he saw Emily standing there. There were tears burning his cheeks, and he felt exposed; vulnerable to her; but he wanted her to see and to know.

'What are you doing here?' he asked, in shock and delight.

He reached out his hand to her and she took it, kneeling gently beside him. His eyes told her everything she needed to know. A look that she had seen on that day in the parlour and which she had for so long mistaken. Now there was no doubt, and she would tell him what he had been unable or unwilling to admit to her or himself.

'Richard', she said, so natural now to say. 'I saw the sunset. And I saw what you feel.'

She gently wiped the tears from his eyes and then she looked down and he could see that she was looking at the book, her book.

'Someone to love---' he began.

'---and someone to love you,' she replied.

She leaned in and kissed him. And as he felt the warmth of her embrace, he knew finally, what those words meant. And he reached into his pocket to find the ring that he still carried there.

Whatever their life would be after this, she thought, holding him tight, it would be truthful, and it would be shared.

Appendix

The real lives behind the story

The feared Form 104/82 which was sent to the next of kin

© River and Rowing Museum

Much of the story of Richard Hansen and his recovery from the trauma of war is based on real people and events, and the symptoms he experiences are also genuinely those reported by soldiers and others who suffer from Post-Traumatic Stress Disorder (PTSD), though his case is particularly severe.

Richard's story

Although largely fictional, Richard's story as a young officer is based on reality. Many university students volunteered to serve and saw themselves commissioned as officers at a young age, often commanding men much older and more experienced than themselves.

Officers were targeted on the battlefield, and the mortality rate was therefore high. Hence promotions could be rapid if they survived. Officers' manuals of the time exhort them to earn the respect of their men and not to be too soft. A distance had to be maintained, and it was a job full of stress, as well as a lot of paperwork. Units were rotated so that they didn't spend too much time in the line of fire. They would spend a week or two at the front before being moved into reserve and then finally for rest away from the trenches.

Soldiers found a comradeship that was difficult to replace in civilian life, and the intensity of the experience and the horrors they saw everyday were not things they wished to share with their families, so many buried their experiences for decades afterwards.

Private Harry Patch, the last Tommy, didn't talk about his experiences until he was in his nineties.

It's likely that most suffered some form of PTSD, and the symptoms Hansen experiences are common, including frightening and disorienting waking flashbacks, often triggered by a sensory memory. They might be brought on by small things, such as a familiar place, smell or sound. Other symptoms might include nightmares, anxiety, tremors, disturbed sleep, depression, mood swings and an inability to see a future for themselves. The condition was not well understood at the time - often called 'shell shock', because it was thought to be a physical effect of the explosions.

The threat of a mental institution was also a real one. The symptoms of shell shock were often mistaken for madness, and soldiers suffering depression, tremors or other physical symptoms might be committed to what were still called insane asylums, some for the rest of their lives. His mother's fear that such madness might be inherited, or that overemotional or eccentric behaviour might leave her vulnerable to the same fate were also not without substance. Women in the nineteenth century could be committed for relatively minor reasons, or even on the strength of evidence from their husbands.

'Talking cures' were pioneered in 1917, based on the work of Sigmund Freud, amongst others, but most soldiers received no treatment. Nowadays drug treatments for depression, counselling and cognitive behavioural therapy (CBT) would be available, but in the First World War, officers might at best be given time off for 'R and R', while their men would get little or nothing. Some were given what we would today call occupational therapies, including traditionally feminine activities like knitting or sewing. They would then be moved onto more masculine activities such as farming, before finally returning to military service. They had hit upon some effective therapies, albeit based on the false assumption that the symptoms were due to the soldiers being less than manly.

The condition can come and go. For some it can disappear with time, but for many it persists, and suicide rates of soldiers with PTSD are high to this day. The charity Combat Stress, who work with veterans, advise that, whatever other treatments are available, the love and support of friends and family is essential for those with PTSD to manage their condition and live a more normal life, and it is this idea that influenced the love story between Hansen and Emily - it is her support and care that helps him to manage the condition, rather than the journey he goes on, but he doesn't realise this until the end.

Emily's story

As a 'maid of all work' in a relatively small, middle class house, there were many thousands of 'Emilys' in the late nineteenth and early twentieth centuries. As a new affluent middle class wished to emulate the aristocracy, they hired servants to support their lifestyle, but could usually only afford one or two. Maids of all work, often called skivvies, and referred to as 'the girl', would be required to do every household job, from answering the door to dusting and cleaning, laundry, laying the fires and in many cases cooking and serving meals as well. Without modern labour-saving devices, it was a long day that started at 5am and often didn't end until midnight, with little time off - usually only Sunday afternoons after church.

They could be dismissed with no warning, their pay was low and conditions could be terrible. Much depended on their employer. Often girls like Emily would be recruited at the age of 12 or 13 from the workhouse. It was deemed to be a good job, and cheap labour for the employer. Frequently employers would not allow them to court men, and their only contact beyond the house might be deliveries from tradesmen, making it a very hard and lonely life.

Mrs Beeton wrote that the life of the maid of all work was the only domestic who should be pitied. In big houses the job could be hard, but there were at least others to share the burden and provide company. As a teenager (although the term was unknown at this time, and she would have been considered an adult) coming into this life still grieving for her mother, and with no family to fall back on, Emily could not expect much from life. She is more fortunate than most in that her mother was educated and literate, and so has given her some schooling and a passion for learning. Her escape therefore comes through reading and dreaming of a better life. Because she lacks other company, her frame of reference for most life experiences comes from books. As the only man of near her own age, it is unsurprising that she develops a crush on Richard, but in time it is also the friendship, intimacy and intellectual challenge that he offers that deepens her feelings for him.

Real events

The 8th and 9th battalions of the Devonshire Regiment fought in France and Belgium as depicted. The 8th battalion, known as 'Buller's Own', after the Boer War General Redvers Buller, was a reserve battalion largely made up of volunteers. Following training they were deployed to France and took part in the Battle of Loos in autumn 1915, where they suffered very heavy casualties. They later took an active role in the actions at The Somme in 1916, and the Third Battle of Ypres (known as Passchendaele) in 1917. They were deployed to the Italian front later that year, where they were involved in successful actions against the Austro-Hungarians.

The 2nd battalion, to which Private Cairns belongs, were a standing battalion serving in Egypt in 1914. They were rushed to France and were involved in many battles. On 27 May 1918 at Bois de Buttes their Brigade was overwhelmed by a huge German attack and, to buy time for the rest of the Corps, the 2nd Devons stood and fought. This action cost them 551 killed and missing – most of the battalion. Among those killed was their Colonel. To recognise their courage the French awarded the Regiment the Croix de Guerre, a unique honour, whose ribbon all Devons wore on their sleeve.

Full scale battles were actually relatively rare events. The everyday reality for most soldiers, most of the time would have been boredom and squalor, mixed with the ever-present threat from gas attacks, which left them scrambling for inadequate masks, as well as artillery bombardments and snipers. Snipers would lurk in shell holes, waiting for any sign of movement, and it gave rise to the superstition, particularly at night, of 'three on a match'. This was the idea that if three soldiers all lit a cigarette from the same match, one would die. It was because the sniper would be attracted by the first flame, aim on the second, and shoot on the third. Soldiers would 'stand to' every dawn and dusk – the times most likely for enemy attack, and there was fear of the enemy taking advantage of the low visibility and panic in a gas attack. Raiding parties would also harry enemy trenches, attacking in small numbers and often using primitive weapons like clubs improvised from sticks and old grenade casings for fear of attracting enemy fire by using rifles. These trench battles became savage hand to hand affairs in a confined space.

Real people

Revd. Ernest Courtenay Crosse

Crosse was the padre attached to the 8th and 9th battalions during the war. Although his character is dramatised in the story, he did tend to the wounded and buried many hundreds of soldiers.

Following the attack on Mansel Copse he buried Captain Martin and as depicted he did erect a wooden sign reading: 'The Devonshires held this trench. The Devonshires hold it still.' It was later turned into a stone memorial (below). Following the war, he moved to New Zealand to become a headmaster.

© The Keep Military Museum

Captain Duncan Lennox Martin

Captain Martin was indeed an artist (although his work is not known), who spent time in Newlyn before the war. Gertrude Harvey was a real artist of the Newlyn School who would go on to have considerable success in later years. She modelled for many of the artists there and it's likely she would have known Martin.

© The Keep Military Museum

As a volunteer at the beginning of the war, Martin was older than most, being already nearly 30, so was quickly promoted to Captain. He constructed a model of Mansel Copse for his superiors to help plan the attack on 1 July 1916 and pointed out an area on the model he called the 'danger spot' where a machine gun emplacement might trap his company if it were not eliminated. Having caught the Germans by surprise in an earlier attack his superiors felt the element of surprise, combined with a heavy artillery bombardment in the hours before, would destroy all opposition. His prediction was proved correct as his company walked into a trap and he was killed with many others. Revd. Crosse buried him later with the memorial mentioned above.

Gertrude Harvey

Gertrude was a Newlyn artist who would later exhibit at the Royal Academy. She modelled for many artists in Newlyn before the war. She may well have known Duncan Martin.

Corporal Albert Allen

Born in about 1883, Corporal Allen was already an old soldier when the war began. For the purposes of the story, his background has been somewhat fictionalised, but he was from Cornwall. He assisted Private Veale in the rescue of Lieutenant Savill from No Man's Land on 16 July 1916 and was shot through the head during the rescue, much as depicted in the story.

Some enlisted men were promoted as officers, but disparagingly termed 'temporary gentlemen' or TGs, by the middle- and upper-class officers around them. Officers were otherwise trained at Officer Training Colleges (OTCs) which were expanded massively during the war to accommodate the recruits that were needed. Nevertheless 'TGs' were also required because the rate of attrition on officers was so high.

Private (later Corporal) Theodore 'Tommy' Veale VC

Private Veale's remarkable rescue of an officer from No Man's Land on 16 July 1916, during the battle of the Somme, happened largely as depicted, except that the officer in question was actually Lieutenant Savill. Following a failed advance, Veale saw a hand waving amongst the corn and went to rescue him, at great risk to himself. The whole operation took a day and saw Veale make the journey into No Man's Land a number of times to take water to Savill, to move him away from enemy lines, and to defend the officer from German patrols. It was an incredibly brave act, which earned him the Victoria Cross, the highest honour for gallantry. Veale survived the war and attained the rank of Corporal. He died in 1980, aged 87.

© The Keep Military Museum

Sergeant Cairns' story

Although he is a fictional character, the raid on the trench which sees Sergeant Cairns lose his life is based on a real story where a

316

supply party disappeared at a place called 'Crucifix Corner' (named because a roadside crucifix remained on the side of the trench). It was a notorious area which soldiers feared to pass through because of sniper attacks, and the party which disappeared was thought to have been attacked by a German raiding party.

'Mons men' like Cairns were professional soldiers who were part of the original British Expeditionary Force (BEF) and served at the Battle of Mons in 1914 - the first action of the war. Part of the small, professional pre-war army, their knowledge and experience were invaluable, especially later as the army ballooned with the addition of Kitchener's volunteers in 1915 and drafted soldiers from 1917. Officers had to be drawn from the middle and upper classes and many, like Hansen, were young and inexperienced. The support of experienced NCOs like Cairns was vital.

Private Challacombe's story

The story of Private Challacombe is also based on real incidents. Some soldiers suffered from a form of PTSD called hyperacusis, an extreme sensitivity to noise, thought to have been brought about by the constant gunfire and artillery. In some cases, the soldiers sought medical attention, which was refused because the condition was not known at the time. Unable to bear the noise, they might refuse to return to the front and were consequently treated as cowards and court-martialled. Although the number of soldiers actually shot for cowardice was relatively low in comparison to the number of convictions (many sentences were commuted), it did happen.

Such was the stigma that wives of those men were treated as pariahs, and if they applied for a widow's pension, could be refused. Widows like Betty Challacombe would have had to go back to work, and in a small community they might have found that hard to come by, especially after the war when a flood of returning men made jobs scarce.

Printed in Great Britain
by Amazon